BLACK THUNDER

D0880570

BY THE AUTHOR

Novels
God Sends Sunday
Black Thunder
Drums at Dusk

Poetry
Personals

Children's Books
Popo and Fifina (with Langston Hughes)
Sad-faced Boy
Fast Sooner Hound (with Jack Conroy)
Chariot in the Sky
Slappy Hooper, the Wonderful
   Sign Painter (with Jack Conroy)
Sam Patch, the High, Wide
   and Handsome Jumper (with Jack Conroy)
Lonesome Boy
The Story of George Washington Carver
Frederick Douglass: Slave, Fighter, Freeman
We Have Tomorrow

Plays
St. Louis Woman (with Countee Cullen)

Biography and History
They Seek a City (with Jack Conroy)
Story of the Negro
100 Years of Negro Freedom

Anthologies
Poetry of the Negro (with Langston Hughes)
Golden Slippers
Book of Negro Folklore (with Langston Hughes)
American Negro Poetry

Black Thunder

By
Arna Bontemps

With an introduction for this edition
by the author

BEACON PRESS   BOSTON

CONTENTS

INTRODUCTION

By Arna Bontemps

Time is not a river. Time is a pendulum. The thought occurred to me first in Watts in 1934. After three horrifying years of preparation in a throbbing region of the deep south, I had settled there to write my second novel, away from it all.

At the age of thirty, or thereabouts, I had lived long enough to become aware of intricate patterns of recurrence, in my own experience and in the history I had been exploring with almost frightening attention. I suspect I was preoccupied with those patterns when, early in *Black Thunder,* I tried to make something of the old major-domo's mounting the dark steps of the Sheppard mansion near Richmond to wind the clock.

The element of time was crucial to Gabriel's attempt, in historical fact as in *Black Thunder,* and the hero of that action knew well the absolute necessity of a favorable conjunction. When this did not occur, he realized that the outcome was no longer in his own hands. Perhaps it was in the stars, he reasoned.

If time is the pendulum I imagined, the snuffing of Martin Luther King, Jr.'s career may yet appear as a kind of repetition of Gabriel's shattered dream during the election year of 1800. At least the occurrence of the former as this is written serves to recall for me the tumult in my own thoughts when I began to read extensively about slave insurrections and to see in them a possible metaphor of turbulence to come.

Not having space for my typewriter, I wrote the book in longhand on the top of a folded-down sewing machine in the extra bedroom of my parents' house at 10310 Wiegand Avenue where my wife and I and our children (three at that time) were temporarily and uncomfortably quartered. A Japanese truck farmer's asparagus field was just outside our back door. From a window on the front, above the sewing machine, I could look across 103rd Street at the buildings and grounds of Jordan High School, a name I did not hear again until I came across it in some of the news accounts reporting the holocaust that swept Watts a quarter of a century later. In the vacant lot across from us on Wiegand a friendly Mexican neighbor grazed his milk goat. We could smell eucalyptus trees when my writing window was open and when we walked outside, and nearly always the air was like transparent gold in those days. I could have loved the place under different circumstances, but as matters stood there was no way to disguise the fact that our luck had run out.

My father and stepmother were bearing up reasonably well, perhaps, under the strain our presence imposed on them, but only a miracle could have healed one's own hurt pride, one's sense of shame and failure at an early age. Meanwhile, it takes time to write a novel, even one that has been painstakingly researched, and I do not blame my father for his occasional impatience. I had flagellated myself so thoroughly, I was numb to such criticism, when he spoke in my presence, and not very tactfully, about young people with bright prospects who make shipwreck of their lives.

What he had in mind, mainly, I am sure, were events which had brought me home at such an awkward time and with such uncertain plans, but somehow I suspected more. At the age at which I made my commitment to writing, he had been blowing a trombone in a Louisiana marching band under the direction of Claiborne Williams. But he had come to regard such a career as a deadend occupation unworthy of a young family man, married to a schoolteacher, and he renounced it for something more solid: bricklaying. Years later when the building trades themselves began to fade as far as black workers were concerned, under pressure of the new labor unions, he had made another hard decision and ended his working years in the ministry.

He was reproaching me for being less resourceful, by his lights, and I was too involved in my novel to even reply. The work I had undertaken, the new country into which I had ventured when I began to explore Negro history had rendered me immune for the moment, even to implied insults.

Had the frustrations dormant in Watts at that date suddenly exploded in flame and anger, as they were eventually to do, I don't think they would have shaken my concentration; but I have a feeling that more readers might then have been in a mood to hear a tale of volcanic rumblings among angry blacks—and the end of patience. At the time, however, I began to suspect that it was fruitless for a Negro in the United States to address serious writing to my generation, and I began to consider the alternative of trying to reach young readers not yet hardened or grown insensitive to man's inhumanity to man, as it is called.

For this, as for so much else that has by turn intrigued or troubled me in subsequent years, my three-year sojourn in northern Alabama had been a kind of crude conditioning. Within weeks after the publication of my first book, as it happened, I had been caught up in a quaint and poignant disorder that failed to attract wide attention. It was one of the side effects of the crash that brought on the Depression, and it brought instant havoc to the Harlem Renaissance of the twenties. I was one of the hopeful young people displaced, so to speak. The jobs we had counted on to keep us alive and writing in New York vanished, as some observed, quicker than a cat could wink. Not knowing where else to turn, I wandered into northern Alabama, on the promise of employment as a teacher, and hopefully to wait out the bad times, but at least to get my bearings. I did not stay long enough to see any improvement in the times, but a few matters, which now seem important, did tend to become clearer as I waited.

Northern Alabama had a primitive beauty when I saw it first. I remember writing something in which I called the countryside a green Eden, but I awakened to find it dangerously infested. Two stories dominated the news as well as the daydreams of the people I met. One had to do with the demonstrations by Mahatma Gandhi and his followers in India; the other, the trials of the Scottsboro boys then in progress in Decatur, Alabama, about thirty miles from where we were living. Both seemed to foreshadow frightening consequences, and everywhere I turned someone demanded my opinions, since I was recently arrived and expected to be knowledgeable. Eventually their questions upset me as much as the news stories. We had fled here to escape our fears in the city, but the terrors we encountered here were even more upsetting than the ones we had left behind.

I was, frankly, running scared when an opportunity came for me to visit Fisk University in Nashville, Tennessee, about a hundred miles away, get a brief release from tension, perhaps, and call on three old friends from the untroubled years of the Harlem Renaissance: James Weldon Johnson, Charles S. Johnson, and Arthur Schomburg. All, in a sense, could have been considered as refugees living in exile, and the three, privately could have been dreaming of planting an oasis at Fisk where, surrounded by bleak hostility in the area, the region, and the nation, if not indeed the world, they might not only stay alive but, conceivably, keep alive a flicker of the impulse they had detected and helped to encourage in the black awakening in Renaissance Harlem.

Each of them could and did recite by heart Countée Cullen's lines dedicated to Charles S. Johnson in an earlier year:

We shall not always plant while others reap
The golden increment of bursting fruit,
Not always countenance, abject and mute,
That lesser men should hold their brothers cheap;
Not everlastingly while others sleep
Shall we beguile their limbs with mellow flute,
Not always bend to some more subtle brute;
We were not made eternally to weep.

The night whose sable breast relieves the stark,
White stars is no less lovely being dark,
And there are buds that cannot bloom at all
In light, but crumple, piteous, and fall;
So in the dark we hide the heart that bleeds,
And wait, and tend our agonizing seeds.

Separately and with others we made my visit a time for declaring and reasserting sentiments we had stored in our memories for safekeeping against the blast that had already dispersed their young protégés and my friends and the disasters looming ahead.

Discovering in the Fisk Library a larger collection of slave narratives than I knew existed, I began to read almost frantically. In the gloom of the darkening Depression settling all around us, I began to ponder the stricken slave's will to freedom. Three historic efforts at self-emancipation caught my attention and promptly shattered peace of mind. I knew instantly that one of them would be the subject of my next novel. First, however, I would have to make a choice, and this involved research. Each had elements the others did not have, or at least not to the same degree, and except for the desperate need of freedom they had in common, each was attempted under different conditions and led by unlike personalities.

Denmark Vesey's effort I dismissed first. It was too elaborately planned for its own good. His plot was betrayed, his conspiracy crushed too soon, but it would be a mistake to say nothing came of it in Vesey's own time. The shudder it put into the hearts and minds of slaveholders was never quieted. *Nat Turner's Confession,* which I read in the Fisk Library at a table across from Schomburg's desk, bothered me on two counts. I felt uneasy about the amanuensis to whom his account was related and the conditions under which he confessed. Then there was the business of Nat's "visions" and "dreams."

Gabriel's attempt seemed to reflect more accurately for me what I felt then and feel now might have motivated slaves capable of such boldness and inspired daring. The longer I pondered, the more convinced I became. Gabriel had not opened his mind too fully and hence had not been betrayed as had Vesey. He had by his own dignity and by the esteem in which he was held inspired and maintained loyalty. He had not depended on trance-like mumbo jumbo. Freedom was a less complicated affair in his case. It was, it seemed to me, a more unmistakable equivalent of the yearning I felt and which I imagined to be general. Finally, there was the plan itself, a strategy which some contemporaries, prospective victims, felt could scarcely have failed had not the weather miraculously intervened in their behalf. Gabriel attributed his reversal, ultimately, to the stars in their courses, the only factor that had been omitted in his calculations. He had not been possessed, not even overly optimistic.

Back in Alabama, I began to sense quaint hostilities. Borrowing library books by mail, as I sometimes did, was unusual enough to attract attention. Wasn't there a whole room of books in the school where I worked—perhaps as many as a thousand? How many books could a man read in one lifetime anyway? We laughed together at the questions, but I realized they were not satisfied with my joking answers. How could I tell them about Gabriel's adventure in such an atmosphere?

Friends from the Harlem years learned from our mutual friends at Fisk that we were in the vicinity and began dropping in to say howdy en route to Decatur or Montgomery or Birmingham. There was an excitement in the state similar to that which recurred twenty-five years later when black folk began confronting hardened oppression by offering to put their bodies in escrow, if that was required. In 1931, however, the effort was centered around forlorn attempts to save the lives of nine black boys who had been convicted, in a travesty of justice, of ravishing two white girls in the empty boxcars in which all were hoboing.

The boyish poet Langston Hughes was one of those who came to protest, to interview the teen-age victims in their prison cells, and to write prose and poetry aimed at calling the world's attention to the enormity about to be perpetrated. It was natural that he should stop by to visit us. He and I had recently collaborated, mainly by mail, on the writing of a children's story, *Popo and Fifina: Children of Haiti.* He had the story and I had the children, so my publisher thought it might work. Perhaps it would not be too much to say they were justified. The story lasted a long time and was translated into a number of languages. The friendship between the two authors also lasted and yielded other collaborations over the next thirty-five years. But the association was anathema to the institution which had, with some admitted reluctance, given me employment.

As my year ended, I was given an ultimatum. I would have to make a clean break with the unrest in the world as represented by Gandhi's efforts abroad and the Scottsboro protests here at home. Since I had no connection or involvement with either, other than the fact that I had known some of the people who were shouting their outrage, I was not sure how a break could be made. The head of the school had a plan, however. I could do it, he demanded publicly, by burning most of the books in my small library, a number of which were trash in his estimation anyway, the rest, race-conscious and provocative. *Harlem Shadows, The Blacker the Berry, My Bondage and Freedom, Black Majesty, The Souls of Black Folk,* and *The Autobiography of an Ex-Coloured Man* were a few of those indicated.

I was too horrified to speak, but I swallowed my indignation. My wife was expecting another child, and the options before us had been reduced to none. At the end of the following term we drove to California, sold our car, and settled down in the small room in Watts in the hope that what we had received for the car would buy food till I could write my book. By the next spring *Black Thunder* was finished, and the advance against royalties was enough to pay our way to Chicago.

Black Thunder, when published later that year, earned no more than its advance. As discouraging as this was, I was not permitted to think of it as a total loss. The reviews were more than kind. John T. Frederick, director of the Illinois Writers Project, read the book and decided to add me to his staff. He also commended it warmly in his anthology, *Out of the Midwest,* and in his CBS broadcasts. Robert Morss Lovett mentioned it in his class at the University of Chicago. But the theme of self-assertion by black men whose endurance was strained to the breaking point was not one that readers of fiction were prepared to contemplate at the time. Now that *Black Thunder* is published again, after more than thirty years, I cannot help wondering if its story will be better understood by Americans, both black and white. I am, however, convinced that time is not a river.

Chicago
April 1968

BLACK THUNDER

BOOK ONE

Jacobins

1

Virginia Court records for September 15, 1800, mention a certain Mr. Moseley Sheppard who came quietly to the witness stand in Richmond and produced testimony that caused half the States to shudder. The disclosures, disturbing as they were, preceded rumors that would positively let no Virginian sleep. A troop of United States cavalry was urgently dispatched, and Governor James Monroe, himself an old soldier, paced the halls of Ash Lawn with quaking knees and appointed for his estate three special aides-de-camp.

It is safe to say, however, that on the night this history

begins, early in June of the same year, Mr. Moseley Sheppard slept well. That night the planter's great house was as dark as death. The rooms, cavernous and deep, were without sound, except when a gray squirrel scampered over the roof or when Ben, the old slave, rattled a plate in the pantry. A tall clock, ticking hoarsely on a landing, changed its tone occasionally and suggested the croaking of a bullfrog. Mr. Moseley Sheppard breathed heavily behind his mosquito netting, turned now and again on his high-piled mattresses, but slept well.

Old Ben twisted a scrap of paper, got a fragment of flame over the pantry lamp and went into the kitchen. There were candles on a table in the corner. He lit one and threw the punk that was burning his fingers into a kettle of ashes.

Following the taper, the old servant's face glowed like a drunken moon behind a star. He was smiling. There was gray wool on the sides of his face as well as on his head. Ben wore satin breeches and shoes with white paste buckles; his savage hair was long and tied with a black string at the back of his neck.

On the landing he opened the clock and began winding it with a brass key. He had placed the candle above his head, and it threw on his shoulders a dull blue radiance weaker than the light a ghost carries. Ben's thin hands kept turning the key, winding the tall clock. He was still turning, still winding, when young Robin Sheppard let himself in by a side door and came quietly through the unlighted great room. He reached the staircase and paused. Ben closed the clock, took his candle and came down. The boy's embroidered cuffs covered his pale hands. There was glossy braid on his knee-length coat.

"Listen, Ben," he said. "You're not supposed to see things, and you're not supposed to hear."

"No, suh, young Marse Robin. I don't hear and I don't see."

"You don't know what time I came in – understand?"

"I don't know nothing," Ben said, "nothing."

"That's it. Have you got anything handy in the pantry, Ben?"

The boy followed him out to the larder, took a stool beneath the pantry lamp and waited while Ben trimmed the breast of a cold roasted duck, opened an earthen jar of preserves and poured wine from a reed-covered jug. Home from the College of William and Mary, Robin seemed strangely unfamiliar to Ben, not at all like the youngster he had seen grow up in that same house; but he was showing his Sheppard blood all right, keeping such hours before he was twenty-one and drinking like a congressman. Ben knew what to expect of the quality.

"You know where I've been, Ben?"

"I don't know nothing, young Marse Robin. Not a thing."

"You know, but you're not supposed to say. I want you to know, Ben. I might need you some time. You see, she's yellow."

"Yes, suh. I know and *don't* know."

"The horse is tied to a tree on the drive."

"I'll put him up myself," Ben said. "No need to call Pharoah."

"Thanks, Ben. You're a good boy."

The old gray-haired Negro smiled. He went through the kitchen and out on the gravel way. His heart fluttered with pleasure; he was a good boy.

Mr. Moseley Sheppard was still asleep behind his mosquito netting, his toes peeping out of the cover, but cocks were crowing. The handsome great house was dark as death inside, but in the fields thousands of gleaming birds were crowing up the sun. Old Ben, a shadow among shadows, wavered on the path that led beneath the walnut trees. He was smoking a corncob pipe, and in his hand there was an empty bowl covered with a napkin. He let himself into the kitchen.

Later, when Drucilla came with her grown daughter and started cooking breakfast, Ben returned to the back steps, bringing the silverware in a plush bag, and commenced polishing the pieces one by one on a bench. It was a big job, one that would take most of the morning, and he was glad to get an early start.

He worked steadily. By and by the sky flushed. There was a blue mist on the world. Ben always felt mellow at that hour. Somewhere, in some hedge or thicket a thrasher called; a thrasher called him somewhere. A few moments passed. The mist stretched and broke like a cobweb, and through it crept Bundy, an extremely thin Negro carrying a fat earthen jug.

"'Mawnin', Ben."

They were near the same age, but Bundy was not gray, had no hair to be gray, in fact, and had no frizzly whiskers on his face.

"What's on yo' mind?" Ben said.

Bundy turned his jug bottom up.

"Look: dry's a bone," he said. "Can't you give me another little taste of that old pizen rum, Ben?"

"You drinks worser'n a gentaman, Bundy. But I reckon maybe Marse Sheppard can spare you one mo' jugful. I'll just fill it anyhow and ask him about it some other time. He sleep now."

"That's the ticket, Ben. You oughta be a mason."

"A mason?"

"Sure. I'm one. You oughta come j'ine."

Ben came out of the cellar a few moments later hammering with his palm on the cork of Bundy's jug.

"There you be."

"Much obliged, Ben. But sure 'nough, you oughta come on j'ine the masons."

"I ain't got time for no such chillun's foolishness as that, Bundy."

"If you come find out what it is, you might change that song."

"Nah, not me, boy."

"Listen. I'm going to come get you next week just the same."

"Don't bother, Bundy. I'm too busy."

"I just want you to talk to Gabriel; I ain't asking you to j'ine no mo'."

"I'm too busy," Ben said. "That's all chillun's foolishness anyway."

"You just wait'll Gabriel 'splains it. I'm going to come get you next week."

"Aw, Bundy —"

"Don't say a word. Just you wait'll you talks to Gabriel. Much obliged, Ben."

"Don't mention it, Bundy. It wa'n't nothing."

Bundy left with his jug. The mist had broken into scraps. Ben could feel the softness of the young day. It amused him to see Bundy making his way across the fields on such unsteady legs with such a fat jug. Join the masons! Lordy, what a notion! Where was it the thrasher called him, to what green clump? Mr. Moseley Sheppard was probably still sleeping, his toes looking out from under the sheet, but bacon was frying in the kitchen and Ben thought he had better go up and wake him now.

2

Mr. Thomas Prosser was waiting beside a water oak in the low field when the sky flushed that morning. His lips were soiled with snuff; his pippin cheeks were bright. He had on a wig, a three-cornered hat and a pair of riding breeches, but he had neglected his shirt, and he stood expanding a hairy chest in the dewy air and smiting his boot with the firm head of a riding whip. His horse whinnied and pawed the earth.

Some Negroes were already in the field hoeing. Old

Bundy came over a knoll, crossed a meadow and climbed a fence. Still toiling with the fat jug, he got in a corn row and followed it. His legs seemed less and less secure.

Mr. Thomas Prosser flung himself into the saddle, drove his horse up to the end of the corn. The lines around his mouth and eyes tightened. A worthless old scavenger, that Bundy. Too old for hard work, too trifling and unreliable for lighter responsibilities. Not worth his keep. No better'n a lame mule. And here coming home from God knows where with a jug of rum as big as himself.

Old Bundy saw something coming and veered away, his arm thrown up to protect his head. He saw it again and started side-stepping. He dropped the jug, threw the other hand up and felt the butt end of a riding whip on his elbow. His arms became suddenly paralyzed. Again he veered anxiously. This time he went down on his knees in a clump of rank polk and began crying like a child.

The jug rolled into the corn row without loosing its cork. The Negroes, hoeing in another field, raised their heads, their faces wrenched with agony. Somewhere the thrashers called. The Negroes cupped their hands, whispered through the tall corn.

Something struck Bundy's head. Was it the horse or the man? Both were above him now; both showed him clinched teeth. Bundy regained his feet and made a leap for the bridle. He grasped something, something... But there was darkness now.

Old Bundy's eyes were open, but he didn't see. His mouth was open, and his face had a tortured look, but he said nothing.

Mr. Thomas Prosser was obliged to use his foot to break the critter's grip on the stirrup. Was Bundy trying to resist? The old sway-backed mule. The lickspittle scavenger. Well, take that. And here is some more. This. And this.

Yes, suh, Marse Prosser, I'm taking it all. I can't prance

and gallop no mo'; I'm 'bliged to take it. Yo' old sway-backed mule – that's me. Can't nobody lay it on like you, Marse Prosser, and don't nobody know it better'n me. Me and my jug has a hard time with you, a hard time. That jug done got to be bad luck for a fact. Every time I puts it under my arm I meets trouble. Lordy, me. Ain't that 'nough, Marse Prosser? Ain't you done laid on 'nough for this one time? You see me crumpled up here in the bushes. Howcome you keeps on hitting? Howcome you keeps on hitting me around the head, Marse Prosser? I won't be no mo' good to you directly. Lordy, what was that? Felt like a horse's foot. Lordy . . .

3

The colt called Araby kicked up his heels in the deep clover. He swept his lowered head, over the sweet green surf that broke and foamed about his knees and struck across the field in a joyous race with his shadow. He was as glossy and black as anthracite; his legs, still a trifle long for his body, twinkled in the sunlight. After the fetid stable, the stale straw for a bed and the damp planks underfoot, after the dark indoor prison and the days and weeks of longing at a tiny window, the meadow seemed too good to be true. He bounded again, inscribed a huge circle in the fine gritty turf and came back to the white-washed gate, the water trough and the cake of salt under the chestnut tree.

The young coachman in varnished hat, high boots and tailed coat turned toward the barn, the halter in his hand. Then he paused, put his foot on the gate again. That jet colt was happiness itself, pure joy let loose. The coachman shook his head. His own eyes were wretched; old Bundy was dying.

"That's all right for you, Araby," Gabriel said. "You

ain't a horse yet, and you ain't a nigger neither. That's mighty fine for you, feeling yo' oats and trying to outrun the wind. You don't know nothing yet. Was you a white colt, I reckon I'd have to call you *mister* Araby."

He took a lump of sugar from a pocket in his coat tail and held it between the crosspieces of the gate. Araby's lips touched the immense boyish hand. Gabriel could have cried with melancholy pleasure at the sudden feeling of this confidence, but instead he smiled.

"Nothing like that," he said. "Get on back there in the clover, you and them monstrous flies. I'm got to drive Marse Prosser to town directly."

The horses were hitched, waiting in the door of the carriage room. Taking Araby to the meadow had been an afterthought. Gabriel was fond of the colt. Criddle, the stable boy, would never have thought of it; he was too busy pitching manure out the back window. His little stupid head was a bullet; his eyes were no more than the white spots on a domino.

All about the place Negroes were whispering. They stood in pairs behind the stable, under the low trees, in the tobacco rows, bowed till their corncob pipes nearly touched, cupped their hands and whispered.

High on the driver's seat Gabriel gave the lines a twitch. He was almost a giant for size, but his head was bowed. The tall shiny hat seemed ready to fall on his knees at any minute. One leg hanging loosely beside the footboard gave a suggestion of his extraordinary length. His features were as straight as a Roman's, but he was not a mulatto. He was just under twenty-four and the expression of hurt pride that he wore was in keeping with his years and station. He was too old for joy, as a slave's life went in Henrico County, Virginia, too young for despair as black men despaired in 1800. The gleaming golden horses were out from under the shed with a leap. The newly painted carriage flashed on the gravel path.

The tallest of three uncommonly tall brothers, Gabriel

was also what they considered a man of destiny. His reputation was about a year old. It dated from an encounter with Ditcher, Negro "driver" on a nearby plantation.

Long before, Solomon and Ditcher had fought. Gabriel was fifteen then, but he remembered well the fierce struggle his oldest brother put up against the powerful barrel-chested black that ruled the Bowler slaves in the place of the usual white overseer. He remembered the shiver of powerful muscles and the blowing of powerful nostrils near the ground, and he remembered the thuds of blows in the darkness after night fell on the contest. Finally, too, he remembered how they brought Solomon home unconscious.

Three years later Martin, the second brother, met Ditcher in the clump of trees behind the barn. He and Ditcher were nearer the same age, but Martin didn't last as long as Solomon against the roaring beast. Two or three years passed, and it was Gabriel's turn, the third of the Prosser giants.

Ditcher, naked to the waist, came to the little grove in the twilight. He carried a whip that had been in his hand all day; and when Gabriel approached him in the clearing, straight and unflinching, he tossed it on the ground and slapped his great chest with a proud air. They locked mighty grips. Again there was that wanton display of strength. Again the muscles tightening till they shivered and the two giants tumbling on the ground.

A score of round-eyed blacks encircled the two. For them the earth rocked. The stars shook like lamps swinging in a storm. They thought: Them three big Prosser boys is *some* pun'kins, and this here Gabriel is just too fine to talk about, but that there Ditcher ain't no man: he's a demon. Yet and still, Gabriel ain't scairt of devils or nothing else, he ain't. Look a-yonder. God bless me, he's giving Ditcher the time of his life.

Suddenly Gabriel shook himself free and sprang to his feet. Ditcher rose slowly. The tide had turned. Gabriel leaped to the attack with a bitter grin on his boyish face. He showered blows on the demon that had whipped his two older brothers. It couldn't last. Ditcher curled up on the ground, and the Bowler crowd carried him home, snickering and giggling as they crossed the fields. One of the youngsters took the whip for a plaything.

"That there Gabriel can whup anything on two feet," an old man said. "He ain't biggity neither."

Gabriel didn't like to think about it any more, because he and Ditcher were friends now. Ditcher wasn't really mean; he simply had a loud ugly way of talking and doing things. He had been somewhat spoiled by the feeling of authority. But Ditcher could be depended on to stand by a friend. Of course Ditcher knew right well who was the biggest and the baddest nigger in Henrico County, but Gabriel didn't see any reason to talk about it or rub it in.

The horses stopped in the drive near the front steps. Gabriel's varnished hat inclined a little forward as he waited. His eyes were sad. Being massive and strong didn't make one happy. Being a great slave made Marse Prosser richer, perhaps, but it didn't put any pennies in Gabriel's pocket. Of course there was some compensation in the fine clothes of a coachman, and it was a pleasure to drive to town occasionally and to sport around in a tall hat instead of working in the fields or the shop. These were compensations, but they were brief, very brief.

Beyond the tall columns the door swung open. A lackey with white stockings stepped out first and stood bowing till the master followed. The pippin-cheeked man with three-cornered hat, knee breeches, a white wig and a cane under his arm came down the path fingering a small sheaf of papers.

"I'm going to the notary first, Gabriel."

"Yes, suh."

"Walk the horses. I have some things to read over."

"H'm."

Having only recently inherited the plantation on the

18

outskirts of Richmond, Mr. Thomas Prosser seemed endlessly occupied with legal papers and long conversations at the notary's office. And it may have been, Gabriel imagined, that these concerns were responsible for his curt manners and quick flashes of indignation. At any rate, he was a hard man to serve.

The morning sun mounted. There were grouse dusting in the road and bluejays annoying squirrels in the low branches of trees. A swarm of sparrows covered a green coppice like flies on a carcass. The horses were eager to be gone; at first Gabriel had to hold them in check. Marse Prosser was still fingering his papers, still belching periodically and periodically snapping the top of his snuffbox.

The road went over a hill and down along the edge of a creek. Later it found another rise and beyond that some green slopes and low fields. At best it gave a jolting ride; but it did not stop the flutter of Mr. Thomas Prosser's papers; it failed even to topple the coachman's varnished hat. In time Gabriel was so deeply absorbed by his daydream that his chin fell against his shirt front, the reins fell slack in his hands and he awakened to hear Marse Prosser shouting in his ears.

"Are you asleep there, billy goat? Or are you trying to turn the carriage over?"

"Nah, suh," Gabriel murmured in a deep voice. "I ain't going to turn you over, Marse Prosser."

"Well, if you can't keep those horses in the road, I have a cane here that I can bloody well teach you with."

"Yes, suh."

Gabriel got his wheels out of the ditch promptly. He drew himself more erect in the seat.

"You can let them take a trot from here in."

"H'm."

The streets had a quiet air in the forenoon. Richmond's six or seven thousand people were so scattered the town seemed even smaller than it was for population. Shops were doing a slow business here and there; carriages and saddle horses were tied at hitching bars, and little groups of free blacks and poor whites lolled at the public watering troughs and under the oak trees. There were slaves too, trusted family servants going through the town on errands, the males trotting in the dusty streets, carrying little mashed-up hats in their hands, the women balancing huge baskets on their heads, slapping their bare feet in the footpaths.

There was always the hum of fiddles at the dancing school and the flutter of clean, crisp-looking children in crinolins with pompous black attendants. The dancing master was a Frenchman, as was also his friend the printer, whose shop attracted Gabriel while he waited for Marse Prosser to complete his conversation with the notary.

M. Creuzot had a visitor, and the two were talking very rapidly and in deep earnestness. The rather young visitor wore thick-lensed glasses; he was short and dark and his hair was thick. M. Creuzot was tall and fair and his hair was thin. The printer had also a hoarseness in his throat and a perpetual cough on his chest. He shook a long nervous finger before his face as he talked.

Gabriel walked over to the window where M. Creuzot's red-haired shop boy was setting type so fast it was scarcely possible to follow his fingers. The boy had moved a case and his copy near the window in order to enjoy the better light and the suggestion of a breeze outside. He did not seem interested in the conversation of M. Creuzot and his Philadelphia visitor. But Gabriel, his eyes on the plump red-haired fellow, was innocent of letters and interested only in the words of the other men.

Presently M. Creuzot grew tired, his voice weak.

"Here in Richmond," he said with an accent, "I am an outsider. I am not trusted too far."

"I know," the younger man said. "I know."

"They have catalogued me with the radicals for some reason. I don't know why. I never talk."

"They have heard of Sonthonaz and the *Amis des Noirs*."

"It is an inconvenience," M. Creuzot said.

They paused. There were blue shadows outside the back window. Through the front, yellow sunlight slanted in shafts. And after a while Alexander Biddenhurst said vigorously:

"The equality of man – there's the pill. You had the filthy nobles in France. Here we have the planter aristocrats. We have the merchants, the poor whites, the free blacks, the slaves – classes, classes, classes ... I tell you, M. Creuzot, the whole world must know that these are not natural distinctions but artificial ones. Liberty, equality and fraternity will have to be won for the poor and the weak everywhere if your own revolution is to be permanent. It is for us to awaken the masses."

"Perhaps," said M. Creuzot weakly. "Perhaps. I do not say. It baffles me. I have read Mr. Jefferson's *Notes on Virginia*, and I understand that Judge Tucker, here at William and Mary College, makes a strong proposal for gradual abolition in his *Dissertation on Slavery*, but it all seems hopeless in this country."

"Never say hopeless, M. Creuzot. Even now the blacks are whispering."

"Perhaps not hopeless entirely. But the blacks are *always* whispering. It baffles me."

"The trouble is that those statesmen you named do not go far enough in the direction they indicate."

They were all just words, but they put gooseflesh on Gabriel's arms and shoulders. He felt curiously tremulous. Standing at the window he felt one chill after another run along his spine. He knew that he was delaying longer than he should, but his feet were planted. He was as helpless as a man of wood. He stood facing the funny little typesetter but seeing nothing; he was bewitched. Here were words for things that had been in his mind, things that he didn't know had names. Liberty, equality, frater – it was a strange music, a strange music. And was it true that in another country white men fought for these things, died for them? Gabriel reeled a trifle, but his feet were hopelessly

21

fastened. So they had noticed the blacks whispering, had they?

The men talked on. After a while the young man from Philadelphia came out, slapped the immense Negro on the shoulder and pointed to the typesetter.

"Would you like to learn things like that?"

Gabriel came out of his trance. He managed to get turned around so that he faced the carelessly dressed visitor.

"I reckon I would, suh. I reckon so."

"Are you a free man?"

Gabriel's shoulders rounded, his arms hung a bit in front of his body, the tall hat tilted forward on his head.

"No." His head went lower. "I ain't free."

Young Mr. Biddenhurst looked at him a long time in silence, looked up at the great stature, the powerful shoulders, looked at the sober melancholy face.

"That's a pity. Listen. Peep in the wine shop by the river bridge some time. I do my reading there. I'll buy you a drink, maybe."

When he had turned away, Gabriel felt the hand on his shoulder again. He was so embarrassed by the white man's attention he could not speak. He was now thinking about Marse Prosser and the danger of keeping him waiting, but that was a small thing as compared to Mr. Biddenhurst's astonishing words.

M. Creuzot went back to the form he was making up on the flat stone in the corner. The red-haired boy threw a glance or two out of the window, but he had not interrupted his work. Across the street and down a few paces the fiddles were still humming. They were upstairs over a tailoring establishment, and there were young girls, dancing pupils, at the windows with fans. Downstairs two black crones sat on a stone smoking corncob pipes. Others, like them, were leaning against carriage wheels, giggling with the glossy males who held the horses. Alexander Biddenhurst carried a book under his arm, but he wore no hat. His long natural hair looked odd and wild, and he walked with a sharp step. Gabriel went the other way, staggering.

Marse Prosser was walking back and forth beside his carriage, the sheaf of papers in one hand, his cane in the other. Gabriel came up like a drunken man.

"You left the horses, fool."

"They wa'n't fidgety. I just walked a little piece."

"But you kept me *waiting*. I'll teach you to gad around when I'm on business. There. Let that be a lesson to you. And that."

Twice the cane whistled. Once it fell on Gabriel's arm, the second time across the side of his face. He raised his head slowly. Something tightened in his shoulders.

"Yes, suh. Yes, suh, Marse Prosser."

Mr. Thomas Prosser took a pinch of snuff and climbed to his seat. His pippin cheeks were no redder than they had been, but his three-cornered hat and the wig under it were sitting a bit off kilter. Gabriel took his place and gave the driving lines a jerk. For some reason he felt less wretched than he had felt earlier. Marse Prosser's licks didn't actually hurt him much; even though they left a long welt on his arm and another on his face, they were really nothing.

4

M. Creuzot's shop apron suggested a huge penwiper. It was inked so thoroughly he must have long ago despaired of making a new smear on a fresh spot. Had the cloth been black from the beginning, the effect might have been less like a stipple job now, but the garment could hardly have been more completely darkened. He stood at the window rubbing his fingers on it sadly and looking out at the shaded street – stood and rubbed as if his sadness were occasioned by his failure to make another impression on the hopeless apron.

Once, apparently, he had chosen to wipe his hands on his cheek, and there he had been more successful. A vivid three-fingered smudge ran downward, reached his chin. But this did not reassure M. Creuzot's despondent eyes. They were as melancholy as if the whole world were blackened and all smears made.

Not that M. Creuzot pined to besmear the earth actually – possibly the picture suggests too much. M. Creuzot longed to see justice prevail. He had come to the new world before the storm broke in his former home, but he had been deeply stirred by the triumph of the third estate, and he often cried in his heart for another sight of the little singing village he had left too soon. In this city where he was not trusted, where the poor man was as wretched as a feudal serf, he stood at his window, hearing violins that seemed to be playing in the branches of the trees across the street, seeing poverty-stricken youngsters flee before the approach of proud horses on the cobblestones, and felt sick for another breath of Norman air, for another night in a little stone house he remembered and another stroll in a field of tiny haycocks.

Yet he did not think, as did the young man with the bushy hair, the thick-lensed spectacles and the copy of the *Dictionnaire Philosophique* under his arm, that there was hope for the masses in Virginia, that white and black workers, given a torch, could be united in a quest. He could not feel hopeful or buoyant as did Alexander Biddenhurst. His own head was usually low. Perhaps, he thought, it was because of his lungs, that confounded barking cough, that persistent rattle in his chest.

There were many who said that a man's thoughts could make him ill; perhaps it was also true that a man's illness could corrupt his thoughts. M. Creuzot turned to the pudgy red-haired boy who was no longer standing before the case of type.

"Have you finished that galley, Laurent?"

"Yes, sir. This is the last."

Even as he spoke he was removing the type from his stick, balancing the orderly pile between his fingers.

"Good. Perhaps I can read the proof before the children bring my lunch."

"I'll take it directly."

The boy inked the type with a small hand roller, took an impression and brought it to the pale man. M. Creuzot moved a stool to the window.

"This is very clear. You might make another one, though, so that we can compare our corrections."

"Yes, sir."

They read a few moments in silence, M. Creuzot on his stool, Laurent standing with his elbows on the sill. Suddenly the older man looked up astonished.

"Something's wrong. This doesn't make sense."

"Where's that?"

"Between the third and fourth paragraphs. He is giving here instances in which great fish have been known to swallow men, in support of the Jonah legend, and then in the next sentence he is speaking of the various ranks of angels."

"I followed copy."

"Yes? Where is that copy?"

The fat, round-faced boy gathered all the scattered pages, assembled them and handed them to M. Creuzot.

"It was all hard to follow."

"Yes, these pamphlet-writing preachers are generally as incoherent as they are dull. They write like schoolboys."

"I thought perhaps the fault was mine."

"Just partly, Laurent. Your wits are normal, but it may be true that some spiritual things elude you for other reasons."

The boy became intensely red. He dropped his eyes as he tried to smile.

"I hadn't thought I was so wicked as all that."

M. Creuzot looked up with a twinkle.

"Perhaps not. Perhaps I misjudged you. But, seriously, if pamphlet-writing clergymen are no credit to letters, they *are* a boon to printers. Here – just what I thought – there *is* a page missing."

"I didn't discover it."

"The pages were unnumbered when we got them. I suppose you had better run over there and ask the Rev. Youngblood if he can supply the other sheet."

Laurent looked out at the sun. It stood almost directly above the street.

"Shall I eat my lunch first?"

"I'd rather not. I can work while you eat if you go now."

The boy put an absurd little round cap on his head and went out, walking reluctantly. The stockings he wore with his knee breeches had been white. They were dust-colored now, and there were holes in them, and they had a tendency to wrinkle on his legs.

On his stool at the window M. Creuzot smiled without mirth and gave his thought once more to the pages in his hand.

The youngsters André and Jean were as dark and rugged as Tartars and nothing at all like M. Creuzot; nothing, that is, except that André was inclined to be a trifle tall for his years and that Jean's eyes were bluish. The little heavy fellow carried the lunch in a basket, and André brought a warm dish with a cover and the bottle of wine, and each had a hoop that he was not able to roll because his hands were too full.

"Papa, there's something here that will surprise you. May I have a little taste of it?"

"Now, what is that? What have you brought that you want to eat from me, little pig?"

"He had one already," André said. "They're tarts."

"Mine was awfully small," Jean protested. "May I have just a taste of yours? You have two big ones."

M. Creuzot uncovered the small basket and divided one of his tarts between his sons. Then he spread the lunch on the stone make-up table in the corner and sat down and blessed himself. The boys went past the window slapping their hoops with one hand, clasping the fragments of their dainty in the other. M. Creuzot coughed behind his napkin, munched his bread sullenly and at intervals drank from the bottle.

For some reason Laurent delayed. He was gone longer than it would ordinarily require for a boy to go and return twice. And when M. Creuzot's bottle was nearly empty, he began throwing anxious glances at the door. He finished the mutton stew and raked the crumbs of bread from the table into the bowl.

The table cleared, he folded his napkin, put the bowl in the basket and went back to the stool at the window with his bottle and tart.

A fastidious young man with fancy riding gloves and frills on his shirt-front went by on a white horse. A poor farmer walked beside his ox cart, and a barefoot boy was sleeping on a sack of meal thrown across a scrawny mare's back. There were people walking too, more of them than there had been an hour or two earlier, but Laurent was not among them. His round, moth-eaten cap was nowhere in sight; his round, pock-marked face was nowhere. M. Creuzot took another bite of his tart, another swallow from his bottle.

When the boy did finally return, his cap was in his hand; he had been running, and he was breathless. His red hair had fallen on his forehead in a shaggy bang.

"You had to run?"

"Yes, sir. Here's the other page of copy."

"But you could have gone and returned three times at the gait of an ox."

"I was detained," Laurent said with embarrassment.

"Not by the Rev. Youngblood?"

"Some town boys."

"The same ones as usual?"

"Some were the same, but there were others. They were

hiding behind a fence. When I passed, they leaped over and gave me a broadside of green apples."

"Were you hurt?"

"Just a little. I ran for it. I was at the Rev. Youngblood's in a wink, but I couldn't stop. They stayed at my heels till I reached the edge of town, and I had to wait there till they went away."

"You should have led them into our own neighborhood and there returned their fire."

"There wasn't time to think."

"Did they call you a Jacobin?"

"Yes, that's always the first thing. Then something about my red hair. Some of the big fellows were really men."

"They are dogs, not men. That's their amusement as mine is my fiddle and a game of chess."

"It's a mean sport," Laurent said.

"Perhaps when they learn that we do not wish to impose our views on them, they may be more willing to tolerate us, Laurent. Even now *some* conditions are improving a trifle."

"You wouldn't have thought so had you been in my shoes a few minutes ago."

M. Creuzot smiled, took a few steps toward the back of the shop.

"I suppose that *was* a hypothetical remark. You'd better eat your lunch now. I'll set that."

5

The impartial sun kept its course. The first pearl-gray flush gave the great Prosser house a silver glow, and the same flush filled the chink holes in Gabriel's cabin with a duller silver. There was still the reek of fried greens, ham hocks and coffee grounds in the hut. Gabriel turned fretfully on his bed of rags. Something like a powerful cobweb constricted his arms, bore down upon his chest. He was neither asleep nor awake; he felt paralyzed, yet he continued to struggle. The same thoughts ran through his mind over and over again and he couldn't stop them. They were like snakes crawling. Suddenly the cobweb tightened, tightened till he thought the breath would go out of him, and he wakened in the arms of Juba, the tempestuous brown wench.

"Go on back to sleep, big sugar," she said. "You ain't slept enough to do a scarecrow."

"I know, gal. I know I ain't slept much."

"Put yo' head on my breast, boy. Sleep some mo'. There, like that. Go on back to sleep now."

"H'm."

A pause.

"Soft?" she asked.

"Soft as goose feathers."

"Well, howcome you can't sleep no mo'? Howcome that?"

"I can't sleep, and I don't know howcome, gal."

Her arms half-around him, she patted his shoulders and looked frightened. Her eyes were bright in the dark corner, her mouth round. She raised her head and saw the dull silver in the chink holes. There was a bitter sweetness in her voice.

"Big sugar?"

"Little bit."

"Maybe it's a yellow woman on yo' mind?"

"No womens but you, gal, no womens."

"That yellow white man's woman that they calls Melody, maybe?"

"No woman they calls Melody; just you."

"Ain't the place where you's laying sweet no mo'? Ain't it sweet and soft no mo', boy?"

"Too sweet, gal, too sweet. Yo' breast, soft. Yo' lips, sweet, sweet as ripe persimmons."

"Sweet, hunh?"

She patted his shoulders with both her hands, rocking a little as she patted.

"Too sweet. Yet and still – I can't sleep no mo'."

He yawned and stretched the length of a giant. The muscles quavered and ran under his skin. He saw the silver welding in the chink holes and wondered why the bell hadn't rung. There was a pig outside, rooting against the bottom log.

"Is you – " She stopped short.

"What you go to say, gal?"

"Ne' mind."

"Go on, say it."

"Is you thinking, boy?" she whispered. "Is that how-come you can't sleep no mo'?"

He looked ashamed.

"I reckon so. I reckon that's it, gal."

"That's bad."

"I know. I can't help it, though."

"What you thinking about, big sugar?"

"Thinking about I don't know my mind and I ain't satisfied no mo'."

"Ain't satisfied?"

"No mo'n a wriggletail."

She clasped him tighter, rocking, patting his shoulders again.

"Stop it, boy; stop thinking like that. It ain't good."

"You say stop, but you don't say how."

"Yo' head on my breast; there.... Yo' arms; there. Stop thinking."

"Soft. Sweet too, but I can't stop thinking."

"Thinking about *what*?"

"Thinking about how I'd like to be free—how I'd feel."

Juba cried. Real tears came in her eyes.

"You thinking it too, hunh? You fixing to leave me soon."

"No, I ain't fixing to run away, and I ain't going to leave you soon. But I wants to be free. I wonder how it'd feel."

"The police'll get you for just thinking like that, boy. It's bad, bad."

"I reckon so, but I can't help it."

The bell rang. Criddle, the short black stable boy with the bullet head and the eyes like white spots on a domino, was already in the barn. The mules were geared. Presently there were little puffs of smoke above each cabin. The sleepy slave folks, as crochety as things scissored from black paper, crept out half-naked. Each had his corncob pipe, his tuft of rebellious wool. Here and there one cupped his hand, threw à glance over his shoulder and whispered to a round-eyed neighbor.

Gabriel and Juba came up from the creek dripping. They lit their pipes at an outdoor fire, and the girl, who wasn't yet eighteen, ran back to the hut. Gabriel walked down toward the shops.

6

Old Bundy was dying when Ben got the word. It was night again, and the old great house was still and dark, but Ben was not alone. While Mr. Moseley Sheppard and his son slept in the large bedrooms at the top of the stairs, the frizzly whiskered major-domo and the female house servants buzzed quietly in the kitchen.

Drucilla was preparing her next day's vegetables by the flicker of a candle, and Mousie, the grown daughter that did the scrubbing, had stayed to help her. Mousie was picking and cleaning greens while her old black mother shelled peas. Ben stood at the lamp table blowing his breath on a smoked chimney and polishing it with a soft cloth. There was an octagonal ring on his finger. It was about the thickness of a woman's wedding band, and it kept clicking against the glass as Ben turned his hand inside the chimney.

Presently there was a little scraping noise at the back door, a sound like the pawing of a dog. Ben opened it and looked out. Criddle was there, terrified and panting, the two little domino spots showing plain on his bullet head.

"Bundy –"

"Hush that loud talk, boy. The white folks is sleep," Ben said.

"Well, I help you to say hush," Drucilla whispered.

"What about Bundy?"

"He's dying, I reckon."

"Dying!"

"H'm."

"Dying from what?"

"From day before yestiddy; from what happened in the field."

They all became silent and looked one at the other. The candle on the table gasped as if catching its breath. Ben put the lamp chimney down, knotted his brow and looked at the boy.

"I ain't heard nothing about day before yestiddy."

"Marse Prosser whupped Bundy about coming here," Criddle said. "He whupped him all up about the head and stepped on him with his horse."

Mousie turned her head petulantly.

"That's one mo' mean white man, that Marse Prosser."

"H'm," Criddle murmured. "That's what Gabriel and the rest of them is saying now. They say it ain't no cause to beat a nigger up about the head and step on him in the bushes with a horse."

"Po' old Bundy," Ben said. "He was worried about making me a mason."

"That's howcome he sent me," Criddle said. "He say don't you stay away on account of him. He want you to talk to Gabriel about j'ining up."

"I wasn't aiming to go," Ben said. "I ain't strong on that chillun's foolishness, but you needn't mention it to Bundy if he's all that bad off."

32

"I reckon he dying all right."

"Bundy used to talk a heap about freedom," Drucilla said. "Used to swear he's going to die free."

"He ain't apt to do that now."

"Nah," Criddle said; "leastwise, not less'n the good Lord sets him free."

"Po' old Bundy," Ben said. "He kept drinking up all that rum because he couldn't get up enough nerve to make his getaway."

"Must I tell him you said yes, Uncle Ben?"

"Tell him I said I reckon. That mason business is chillun's foolishness."

Criddle slipped away, dissolved in the shadows. Ben took a candle and went through the dark house trying the doors, adjusting the windows and hangings. His hand trembled on the brass knobs. Old Bundy was dying. A squirrel sprang from a bough, ran across the roof. Poor old Bundy. It seemed like just the other day since he was a young buck standing cross-legged against a tree and telling the world he was going to die free. He had grown old and given up the notion, it seemed, but Ben could well imagine his feelings. A slave's life was bad enough when he belonged to quality white folks; it must have been torment on that Prosser plantation.

They were praying for old Bundy's life when Criddle returned. Moonlight made shadows of uplifted arms on the wall above his heap of rags. There was a chorus of moaning voices. There were faces bowing to the earth and bodies swaying like barley.

Oh, Lord, Lord-Lord ... Knee-bent and body-bound, thy unworthy chilluns is crying in Egypt land ... La-aawd, Lord ... Wilt thou please, Oh, Massa Jesus, to look upon him what's lowly bowed and raise him up if it is thy holy and righteous will. Oh, La-aawd. La-aaaawd-Lord! ...

"Amen," old Bundy said feebly. "*Amen*!"

33

They were praying for old Bundy's life, but there was one who didn't pray. He stood naked to the waist in the hot cabin, stood above the others with hands on his hips and head bowed sorrowfully. His shadow, among the waving hands on the wall, was like a giant in a field of grain.

Old Bundy's eyes opened; he looked at the big fellow.

"That there head of yo's is mighty low, long boy, mighty low."

"Yeah, old Bundy, I reckon it is," Gabriel said.

"And it don't pleasure me a bit to see it like that neither."

"I'm sorry, old man; I'm sorry as all-out-doors. I'd lift it up for a penny, and I'd pleasure you if I could."

"It's that yellow woman, I 'spect, that white men's Melody waving her hand out the window."

"No woman, old Bundy, no woman."

"That brown gal Juba then – her with her petticoats on fire?"

"She belongs to me, that Juba, but she ain't got my head hung down."

"Not her? Well, you's thinking again, boy."

"Thinking again. It's all like we been talking. You know."

"H'm. I was aiming to die free, me. I heard tell how in San Domingo – "

"Listen, old man. You ain't gone yet."

"I don't mind dying, but I hates to die not free. I wanted to see y'-all do something like Toussaint done. I always wanted to be free powerful bad."

"That you did, and we going to do something too. You know how we talked it, you and me. And you know right well how I feel when my head's bowed low."

"Feel bad – I know. I feel bad too, plenty times."

One of the moaners on the ground raised a fervent voice, cried in a wretched sing-song.

"When Marse Prosser beat you with a stick, how you feel, old man?"

34

"Feel like I wants to be free, chile."

Gabriel gave the others his back, strolled to the door, rested one hand on the sill overhead. The chant went on.

"When the jug get low and you can't go to town, how you feel?"

"Bound to be free, chillun, bound to be free."

Gabriel left the others, walked outdoors.

"When the preacher preach about Moses and the chillun, about David and the Philistines, how you feel, old man?"

"Amen, boy. Bound to be free. You hear me? Bound to be free."

Gabriel did not turn. Even when the moaning and chanting stopped, he continued to walk.

7

Then the days hastened. M. Creuzot and his friend the dancing master were at a game of chess when sharp heels clicked on the doorstep. Both of them paused, looked up and waited for the knocker. When it sounded, M. Creuzot rose slowly. Hugo Baptiste took the board. The two men had been holding it on their knees, but now M. Baptiste placed it on the edge of a table. The eager, hopeful voice of Alexander Biddenhurst came from the vestibule. Laurent, the red-haired boy, was with him.

"We had a bottle of wine at the *Dirty Spoon*," Biddenhurst said. "All the blacks have the jumps. Something's up."

"It's nothing. The Negroes are always jumpy, always whispering."

"I think they're waking up. I really do."

"More's the pity," M. Creuzot said. "They are far better off asleep."

M. Baptiste stroked his fine chin whiskers with a wan hand.

"Better to sleep," he echoed.

"But I disagree," said Biddenhurst. "Think of the white peasantry, our own poor."

"Yes, do," said M. Creuzot, "but it is better to sit while thinking of them. Laurent, go in the kitchen and ask my wife to put one of her aprons on you. You know your job."

M. Creuzot pushed open the tall shutters of his living room. There was a light flutter of hangings before a frame of stars. M. Baptiste reclined in a straw-stuffed seat; Biddenhurst took a straight-backed chair, tilted it on its hind legs. In the kitchen Angelique and her small sons were laughing boisterously at Laurent.

"This may interest you," Biddenhurst said, taking a handbill from his pocket.

The dancing master read it aloud.

"Slavery and the Rights of Man."

"More of that stuff intended to incite the proletariat," the printer said, bowing over the other's shoulder. "Trouble is the proletariat is innocent of letters. They know of only one use for clean sheets of paper like this."

"A boon to the outhouses – that's what they are. Especially at a time when cornshucks are not plentiful."

Biddenhurst laughed with them.

"But there is a striking thing about this one," he said seriously.

"The subject is trite."

"That's true. But the gossips in town have it that this one was written by Callender."

"Callender?"

"Yes, sir, Thomas Callender, Jefferson's friend, right here in the Richmond prison where he's serving time for sedition. They are saying everywhere that he's the anonymous author."

"What a mad thing to distribute at a time like this," M. Baptiste said. "Where did you get this copy?"

"Two French Negroes, boys from Martinique, were distributing them among the free colored folks and the slaves – who probably took them for wedding certificates or something of the sort. The boys were assisted by a United Irishman. All there were strangers. The boys were from the French boat that was docked here yesterday. They have just sailed."

"Do you suppose they knew what they were scattering?"

"Of course not, but they knew to whom they should give them. I had the devil's own time wrangling them out of one."

Laurent came in with bottles and tall greenish glasses. He looked grotesque in the white apron Mme. Creuzot had pinned around him. Beyond the dining room the faces of Jean and André could be seen in the candlelight, giggling in the kitchen door. They felt sure they had made a clown of Laurent, but the men did not notice the apron or the way the boy's red hair had been ruffled. M. Baptiste continued to read, M. Creuzot looking over his shoulder and both holding full glasses.

"I doubt that Callender would be guilty of an attempt to incite the Negroes," M. Creuzot said.

"Possibly not," said Biddenhurst, "but it gives you an idea what they're whispering about. *Some*body published it, you know."

"It mentions the San Domingo uprisings, I see."

"Yes, the Negroes talk about that too. It's one of the things that makes me suspect they're awakening."

M. Creuzot emptied his glass and held it out for the boy to refill.

Then something occurred to him. A twinkle came into his eye.

"It would be too bad for poor Laurent should we live to see any real discontent among the masses here. They call him a Jacobin on the streets now, and sometimes they pelt him when he passes."

Laurent blushed a deeper red.

"That's partly because of his red hair," said M. Baptiste laughing. "But it is true that all Virginians have a tendency to associate the slogans of the *States-Général* with every show of discontent among slaves. They blame those principles for the San Domingo uprisings, and they resent the resumption of commercial relations with that country. Such things as that possibly come into their minds when they see poor Laurent with his round face and run-down stockings. He is just the type. He could scarcely suit them better if he had a shaggy beard. A Jacobin, they fancy, is an abandoned, villainous person with a foreign accent and a soiled shirt."

"I hadn't thought of that," Laurent lamented. "I'll have to spruce up."

"Don't grieve, Laurent," Biddenhurst said lightly. "The worm can turn. You may well pelt them some day."

"Let us hope that M. Baptiste and I, poor souls like us with our less combative spirits, have moved on by then. There'll be bitter days ahead when Laurent pelts the town boys in Richmond. It will be an omen."

They all laughed. Laurent went into the kitchen and returned with a tray of cheese, cold meat and bread. The men laughed again. Young Biddenhurst threw out his feet with hearty pleasure.

"Will John Adams be re-elected this fall, Mr. Biddenhurst?"

"No, I think not. Mr. Jefferson's popularity is increasing. This sliced turkey – it *is* good M. Creuzot. Where do you shoot these days?"

"There's a bottom out of town, a place where the creek broadens and the thicket is dense. The Brook Swamp."

"Well, now, that's a fortune."

"One can't amuse himself with the fiddle *all* the time, and M. Baptiste is occasionally unavailable for chess."

"By the by," M. Baptiste said, "you were in Paris last year?"

"Yes."

"Ah –"

"One gets homesick some time, I daresay?"

"Homesick? *Mon Dieu!* Who is seen at the old Procope nowadays, Mr. Biddenhurst?"

"A very interesting crowd. Poets, musicians, artists, and a great many others who'd like to be poets or musicians or artists. They were mostly young. Perhaps they're a new crowd, a younger generation than you knew."

"Yes, yes. Of course, they are. What memories that café holds! I can remember seeing Voltaire there when I was a student in the Latin Quartier. Murat and Danton and Robespierre came too. Time flies, Mr. Biddenhurst. You do not know yet. Wait till you pass fifty-five."

"I shall not mind passing fifty-five at all if I am as nimble as M. Hugo Baptiste, the dancing master, is at that age."

They all laughed. Laurent stumbled going into the kitchen with his empty tray, but he did not fall. The small boys came to the kitchen door again, laughing hard. Laurent had stepped on his apron.

8

Melody, the apricot-colored mulattress, swept her rooms with a sage-straw broom, dusted the chairs and table with a spray of turkey feathers. The windows were open, the curtains knotted high and the shutters thrown out as she cleaned, and through the house there went an early morning breeze from the river. Her skirt was folded up and caught at the back, and her leaf-green petticoat kept turning at the bottom, turning up the frill of a yellow one underneath. Melody's headcloth was a faded red, but beneath it there was enameled black hair and barbarous hoops in her ears.

The broom, a handful of straw bound to the stick with a

cord, was in her hand when she stood at the window looking down at the quiet street. She nipped a twig with her fingernails and chewed it a moment. Then she dipped the frayed tip into a snuffbox on the table and put it in her mouth against the gums.

A few minutes passed. Melody twirled the broom. She thought: He's a funny one with them thick specks of his'n and that book underneath of his arm all the time. Favors a Jew more'n he does a Englishman. I reckon he reads too much. One thing's mighty sure, though: Him and his equality of mens, his planter aristocrats as he calls them, and all like of that is going to get his Philadelphia pants hung wrong-side-out on a sour apple tree if he don't mind out. And it's worse'n a shame, too, because he talks like he mean what he say, and I thinks he likes poor folks a heap.

Another thing too: My name'll be mud if folks start saying he come up here to get drunk on peach brandy and to big-talk about how all the money in the country ought to be divided up equal amongst everybody. The rich white folks in this here town, leastwise the menfolks, ain't going to put up with no such running on. Next time he knock on the door, I'm going to have company, full house. If I don't, I'm going to come across myself leaving town one of these fine mornings.

The old slave called General John Scott was cutting weeds in the back yard with a scythe. He had no teeth, strictly speaking, only a half-dozen crooked brown fangs in front, and it was a miracle how he managed a chew of tobacco. Yet there was always that lump in his cheek, that busy gnawing of his lower jaw and that periodic dark spout. His whiskers were gray and frizzled, and his butternut pants, suspended from his shoulder by a single strap, were perhaps the most thoroughly patched homespuns in Virginia. His old arched body was as scrawny and shriveled as a dead oak leaf. He paused once, fished into a pocket that dropped below his knee and brought out a whetstone with which he touched up his blade. In a moment, the edge restored, his lower jaw was busy again, his sharp blade was whispering to the grass roots.

"How you come along, Gen'l John?" Melody called from the back window.

"Tolerably, Miss Melody," he said. "Just tolerably."

"Well, did you hear all that commotion down by the river just now?"

He straightened up as best he could, let the blade touch the ground.

"I ain't heard a thing," he said. "Did it sound like something to you?"

"Indeed it did, Gen'l. Some of them was hollering loud enough for it to of been a boat coming up."

"Well, bless me, I ain't heard a thing. There was a Norfolk boat just the other day."

"I know," she said. "There it is again. Hear them, Gen'l? Hear that hollering?"

"I'm got both ears pricked."

"Run down to the river road and see what it is."

"I'm gone already, Miss Melody. I'll tell you about it directly."

Melody's rooms were upstairs over an abandoned shop; weeds were high on either side, and there were no other houses near. The place had once been a grove, and still many trees were standing, but people passed on a carriage path now, and only a stone's throw away was the big road that ran by the river.

General Scott snatched the tiny crown of a hat off his head and shambled around to the front.

Melody was there looking out of her little plush parlor when he got on the path. A lock of the enameled black hair had fallen down on her neck; one end of the red headcloth was hanging.

Her smile, compounded not only of excitement and pure pleasure, was no less comely. She leaned over the row of tiny plants in earthen pots and watched the ragged old slave scuffling the dust on the footpath.

Partly, General John Scott came to cut weeds in Melody's back yard because he was too old to do a real day's work in the field where the other slaves were cutting tobacco, and partly he came because his tipsy middle-aged master wanted to do something handsome for a rosy buff-colored girl. It made no difference at all to General John. He didn't have to work any harder than he was pleased to work; Melody usually put a shilling in his hand when he finished, and just a short way down the river road was the rum shop beloved of the black folks. Melody had a habit of sending him there before the day's work was done.

The old fellow couldn't run, his time for that sort of kicking up had passed, but he swung his arms gingerly as he went and threw enough dust with his excited heels to represent well a running man. A boat! Children dancing along the river. Black folks opening their eyes in the warm sunlight, rousing from sleep on the stacked boxes at the landing, coming out of the *Dirty Spoon,* whistling, waving their hands.... It was mighty fine. The old man's heart fluttered.

Yes, sir, that was it; a boat was coming up the river just as Melody suspected. General John crossed the road and went on to the crest of a slope. There he stood, hat in hand, mouth open and eyes fixed. The patches in his pants were as bright as stars. He had lost his chew of tobacco, perhaps swallowed it, but that didn't matter now. He was busy thinking.

Yonder she come. And a pretty one she is, I thank you. Them white sails and that rigging. They ain't giving her much canvas now, just enough to bring her upstream easy and slow-like. Them flags – well, what kind of flags *is* them? Aw, sail it, Cap'n Bud, sail it.

A finger touched General's elbow, touched it a second time, then a third. He felt it. It was just a little push, nothing to hurt a body. He didn't mind it; he was looking at the boat. There were children scampering around, and the air was full of voices. He didn't mind them either; he was looking at the boat, thinking.

There's some black boys on her too, hauling at them ropes. Well, bust my breeches, what kind of nigger is that one? Red pants fastened at the ankles like a woman's bloomers, bare feet, no shirt and a pair of earrings in his ears. And will you look at that head? Just like a briar patch. He oughta cut some of that mess off if he don't aim to keep it combed and plaited. But he sure looks sassy in that pretty boat. She's fixing to land, too.

That finger on his elbow pushed again, pushed so hard General John dropped his hat and turned to see what touched him. He smiled when he saw the huge young fellow standing beside him in a two-foot hat.

"Quit yo' foolishness, boy," he grinned.

"Was you visioning, Gen'l John?"

"Sure I's visioning. I visions all the time."

Gabriel laughed.

"That's the boat from San Domingo," he said. "Indigo, coffee, cocoa and all like of that."

"Howcome it ain't stopped at Norfolk?"

"I reckon it did stop there. What you doing here?"

"Melody wanted me to find out what all the noise was about. How you come?"

"Taking a walk," Gabriel said. "Just strolling-like."

"Where'bouts yo' Marse Prosser?"

Gabriel shrugged insolently.

"I'm bigger'n him, ain't I?"

"Yes, you's bigger, but you might ain't so loud."

"They're pulling her up at the landing."

"H'm."

"How much money we got in the treasury now, Gen'l?"

"Well, sir, I ain't spent nothing this week, and I laid hands on ten dollar more."

"That's good."

The two started down toward the landing and toward

the *Dirty Spoon* that wasn't far away. There was a good crowd in the road, all hurrying. They quickly rushed past old General John and Gabriel. But after them came one who did not rush. She carried a leaf-green parasol, and she had changed to a plum-colored dress. And when the two men stopped by the lamp post to talk, she went past them, walking with a languid and insolent twitch, and entered the wine shop called the *Dirty Spoon*.

"Money ain't nothing to us," Gabriel said. "We going to have plenty to eat from crops and cattle and hogs and all. But you and Ben'll need a little for expenses. Pharoah, too."

"Pharoah?"

"Yes. I made up my mind to send Pharoah up to Caroline County with Ben."

"Howcome?"

"I don't trust that pun'kin-colored nigger."

"I thought he was hankering to lead a line."

"He was. I don't trust him, though."

"Well, maybe you did right. Get him far way as you can if his eye ain't right."

The ragged old man looked at Gabriel long and earnestly. His own eyes rounded, then sharpened. Now, take Gabriel here – there was an eye you could bank on. He'd stand up to the last, that Gabriel; he was a nachal-born general, him. General John's mouth dropped open, but he did not speak.

Some noisy sailors came up from the boat, went into the *Dirty Spoon*.

9

Mingo knew how to read. He held the Book on his knee and fluttered the crimped leaves with a damp forefinger. A freedman and a saddle-maker, Mingo was also a friend to the slaves. They came to his house on Sundays because he welcomed them and because they liked to hear him read. The room was hot and small, and Gabriel stood in the midst of the tattered circle that surrounded the reader's chair with his coachman's hat pushed back, his coachman's coat flung open.

"There, there," he said abruptly. "Hold on a minute, Mingo. Read that once mo'."

Mingo looked over his square spectacles. A cataracted left eye blinked. He smiled, turned the page back and repeated.

"He that stealeth a man and selleth him, or if he be found in his hand, he shall surely be put to death. . . ."

"That's the Scripture," Gabriel said. "That's the *good* Book what Mingo's reading out of."

The Negroes murmured audibly, but they made no words. Mingo fluttered a few more pages.

"Thou shalt neither vex a stranger nor oppress him; for ye were strangers in the land of Egypt. . . . Thou shalt not oppress a stranger, for ye know the heart of a stranger. . . .

"Therefore thus saith the Lord: Ye have not harkened unto me, in proclaiming liberty, every one to his brother, and every one to his neighbor: behold, I proclaim a liberty for you, saith the Lord, to the sword – "

"Listen!" Gabriel said.

" – to the pestilence, and to the famine; and I will make you to be removed into all the kingdoms of the earth. And I will give the men that have transgressed my covenant, which have not performed the words of the covenant which they had made before me, when they cut the calf in twain, and passed between the parts thereof, the princes of Judah, and the princes of Jerusalem, the eunuchs, and the priests, and all the people of the land, which passed between the parts of the calf; I will even give them into the hand of their enemies, and into the hand of them that seek their life; and their dead bodies shall be for meat unto the fowls of the heaven, and to the beasts of the earth. . . ."

Mingo thumbed the crimped pages awkwardly.

"Don't stop, Mingo. Read some mo'," Gabriel said. "That's the Scripture, ain't it?"

"Scripture," Mingo said. "Scripture – "

"Is not this the fast that I have chosen to loose the bands of wickedness, to undo the heavy burdens, to let the oppressed go free, and that ye break every yoke?"

"Read some mo', Mingo. Keep on reading some mo'."

"He sent a man before them, even Joseph,

"Who was sold for a servant;

"Whose feet they hurt with fetters:

"He was laid in iron – "

"Lord help; Lord help."

"Mm-mm. Do, Jesus. Do help."

" – Until the time that his word came,

"The word of the Lord tried him.

"The king sent and loosed him –

"Even the ruler of the people, and let him go free."

"Yes, Jesus, let him go free. Let him go free."

Mingo cleared his throat.

The black folks in chairs, on boxes, kneeling with folded arms, sitting on the floor, rocked reverently as they murmured.

Gabriel flipped his coat a little self-consciously and went to the window, giving the others his back.

"One is your master, even Christ; and all ye are brethren . . .

"Rob not the poor because he is poor; neither oppress the afflicted in the gate: for the Lord will plead their cause, and spoil the soul of those that spoil them. . . .

"The people of the land have used oppression, and exercised robbery, and have vexed the poor and needy; yea they have oppressed the stranger wrongfully. And I sought for a man among them that should make up the hedge, and stand in the gap before me in the land, that I should not destroy it: but I found none. Therefore have I poured out mine indignation upon them. . . .

46

"Woe unto him that buildeth his house by unrighteousness, and his chambers by wrong; that useth his neighbor's service without wages, and giveth him not for his work. . . .

"Behold the hire of the laborers who have reaped down your fields, which is of you kept back by fraud, crieth; and the cries of them which have reaped are entered into the ears of the Lord of Sabaoth. . . .

"And I will come near you to judgment; and I will be a swift witness against the sorcerers, and against the adulterers, and against false swearers and against those that oppress the hireling in his wages. . . ."

Gabriel swung around, one hand at his side, the other still on his hip.

"God's hard on them, Mingo. He don't like ugly, do he?"

Mingo shook his head.

"God's hard on them, and he don't like ugly," he said.

"It say so in the book, and it's plain as day," Gabriel said. "And, let push come to shove, He going to fight them down like a flog of pant'ers, He is. Y'-all heard what he read. God's aiming to give them in the hands of they enemies and all like of that. He say he just need a man to make up the hedge and stand in the gap. He's going to cut them down his own self. See?"

The Negroes stopped rocking and looked up. There was a glint of something bright in Gabriel's eye. Their mouths dropped open; they gazed without speaking.

10

Mr. Moseley Sheppard, slim, silvered, a man with a military air, waited at the foot of the stairs for his candle. Ben brought it to him in a saucer with a handle like a teacup. The old Negro bowed gravely in the shadows.

"All the black folks are terribly nervous, Ben. What's the trouble?"

Ben shook his head slowly.

"I don't get round a heap, Marse Sheppard. I don't hear much talk."

"There must be *some*thing. Why, you see little groups of them whispering under every tree. When you start toward them, they bow their heads and break up."

Ben thought for a long moment. Then he looked up.

"Old Bundy's dead," he said. "You reckon it's that?"

"Who's Bundy?"

"Marse Thomas Prosser's old Bundy. He died from a whupping he got for slipping away, and they's aiming to bury him tomorrow."

"Oh, him."

"Yes, suh, him."

"Well, I suspect that's it. I reckon the niggers are learning that Mr. Prosser doesn't take the foolishness from his slaves that some of us take."

"H'm. They's learning that, Marse Sheppard."

"Good-night, Ben."

"Good-night, suh."

Ben stood at the foot of the stairs till the frail, slim man closed a door overhead. Then he went into the front room and started trying the doors and windows. He remembered that young Marse Robin wasn't in yet, so he left the bolt unfastened on the side door.

Drucilla and Mousie were still slipping about softly in the kitchen and pantry. Ben heard the click of plates they touched, heard the chair legs drag when they moved. He was standing at a tall window, looking out through a lace-work of shadows on the lawn.

Marse Sheppard must be the most lonesomest old man in the country, he thought. He must of been that for a fact, what with no mo' womens in the house and him going to bed early like he did because he didn't have nobody to sit around and drink and talk with. And it was just like him to worry hisself about a lot of niggers that didn't even belong to him and that wasn't no ways as lonesome as him.

Ben's heart melted.

And there was young Marse Robin that wasn't a heap of comfort to the old man neither. That college boy had his daddy's quality and manners all right, but he went in stronger for merry times. His heart was a leaf. There he was this very evening out getting hisself drunk with a yellow woman with enameled black hair and hoops in her ears. He wasn't a heap of comfort to his daddy – leastwise, not when the old man felt his lonesomeness coming down.

A small wind fluttered the curtain. Ben closed the window and went through the large dining hall to the kitchen. Mousie was peeling peaches, fishing them out of a bucket of water. Drucilla was getting ready to set her light rolls before leaving for the night. Her hands were full of dough. Ben went into the pantry and came out with a plate of food he had left there half-eaten. He placed it on the kitchen table across from Mousie and went back for his coffee.

"Maybe I can get through eating now," he said.

"I reckon so," Drucilla smiled. "Here, let me set yo' coffee on the back of the stove. I bound you it's stone cold now."

"You's right about that. Thanks."

There was a pone of bread on the plate in a puddle of pot liquor. A small ham hock, partly demolished, stood at the side like a mountain. There had been a half-dozen pots from which to choose, but Ben knew his own mind and he knew his own palate. Let others tear at the tenderloin steaks; let them mop up the gravy and devour the garnishings; let them lick the artichoke's succulent petals if they chose; he would bear them no malice and no envy. He crushed his pone quietly in the puddle of pot liquor and smiled somewhere amid his frizzly whiskers.

"Old Bundy's dead," Mousie muttered over her peaches.

"Lord, it don't seem real."

"The last thing I heard him say was something another about rum," Drucilla said.

Ben's mouth was full, but not too full for him to talk.

"He was worrying me to be one of them colored masons, and I reckon he died with it on his mind."

"H'm," Drucilla answered. "And he'll come back to you with it, if you don't mind out."

"He didn't 'zactly ask me to j'ine up," Ben said. "He ended with asking me to see Gabriel and listen to him talk. He didn't say j'ine, not 'zactly."

"Was I you, Ben, I'd do just about like Gabriel say do about that when you see him. That is, I'd do it if I didn't want to be pestered by no dead mens. It won't cost nothing to oblige him that little bit on account of his last request."

"I reckon it won't cost nothing, but it's a peck of trouble. Yet and still, I ain't after having trouble with no devilish hants and the like of that."

Mousie looked up sharply, her eyes round.

"Lordy, what was that noise I heard?"

"Nothing," Ben said. "Just a squirrel jumped on the roof, I reckon."

They all waited a moment without speaking or moving. Then there was something again.

"Squirrel nothing," Drucilla said. "It's upstairs, Ben."

"Upstairs, hunh?"

"Sound like Marse Sheppard stumbling."

Ben got his feet from under the table as quickly as he could, snatched one of the candles and started through the dining room. When he reached the stairs, he heard the old man opening the bedroom door. Ben rushed up.

Marse Sheppard came into the hall supporting himself by keeping one hand on the door frame. He was pale and his candle trembled in his hand. He looked like an old woman in his nightcap and his long sleeping shirt, but Ben saw only the distressed face.

"My God," he said, "my knees gave away, Ben."

"Yes, suh, Marse Sheppard. Here, lean on me. You

oughta be laying down. There, now, suh. Easy. Lean on me, Marse Sheppard, you be all right."

"Get me the salts, Ben."

"Yes, suh. Lay down there; I'll get them directly. There . . . now."

Ben darted around the room while the old silvered man lay in his nightcap. He held the smelling salts to Marse Sheppard's nose, then poured a peg of whiskey into a small glass. The old man tossed it off and leaned back on his pillow. Ben lit two long rows of candles in the room and picked up a coat his master had dropped on the floor.

"Funny, these confounded spells. I'm not as old as you, am I, Ben?"

"No, suh, Marse Sheppard, but you got so much mo' to think about. That's howcome I don't have no spells like you. I got *you* looking out after me, but who's you got?"

The old man smiled a little.

"You're a good boy, Ben, but you're an awful liar about some things."

"Nah, suh, that ain't no tale."

"You'd make me feel good if you could, Ben."

Ben was glad to hear that; glad, too, that Marse Sheppard had called him a good boy.

Drucilla and her grown daughter were in the door now, gawking foolishly, waiting for a word from Ben. But he didn't need them, and after a few moments they went back downstairs. Ben took a seat near the bed and prepared to sit up with the sick man. Half an hour later young Marse Robin crept upstairs on unsteady legs, went directly to his own room. Ben did not call him. That tipsy boy wouldn't be able to help any, he thought; besides, Robin was too young for troubles like sickness in the family, too young, too merry.

11

They were burying old Bundy in the low field by the swamp. They were throwing themselves on the ground and wailing savagely. (The Negroes remembered Africa in 1800.) But there was one that did not wail, and there were some that did not wail for grief. Some were too mean to cry; some were too angry. They had made a box for him, and black men stood with ropes on either side the hole.

Down, down, down: old Bundy's long gone now. Put a jug of rum at his feet. Old Bundy with his legs like knotty canes. Roast a hog and put it on his grave. Down, down. How them victuals suit you, Bundy? How you like what we brung you? Anybody knows that dying ain't nothing. You got one eye shut and one eye open, old man. We going to miss you just the same, though, we going to miss you bad, but we'll meet you on t'other side, Bundy. We'll do that sure's you born. One eye shut and one eye open: down, down, down. Lord, Lord. Mm-mm-mm-mm. Don't let them black boys cover you up in that hole, brother.

They had raised a song without words. They were kneeling with their faces to the sun. Their hands were in the air, the fingers apart, and they bowed and rose together as they sang. Up came the song like a wave, and down went their faces in the dirt.

Easy down, black boys, easy down. I heard tell of niggers dropping a coffin one time. They didn't have no more rest the balance of their borned days. The dead man's spirit never would excuse a carelessness like that. Easy down, black boys. Keep one eye open, Bundy. Don't let them sprinkle none of that dirt on you. Dying ain't nothing. You know how wood burns up to ashes and smoke? Well, it's just the same way when you's dying. The spirit and the skin been together like the smoke and the ashes in the wood; when you dies, they separates. Dying ain't nothing. The smoke goes free. Can't nobody hurt smoke. A smoke man – that's you now, brother. A *real* smoke man. Smoke what gets in yo' eyes and makes you blink. Smoke what gets in yo' throat and chokes you. Don't let them cover you up in that hole, Bundy. Mm-mm-mm-mm.

Ben crossed a field and came to the place. The sun was far in the west; it was slipping behind the hills fast. But there were small suns now in every window on the countryside, numberless small suns. A blue and gold twilight sifted into the low field. The black folks, some of them naked to the waist, kept bowing to the sun, bowing and rising as they sang. Their arms quivered above their heads.

That's all right about you, Bundy, and it's all right about us. Marse Prosser thunk it was cheaper to kill a old wo'-out mule than to feed him. But they's plenty things Marse Prosser don't know. He don't even know a tree got a soul same as a man, and he don't know you ain't in that there hole, Bundy. We know, though. We can see you squatting there beside that pile of dirt, squatting like a old grinning bullfrog on a bank. Marse Prosser act like he done forgot smoke get in his eyes and make him blink. You'll be in his eyes and in his throat too, won't you, Bundy?

Ben knelt down and joined the song, moaning with the others at the place where the two worlds meet. He watched the young black fellows cover the hole, and he kept thinking about the old crochety slave who loved a jug of rum. Bundy wanted Ben to talk with Gabriel, and Ben knew now he would have to do it. There was something about a dead man's wish that commanded respect. The twilight thickened in the low field. Two or three stray whites who had been standing near by walked away.

Dead and gone, old Bundy. Something – something no denser than smoke – squatting by the hole, grinning pleasantly with one eye on the jug of rum.

The Negroes became still; and Martin, the smaller of Gabriel's two brothers, stood up to speak.

"Is there anybody what ain't swore?"

Ben wrinkled his forehead, scratched his frizzly salt-and-pepper whiskers.

"Swore about what?" he murmured.

"I reckon you don't know," Martin said. "Here's the Book, and here's the pot of blood, and here's the black-cat bone. Swear."

"Swear what?"

"You won't tell none of what you's apt to hear in this meeting. You'll take a curse and die slow death if you tells. On'erstand?"

Ben felt terrified. All eyes were on him. All the others seemed to know. Something like a swarm of butterflies was suddenly let loose in his mind. After a dreadful pause his thought became clear again. Well, he wouldn't be swearing to do anything he didn't want to do; he would just be swearing that he'd keep his mouth closed. It was no more than he'd have done had he not come to the burying. And by now, anyhow, so great was his curiosity, he couldn't possibly resist the desire to hear. Gossip was sweet at his age.

"I won't tell nobody. Martin," he said. "I swears."

There were a few others to be sworn. This done, Martin knelt quietly, and Gabriel took his place in the center of the circle. Near him on the ground was Ditcher, powerful and beast-like. General John Scott knelt in his rags. Criddle looked up, his mouth hanging open, the domino spots bright in his bullet head. Juba, the thin-waisted brown girl with hair bushed on her head, curled both feet under her body and leaned back insolently, her hands behind her on the ground. Solomon, Gabriel's oldest brother, sat with his chin in his palm like a thinker. His head was bald in front, and his forehead glistened. Something imaginary, perhaps the smoke of old Bundy, squatted beside the hole that the black boys had covered, squatted and grinned humorously,

54

one eye on the jug of rum. Gabriel called for a prayer.

Oh, battle-fighting God, listen to yo' little chilluns; listen to yo' lambs. Remember how you brung deliverance to the Israelites in Egypt land; remember how you fit for Joshua. Remember Jericho. Remember Goliath, Lord. Listen to yo' lambs. Oh, battle-fighting God . . .

"That's enough," Gabriel said. "Hush moaning and listen to me now. God don't like ugly. Some of y'-all heard Mingo read it."

He gave a quick summary of the Scriptures Mingo had read. Then he paused a long time. His eye flashed in the growing dusk. He looked at those near him in the circle, one by one, and one by one they broke their gaze and dropped their heads.

Another sweeping gaze.

Then he spoke abruptly.

"We's got enough to take the town already. This going to be the sign: When you see somebody riding that black colt Araby, galloping him for all he's worth in the big road, wearing a pair of Marse Prosser's shiny riding boots, you can know that the time's come. You going to know yo' captains, and that's going to be the sign to report. You on'erstand me?"

Ben caught his breath with difficulty. Lordy. The young speaker was deeply in earnest, but Ben couldn't make himself believe that Gabriel meant what his words seemed to mean. It sounded like a dream. Two or three phrases, a few words, fluttered in his mind like rags on a clothes wire. Take the town. Captains . . . Ben shuddered violently. Somebody wearing Marse Prosser's riding boots, galloping Araby in the big road. Where would Marse Prosser be when they took his shiny boots off him? Did they mean that they were going to murder?

And so this was what old Bundy wanted him to hear from Gabriel, was it? Did he think Ben would get mixed up in any such crazy doings? Ben's lips twitched. His thought broke off abruptly. Something squatting beside the covered hole turned a quizzical eye toward the frizzly whiskered house servant. Ben wrung his hands; he bowed his head, and heavy jolting sobs wrenched his body. He wasn't in for no such cutting up as all that. The devil must of got in Bundy before he died. What could he do now with that eye on him? Ben bowed lower.

"Oh, Lord Jesus," he said, crying.

A powerful elbow punched his ribs, and Ben raised his head without opening his eyes.

"What's the matter, nigger, don't you want to be free?"

Ben stopped sobbing, thought a long moment.

"I don't know," he said.

Gabriel was talking again by now.

"This the way how you line up: Ditcher's the head man of all y'-all from across the branch. Gen'l John is going to –"

He stopped talking for a moment. A little later he whispered, "Who that coming across that field?"

"Marse Prosser."

"It is, hunh? Well, strike up a song, Martin."

They began moaning softly. The voices rose bit by bit, a full wave. Again there was the same swaying of bodies, the same shouts punctuating the song. Gabriel faced the west, his hands locked behind him, his varnished coachman's hat tilted forward. Ben fell on his face crying. It became quite dark.

12

Melody watered the pot plants between the green shutters of her upstairs window. A lock of the enameled black hair fell against her cheek and the large earrings jangled beneath the rose-colored headcloth. General John came around from the back, passed beneath the window and walked toward the river road. There was no bounce in his stride, but he stepped briskly and walked with an air of great importance despite his hopeless rags. He was the busiest man in Richmond.

Three languid blacks lolled in front of the *Dirty Spoon,* one on a chair tilted against the brick wall, one on the doorstep and one standing with legs crossed and hands thrust into the pockets of tattered jeans. There was only the ghost of a breeze in the bright, quiet morning, but the old lamp post swayed in its place a few steps from the door of the wine shop. A tall three-master, its canvas all in, rocked against the river wharf.

General John purchased the wine for which he had been sent and hurried back to Melody's upstairs rooms. She poured him a drink in a tumbler. He stood at the head of the back steps, his mashed-up hat in his hand, and tossed it off.

"Well, if you ain't got nothing else for me to do, I reckon I'll trot along, Miss Melody."

"No need to hurry, Gen'l John. You can sit on the bench under my fig tree and rest yourself some."

He looked at her earnestly.

"Can't rest," he said. "Leastwise, not yet nohow."

She had a slow eye, that yellow woman called Melody. She had finished her sweeping and dusting, and she stood against the door in her billowing furbelows.

"It's mighty funny about you and Gabriel getting so busy all of a sudden."

"It ain't nothing, Miss Melody. Just I'm got to see a friend of mine about something another this morning."

"I ain't seen that Gabriel standing still since I-don't-know-when."

"A brown gal named Juba – that's all."

"His head been mighty low for a nigger what's got the gal he wants. You better tell me right, Gen'l John. You and Gabriel got something up yo' sleeve."

"Just thinking, maybe," he said. "Just thinking how it would feel to be free, I reckon."

57

"See there. You been talking to that Philadelphia lawyer, ain't you?"

General John shook his head.

"I ain't talked to no white man about nothing," he said. "But you couldn't on'erstand like us. Things ain't the same with you. You's free."

"I got a good mind how you feels," she said. Then after a pause, "That ain't telling me howcome you always keeps so busy, though."

General John just grinned a wide crooked-toothed grin.

"I'm got to trot along."

He hurried down the stairs and around the house to the street.

Suddenly Melody thought of something. She ran through her rooms to the front window and called down to General John.

"Wait a minute," she said.

She went quickly to a table and dipped a quill into an ink pot. Then she began writing hastily on a sheet of note paper. When she had finished and sealed the brief missive, she returned to the window and tossed it down to General John.

"Mail it?" he asked.

"No, leave it with M. Creuzot at his printing shop. Ask him if he will deliver it, please."

"H'm."

She remained at the window, watching the old black man out of sight.

13

The days were not long enough now. Gabriel and a young fellow called Blue went to get Ben at night. They left a group whispering on the floor of a hut, crept silently down a corn row, climbed a fence and went over a low hill. Then, finding a wagon path beneath a line of poplars, they walked another half-mile.

Ben was not in his cabin yet, so they started up toward the big house and met him on the path.

"Did Criddle give you the word?" Gabriel said.

Ben quaked.

"Yes, he been here."

"Well, ain't you coming?"

"I reckon so. But I ain't fit for a lot of cutting up now. I ain't young like y'-all."

"Don't you want to be free, fool," Blue said.

"I reckon I does."

"You *reckon*?"

"Listen," Gabriel said, "you ain't got to fight none. We got something else for you to do. Come along."

Ben walked between the other two.

Solomon, General John and Ditcher lay on their bellies in the hut. They were whispering with their faces near the dirt floor. Gabriel and Blue came in with Ben. No greetings, no useless words passed. The three got down and made a circle. An eery blue light pierced a crack in the wall, separated the dull silhouettes. No preliminary words, no Biblical extenuations preceded the essential plans this time. Ben knelt beside Gabriel and saw the huge young coachman touch the earth with his extended index finger.

"Listen. All the black folks'll j'ine us when we get our power. This here thing'll spread like fire. That's howcome we's sending Gen'l John down to Petersburg. He's aiming to get up a crowd there and start kicking up dust directly after we done made our attack. We want Ben to go to Caroline County. Him and Gen'l John can get off and travel 'thout nobody thinking nothing. They's old and trusted-like. Nothing much they going to have to do; just be there to tell folks what's what when the time come.

"But the main plan is right here. We going to meet at

59

the Brook Swamp where the creek go through the grove. On'erstand? There ought to be about eleven hundred of us by then. Mingo's got the names. We going to divide in three lines. One'll go on each side the town; one'll take the old penitentiary what they's using for a arsenal (they ain't but a handful of guards there), and the left wing'll hit at the powder house. The third band is the one that carries the guns and the best of the pikes and blades. Them's the ones that's got to hit the town in the middle and mop up. They ain't going to spare nothing what raises its hand – nothing. By daybreak, and maybe befo', every one of us'll have a musket and all the bullets and powder we can shoot. The arsenal is busting open with ammunition.

"The middle column is going to break in two so it can come in town from both ends at the same time. They's been some talk about not hurting the French folks. We'll find out about that later on. But we's aiming to make one of the biggest fires these here white folks is ever seen. Ditcher and Blue is captains of them two lines, and we can let them carry all the guns we got, all the scythe-swords, all the pikes, everything like that. I'm leading the wing what goes after the arsenal. That's a touchy spot. Everything hangs on that. But we can take it with sticks about as well as we could with guns. We got to move on cat feet there and take the guards by surprise. We got to be all around them like shadows, snatching the guns out of they hands and bashing they skulls with sticks. Solomon will take the powder house the same way."

Ben tried hard to keep his lips moist, but they kept drying up like paper. His breath made so much noise he felt ashamed. He imagined the others were listening to it and judging him harshly. Suddenly there were tears in his eyes and a moment later he cried audibly, his face in his hands.

"I can't do it," he said. "Lordy, it's killing and murder and burning down houses. I can't do it."

Gabriel turned sternly, paused and then spoke.

"It's the onliest way. Besides, I reckon that wa'n't murder when Marse Prosser kilt old Bundy."

Ben sniffled and became silent again. The picture of that scrawny old good-humored ghost squatting near his fat jug came into his mind again and his flesh quaked, but he made no other sound. Then there was another man in his thoughts, too, a man whose feet they hurt with fetters, according to the Book, who was laid in irons – *until the time that his word came.*

Curiously, at the same instant Gabriel said, "This here is the time. There ain't no backing up now. Is you going to Caroline County or must we get somebody else?"

"I reckon I'm going," Ben said faintly.

"Well, that's settled. Gen'l John is carrying the money. He'll give you some for expense. We got a peck of bullets and about a dozen scythe-swords now. Solomon's fixing these in the blacksmith shop and I'm making the handles. They'll do the work."

"We need mo' weapons," Blue said.

"We can have them too," Gabriel answered. "But we don't need many's you reckon. They ain't mo'n twenty-three muskets in the town, and we ain't going to give them time to put they hands on them what they's got. What's mo' God's going to fight them because they oppresses the poor. Mingo read it in the Book and you heard it same as me."

"H'm."

They all murmured. Their assent, so near the ground, seemed to rise from the earth itself. H'm. There was something warm and musical in the sound, a deep tremor. It was the earth that spoke, the fallen star.

Ben's eyes burned for sleep. He went from window to window raising blinds and throwing open shutters, but there was no sun and the handsome high-ceilinged rooms remained dull and cheerless. Ben was tortured with the vision of filthy black slaves coming suddenly through those windows, pikes and cutlasses in their hands, their eyes burning with murderous passion and their feet dripping mud from the swamp. He saw the lovely hangings crash, the furniture reel and topple, piece by piece, and he saw the increasing black host storm the stairway. In another moment there were quick, choked cries of the dying, followed by wild jungle laughter. Then it occurred to Ben which side he was on, and he covered his eyes with his hand. It was going to be an impossible thing for him to do, a desecrating, sinful thing.

14

M. Creuzot stopped in the open door of Mingo's saddleshop. Outside a horse hitched to a small buck wagon was tied to the crossbar. The printer rested his musket and held a wild turkey up for the free Negro to inspect.

"He one mo' beauty," Mingo said, passing his hand over the enameled feathers. "Where'bouts you shoot him, Mistah Creuzot?"

"Out on the creek. I prefer duck, but you don't see many of them this early."

"I reckon not. They start coming this way about October."

"Yes, or possibly later. I want to hang the bird behind your shop here, Mingo. When Laurent comes, I'll have him carry it home."

"Yes, suh. Help yo'self," Mingo said.

"Thanks."

M. Creuzot went out into the small yard behind. Weeds were tall, and there was a rubbish pile that had grown remarkably. He tied the feet of his turkey to a hook as high as he could reach on the wall. Mingo was busy with an awl when he returned.

"How about leaving that there musket here a few days

too?" the Negro suggested.

"Well, I don't mind. You want to try your luck?"

"H'm. I might."

"You'll have to get some small shot."

When he was gone, something Alexander Biddenhurst had said occurred to M. Creuzot. The blacks are whispering ... something's up. Suddenly, and for the first time, the Frenchman seriously wondered if there were reason for the observation. Actually, *could* it be? Could these tamed things imagine, liberty, equality? Of course, he knew about San Domingo, many stories had filtered through, but whether or not the blacks themselves were capable of that divine discontent that turns the mill of destiny was not answered. There had been, or so he had been told, strong forces at work in France; there had possibly been paid and experienced agitators supported by groups of people who sometimes had political as well as humanitarian aims. Young mulattos had been to Paris to school and had met certain of the *Amis des Noirs* ... M. Creuzot found the long thread tiresome. The blacks were not discontented: they couldn't be. They were without the necessary faculties.

He let himself into his printing shop, picked up two small jobs that had been slipped under the door with written instructions and went to the back windows to let in light and air. The morning was fine, and a shaft of yellow sun fell across the room. M. Creuzot tied on his ink-spattered apron and began clearing the composing stone.

Laurent looked drowsy when he came in a little later. His hair had not been combed and the queer little cap seemed ready to fall at any moment.

"Shame," said M. Creuzot. "You look as if you could hardly drag your feet. And such a fine morning it is. Why, I've been out to the grove and shot a turkey already."

"I didn't sleep well," Laurent said weakly.

"Too much rum?"

"No, I only took a trifle."

"That was too much. Did you see Biddenhurst last night?"

"Yes, it was he that bought the drink."

"Well, I hope you reminded him that we have a note for him here."

"He said he'd be by this morning. Where's the turkey?"

"Hanging behind Mingo's saddle-shop. I want you to carry it home for me when you deliver that job to the greengrocer on our corner."

A little later M. Creuzot looked up from the job he was locking in the form. Laurent had taken his place on a stool in front of his case and his fingers were darting rapidly.

"I keep remembering what Biddenhurst said about the Africans."

"They do whisper a lot," Laurent said. "Has some one else mentioned the same thing?"

"No, I don't know what put it in my mind."

They became silent again, but after a short time M. Creuzot did conclude what suggested the thought to him. It must have been Mingo. He had thought about it first when leaving the saddle-shop. Mingo had mentioned or inferred nothing suspicious, of course; it must have been his asking to use the musket. That *was* it. M. Creuzot rejoiced to trace his thought successfully to its source.

It would surely be a grave thing for Alexander Biddenhurst, following his bold quotations from Voltaire and other makers of the French Revolution, should discontent be manifest among the proletariat and particularly among the blacks. They bore so many insults that might call forth horrible retaliation. It would be miserable for Laurent, whom the town boys already, quite absurdly, called a Jacobin. The ground might even get hot under the feet of M. Creuzot and his friend the dancing master, what with the Presidential election approaching and with the Federalist press accusing the party of Thomas Jefferson of getting its philosophy from the *States-Général* and inclining very radically toward the left. No Federalist paper, wishing to win votes, missed an opportunity to hurl the anathema of that dreaded word *Jacobin* into the air. They didn't bother to analyze or define carefully. They were glad to have the public catch the misleading implications they had succeeded in putting into the term: redistribution of wealth, snatching of private property, elevation of the blacks, equality, immediate and compulsory miscegenation. The masses were pitifully abused and frightened, M. Creuzot thought. But the fact that he had a more temperate burden for their rise than had Alexander Biddenhurst would help him little in a moment of general passion. The same mark was on him. He was sorry that he had let Mingo have his gun; it gave him unpleasant thoughts, made him nervous. He would get it back as soon as possible.

The writing on the envelope was an illiterate scrawl. Alexander Biddenhurst read the misspelled name, smiled and dropped it into his pocket.

"It is just for laughter, M. Creuzot. Nothing important."

The sunlight was so fine in the back of the shop that Biddenhurst removed his coat, took a chair beneath the window and opened his book. A customer came in and engaged M. Creuzot in the front doorway. Biddenhurst read from his book with quiet absorption.

Man is a stranger to his own research;
He knows not whence he comes, nor whither goes.
Tormented atoms in a bed of mud,
Devoured by death, a mockery of fate;
But thinking atoms, whose far-seeing eyes,
Guided by thoughts, have measured the faint stars.
Our being mingles with the infinite;
Ourselves we never see, nor come to know.
This world, this theatre of pride and wrong,
Swarms with sick fools who talk of happiness . . .
Seeking a light amid the deepening gloom. . . .

15

Brothers and Friends:

I am Toussaint l'Ouverture; my name is perhaps known to you. I have undertaken to avenge your wrongs. It is my desire that liberty and equality shall reign. I am striving to this end. Come and unite with us, brothers, and combat with us for the same cause.

Your very humble and obedient servant,
Toussaint l'Ouverture,
General for the Public Welfare.

The brown girl curled on the floor in front of the circle of men. Mingo sat on a stool; the others had drawn up benches, work tables and boxes. They were meeting in the saddle-shop because Mingo had said, "Never twice in the same place – on'erstand? Here this time and somewheres else the next."

"That's enough reading this time," Gabriel said. "We going to have all the help we needs once we get our hands in. It's most nigh time to strike, and we got to make haste."

Gabriel, silent and dreamy usually, spoke with a quick excitement these days. There was an urgency in his manner that got under the skin at once. He didn't talk in a loud voice; in fact, he didn't talk at all. He simply whispered. Yet Ditcher's mouth dropped open as he listened; he leaned forward and the muscles tightened on his shoulders. His huge hands, dangling at his sides, closed gradually and gradually opened again. He was ready to strike. Blue, hearing every word, pulled the heavy lips over his large protruding teeth, hunched himself somberly on his box. General John Scott, as scrawny and ragged as a scarecrow, rubbed his brown bark-like hands together, blinked nervously. Ben, wearing gloves, stood with a new Sunday hat in his hand, his head bowed. Some of the group trembled. They were all ready.

They had come into the shop through the back way.

They had selected this place for their Sunday gathering because the shops on either side were closed and they were able to feel safely secluded.

"What's going to be the day?" Ditcher said.

"The first day in September," Gabriel told him.

"That falls on a Sad-dy," a pumpkin-colored fellow said quietly.

General John showed his brown fangs without malevolence.

"Sad-dy, hunh?"

"Yes, the first day of September come next Sad-dy," Ben said.

"I's just thinking," the yellow Negro muttered. "I's just thinking it might be better to strike on a Sunday."

"Howcome that?" Gabriel asked.

"Well, it's just like today. The country folks can leave home and travel mo' better on a Sunday. Nobody's going to ask where they's going or if they's got a note. That's what I's thinking. Sunday's a mo' better day for the back-country folks to get together."

"We don't need none of them what lives that far in the country – not right now nohow. We done set Sad-dy for the day and Sad-dy it's going to be – hear? We got all the mens we need to hit the first lick right round here close."

"Well, I reckon maybe that's right too. That other was just something what come in my head."

"This what *you* got to remember, Pharoah: You's leaving for Caroline County with Ben next Sad-dy evening. You can send word up by the boys going that a-way so everything'll be in shape. We going to write up something like that what Mingo read from Toussaint, soon's we get our power, and you ain't got to do nothing up there but spread the news. Them's all our brothers. I bound you they'll come when they hears the proclamation."

"H'm. They'll come," General John said. "They'll come soon's they hears what we's done."

Ben turned the new Sunday hat round and round in

his hands. He was nervous and tremulous again. He turned General John's words in his mind: They'll come. Any thing wants to be free. Well, Ben reckoned so; yet and still, it seemed like some folks was a heap mo' anxious about it than others. It was true that they were brothers – not so much because they were black as because they were the outcasts and the unwanted of the land – and for that reason he followed against his will. Then, too, there was old Bundy buried in the low field and that something else that squatted by the hole where he lay.

"They'll come," Ben echoed weakly. "Anything wants to be free – I reckon."

"You mighty right," Gabriel whispered. "Some of y'-all can commence leaving now. Remember just two by two, and don't go till the ones in front of you is had time to get round the square. That's right, Criddle, you and George. You two go first. Ben and Pharoah – you next. Keep moving and don't make no fuss."

Now they were getting away slowly. They were slipping down the ally by twos and the saddle-shop was emptying gradually. Gabriel stood above the thin-waisted brown girl, his foot on the edge of the bench, one elbow on his knee.

"It's a man's doings, Juba. You ain't obliged to keep following along."

"I hears what you say."

"The time ain't long, and it's apt to get worse and worser."

"H'm."

"And it's going to be fighting and killing till you can't rest, befo' it's done."

"I know," she said.

"And you still wants to follow on?"

"Yes."

"Well, it ain't for me to tell you no, gal."

"I'm in it. Long's you's in it, I'm in it too."

"And it's win all or lose all – on'erstand?"

"I'm in it. Win all or lose all."

Mingo stood by listening. His spectacles had slipped down on his nose. He had a thin face for a black and a high receding forehead. He listened to Gabriel's words and Juba's short answers and tried to tear himself away. Somehow he couldn't move. It was win all or lose all. He became pale with that peculiar lavender paleness that comes to terrified black men. There was death in the offing, death or freedom, but until now Mingo had thought only in terms of the latter. The other was an ugly specter to meet.

He looked at Gabriel's face, noted the powerful resolution in his expression. Sometimes, he thought, the unlearned lead the learned and teach them courage, teach them to die with a handsome toss of the head. He looked at Juba and saw that she was bewitched. She would indeed follow to the end. He was a free Negro and these were slaves, but somehow he envied them. Suddenly a strange exaltation came to his mind.

"Yes," he said, breaking into their conversation. "It's win all or lose all. It's a game, but it's worth trying and I got a good notion we can win. I'm free now, but it ain't no good being free when all yo' people's slaves, yo' wife and chilluns and all."

"A wild bird what's in a cage will die anyhow, sooner or later," Gabriel said. "He'll pine hisself to death. He just is well to break his neck trying to get out."

16

The pumpkin-colored mulatto was outside, standing beneath a willow tree near the back doorstep. Ben could see him from the kitchen window, and at first he was puzzled, but in a moment he recognized that it was Pharoah. He was a field-hand, that Pharaoh, and his jeans were encrusted with earth. He was obsequious beyond reason, and he had a wide, open-mouth smile and little obscure eyes like the eyes of a swine. He belonged to Marse Sheppard, but Ben saw him rarely.

Standing over the lamp table, cleaning chimneys with a silk cloth, Ben could watch him from the window without even rising on his tiptoes. Pharoah waited patiently in the dusk, his back against the willow, his hands in his pockets. And Ben could have gone out promptly, but he delayed. He felt certain that Pharoah had come on some mission connected with the bloody business just ahead, and for that reason Ben was in no hurry.

Drucilla was at the stove, her head tied in a cloth, bowing over a pot of something she was stirring with a long wooden spoon. Presently she went into the pantry for a pinch of salt, and Ben put down his lamp chimney and slipped out of doors. Pharoah began to grin and bow almost as if he had forgotten that it was not a white person who was approaching him.

"S-sorry, Uncle Ben," he said. "I didn't go to disturb you."

"You ain't disturbing me. What's on yo' mind?"

"Well, I been thinking a heap, Uncle Ben."

"Too late to be thinking now, ain't it?"

"I don't know if it is or if it ain't. I been thinking just the same. Is you going to let them send you up to Caroline County, Uncle Ben?"

Ben averted his face. Pharoah came a step nearer, his shoulders hunched, his mouth open.

"You heard the plan well as me. There ain't nothing else left for me *but* go."

"Gabriel's getting biggity," Pharoah said. "You ain't obliged to do *everything* he says, is you?"

"It'll be better going there than staying here. It'll be murder and killing here. Up there it'll just be – "

"I don't know," Pharoah said. "I can't help thinking sometimes, though. Here. Gabriel sent this here."

"Three shillings, hunh?"

"Yes. It's the money for our expense in Caroline County."

"Kind of skimpy change."

"That's what I been thinking. Gen'l John had a roll of bills in his old raggety pockets fit to choke a crocodile. They could of give us a little mo'n this."

Ben kept looking at Pharoah and trying to make out what he meant by talking that way. But he learned nothing. Pharoah just naturally seemed dissatisfied and peeved and possibly sorry he was involved in the plot at all.

"I reckon we can make out," Ben said absently. "When do we go?"

"Sad-dy evening, I reckon. That's the last thing Gabriel said at the meeting. We is supposed to get up a good crowd that'll rise up like a flock of sparrows in a wheat field soon's they get the news that Richmond's in Gabriel's hands."

"If we don't get no news, they don't rise up?"

"I reckon they don't." Then after a pause, "I wanted to lead a line into Richmond, me. Gabriel's so biggity he won't listen to nobody. He say I got to go with you."

"You can lead the Caroline County crowd," Ben said.

Suddenly twilight came to the trees behind the great house. The fat, pumpkin-colored Negro crossed the yard and followed the gravel carriage path out to the big road. Ben returned to the kitchen.

Ben placed the candles on the supper table and touched a small brass gong on the sideboard. He had an eye for niceties, that Ben, and he refrained from drawing the blinds against the blue dusk till Marse Sheppard and young Marse Robin were seated at the table. When grace had been said, he served the soup. This done, he hung his cloth neatly across his left wrist and made the rounds of the windows. Ben knew that that was as it should have been. He could even feel the warmth and security that came to Mr. Moseley Sheppard's supper table. Ben stood in a corner of the room, the white cloth on his wrist, his back against an old-rose hanging. There, without warning, the devil spoke to his mind.

What cause you got feeling sorry for a rich old white man that God don't even love? You ought to know them kind by now. They oppress the stranger, and they oppresses the poor. They kills the old horse when he gets wind-broke. Wa'n't it Marse Prosser that said it's cheaper to kill a wo'-out nigger than to feed him? Leastwise, he must of thought it if he didn't say it. He kilt old Bundy with his riding whip, stepped on him with his horse. Old rum-drinking Bundy with his spindle legs and his laughing and his cutting up. Lord, it was a shame; it was a shame befo' Jesus.

Robin waited for his father to finish his soup, and Ben promptly carried the two bowls into the kitchen. The food was ready; Drucilla was waiting, slightly provoked at the lazy tempo of things. Ben took the steaming platters out to the table. It was a routine that called for little thought. Yet in doing it he did reflect upon the trustfulness of masters who eat food prepared by servants they have despitefully used. Of course they had no reason to fear; he had heard of attempts by slaves to poison their masters, but he had never witnessed an instance. Well, it was good that folks couldn't read one another's minds. Yes, suh, and that wa'n't no lie. Ben returned to the kitchen when he had placed the food on the table. Once he came back with warm rolls and again with warm gravy, but he tried to be inconspicuous while the father and son talked across the platters and candles.

In the kitchen Drucilla's glossy round face became increasingly serious. Her forehead wrinkled.

"Marse Sheppard didn't clean his soup dish."

"No, he left some," Ben said.

"That ain't his way. He ain't supposed to turn away from no oyster soup."

"He ain't got the appetite he used to had. He ain't as young, I reckon."

72

"Maybe he ain't as well, neither. Them spells – "

A little later Ben went in with the sweet dish. Marse Sheppard looked at his and shook his head. Then while young Robin was at his, the old man pushed his chair back and started to rise. But something stopped him, a sudden weakness and a constriction near the base of his ribs on the left side. Robin didn't see it, didn't even raise his eyes, but Ben was by the old planter's side in a wink, saying nothing, but lending his arm and leading Marse Sheppard toward the staircase. They climbed the steps slowly, and Ben blinked with sorrow in his eyes.

He was playing out, Marse Sheppard was, like some old plush-covered music box running down. Yes, suh, his days was few and they was numbered. Ben was getting old too, but somehow he seemed to be lasting a little bit better, thanks the Lord. Nobody couldn't tell, though. He might kick the bucket hisself befo' long. Time didn't stand still. Funny too: it didn't seem long. Yet he had been a full-grown man when Marse Sheppard bought him from old Sol Woodfolk, and that was yonder about fifty year ago. Marse Sheppard had outlived two young wives since then, but he wouldn't outlive nara another two. No, nor one either.

It was right sad to think about it all. And it was going to be hard to go away to Caroline County and leave him like this. But it would be a heap better'n staying home and seeing the crowd of mad savages coming through the windows with scythe-swords and pikes. Lordy!

They reached the top of the stairs.

"I'm going to be all right," Marse Sheppard said. "Fix the candles."

"Yes, suh."

But Ben knew that when Marse Sheppard became so anxious about light in his room it was because he feared he *wasn't* going to be all right.

17

Alexander Biddenhurst hastily took the coach to Fredericksburg. Something was in the air. There was no longer room for doubt. It was leaving time. The Negroes were whispering, and some had whispered a bit too loudly. Nothing was certain, of course, but the prudent act for a stranger who had quoted Rousseau quite freely on the equality of man was to secure passage on the first public conveyance going north.

Laurent was outside, standing on the cobblestones when the horses pulled away. The stagecoach was filled, and there were other people at the junction for saying farewells. They bustled noisily in the street, waving handkerchiefs and, in one case at least, throwing kisses. There were two women with small bright parasols; they wore furbelows and little dainty hats that didn't cover the back of the head. There was a young man with white stockings and a three-cornered hat. And there were others, like Laurent, whose clothes were plain and whose appearance left no remarkable impression.

Laurent followed the footpath beneath the trees along the street. The dust was deep. It had powdered the trees, and Laurent recalled that there had been no drop of rain in more than seven weeks. The earth thirsted. Some small birds rested beneath a shrub, their wings hanging, their tiny throats quavering.

In the shop door he confronted the tall, gentle printer.

"Biddenhurst just took the stage to Fredericksburg."

"So? Is he returning directly?"

"Hardly. He said it was becoming unhealthy for him here."

M. Creuzot looked at his ruddy apprentice with a long puzzled gaze. Then his mouth dropped open. Laurent heard the breath wheezing between the older man's teeth.

"So there *is* something up?"

"He didn't say so to me, well, not as pointedly as that, anyway."

"He'd have no other reason to flee. He's gotten himself involved in mischief all right. Are you in it too, Laurent?"

"There is nothing that I know, nothing more than I've talked with you."

Again that look on M. Creuzot's face, that serious, intent gaze. But when he spoke finally, his voice was tired and it seemed that he would presently cry.

"Anything may happen, Laurent. They think we're Jacobins and revolutionaries. If the mob spirit is aroused, we'll just have to be ready for the worst."

The two went to the front window and looked out on the parched leaves and the dusty street. Heavy green flies boomed above a puddle of filth beside the nearest hitching bar. There were fiddles overhead, sounding through the trees that shaded M. Baptiste's dancing school.

"We're innocent, though," Laurent murmured. "We've done nothing to injure anyone."

"It's all the same. If they say we're Jacobins, that's quite enough to put them on us."

Alexander Biddenhurst reread Melody's letter as the stagecoach lumbered over the difficult road. The dust and heat made a vile journey of it, and the large woman and her handsome daughter, who shared the coach with the young lawyer and an older gentleman, kept their handkerchiefs before their faces most of the time. The traveling bags jostled in their carrier overhead. Disregarding the faces around him, Alexander Biddenhurst read:

I think you're right about what you said the other night. Something is up among the slaves. And if you been talking round town like you talked here when you was drinking I think you best to lay low till it quiets down. If anything was to happen somebody might be apt to blame you beingst your're a stranger and all and throw up to you all that book reading about the natural-born equality of men and all like of that I never did hear no such talking as that amongst the rich white men down here and I reckon as to how they'd hate it a plenty so don't come here again whilst all this whispering is going around and if you are bound and determined to stay in town and see it through it might be healthy to lay mighty low something is up amongst the colored folks and that's a fact as sure's you born. I never before seen them carrying on like now and I'm scared a little myself so don't come here again till it all blows over. Somebody is apt to start looking at me funny too. . . .

Biddenhurst folded his arms tightly when he settled back into his seat. If the town boys pelted Laurent with green apples and called him Jacobin just because he was a Frenchman with red hair, the men were likely to have little mercy on a stranger whom they suspected of inciting slaves to rise against their masters. It was definitely leaving time. Yet the signs were hopeful, in one way of thinking, Biddenhurst thought; there was a definite foment among the masses in this state. The revolution of the American proletariat would soon be something more than an idle dream. Soon the poor, the despised of the earth, would join hands around the globe; there would be no more serfs, no more planters, no more classes, no more slaves, only men.

The stagecoach lurched; dust poured in the open windows.

18

Nobody questioned Criddle's presence in the stable after dark. Even Marse Prosser, slapping his boots with a riding whip, went by without raising his head. But the domino spots in the boy's black face were like silver dollars now. Criddle set the lantern against a stanchion wall and crept into the next room. There he went to a loose floorboard that he knew by sound, removed it and, falling on his belly, ran his arm far back underneath and brought out a monstrous hand-made cutlass with a well-turned handle. Criddle got his hands on a whetstone, and in the dark alone he worked on the edge of his blade.

Everything what's equal to a ground hog want to be free, he thought.

Ditcher spat on the ground in the door of his cabin. A round orange moon confronted him on a low hill. He was without a shirt, and his jeans were frayed away at the knees. But he carried a driver's whip and wore leather bands on his wrists.

"Pretty night, woman," he said, addressing the moon.

A voice in the black hut said, "Yes, I reckon so."

A pause, the earth whispering, the thrashers speaking in the thickets.

"Tomorrow's our night, woman."

"Yes, I knows. You better be getting yo'self together, too."

"H'm. *You* better be having that there baby, you."

"Soon be daylight, son."

The dreamy mulatto boy was fishing in the creek. A few paces away sat his old black mammy. The moon was gone now.

"Yes, mammy."

"I'm going to cook you a breakfast what'll make yo' mouth water, dreamy boy."

"You always cooks good, mammy."

Silence, the earth whispering, the water lapping the bank with a black tongue . . . .

"What you thinking about, son?"

"A heap of things, mammy."

"You ain't fixing to go with Gabriel tomorrow night, is you?"

"I's just thinking, that's all. Didn't you ever want to be free, mammy? Didn't you ever wonder how you'd feel?"

"Hush, boy. Hush that kind of talk."

"Yes, mammy."

Mingo, the freed Negro, locked the door of his shop and said farewell to the stimulating odors of new saddles and leather trimmings. The whole adventure was going to be a plunge into the dark, he reasoned, but at least one thing was certain – nothing would be the same thereafter. The saddle-shop, if he returned to it again, would hold a new experience. His slave wife and children out on Marse Prosser's place – well, they could count on something different. It looked like win all or lose all to Mingo, but he was ready for the throw. Anything would be better than the sight of his own woman stripped and bleeding at a whipping post. Lordy, anything. He raised a hand to cover his eyes from the punishing recollection, but he failed to put by the memory of the woman's cries.

"Pray, massa; pray, massa – I'll do better next time. Oh, pray, massa."

Mingo locked his shop with a three-ounce key, turned away from the familiar door and hurried down the tree-shaded street. Nothing was going to be the same in the future, but anything would be better than Julie stripped and bleeding at a whipping post and the two little girls with white dresses and little wiry braids growing up to the same thing. Lord Jesus, anything would be better than that, anything.

"Well, here's where us parts company, boy," Blue said. He unhooked the mule's collar and slapped the critter's flank. "Kick up yo' heels if you's a-mind to. Sun's going down directly and it might not rise no mo'. Right here me and you parts company for keeps."

He tossed the harness on the barn floor and hurried down the path to the cabins. Fast moving clouds streaked the mauve sky. The other field Negroes were knocking off too; they followed the line of mules up the narrow path.

Blue tried to imagine how it would feel to be free. He could see himself, in his mind's eye, shooting ducks in the marsh when he should have been following a plow, riding in a public stagecoach with a cigar in his mouth, his clothes well-ordered, his queue neatly tied, drinking rum in a waterfront tavern, his legs crossed, one foot swinging proudly, but he couldn't imagine how it would feel.

"About time to stir now," he said aloud.

Old Catfish Primus was busy all day.

"Here, boy, tie this round yo' neck likea that – on'er-stand? It'll do the work. Leastwise, it'll do the work if somebody else ain't already put a bad hand on you."

"Thanks a heap, Old Primus. What I really needs is a black cat bone, but it's too late to get one now."

"Ne'mind, this'll do the work. This a fighting 'hand.' You heard tell about a money hand, a gambling hand, a woman hand and all like of that to help a man out? Well, this fighting hand is just the thing now. I don't reckon nobody else is done put a bad hand on none of y'-all."

"Thanks a heap."

"You other boys – you want the same kind?"

"Same kind, Catfish."

"Well, wait outside then."

"Us ain't got long to wait."

"I knows. Look kinda like rain, don't it?"

"H'm. Mind out what you's doing there, Old Primus. Don't get yo' conjur mixed up, hear?"

"Hush, boy."

"Well, I just don't want no hand to make the womens love me when I needs to be fighting. That's all."

The streaks moved faster and faster across the sky. Then suddenly there were flashes playing on the rushing clouds. Araby whimpered, his lovely head at the open window of his stall. He was bridled and ready. The stables were peopled with shadows slipping from place to place.

Outside a few dry leaves were gathered up in a quick swirl. They danced for a moment like tiny wretched ghosts on the barn roof, then fled.

There was a girl's hand on the colt's bridle.

She wore a shiny pair of men's riding boots and a cut-off skirt that failed to reach her knees.

"Not yet," she said, seeking the colt's forelock. "Not yet, boy."

A taller shadow bowed its head and entered the door.

"You, Juba?"

"H'm."

"I's just seeing was everything ready."

"Everything ready," she said.

"Good. I'll be back directly, then."

Gabriel hurried out. The lightning crackled around him like the sound of a young pine fire. The clouds were growing darker.

19

A little rain won't hurt none," Gabriel kept saying. "Let it rain, if that's what it's up to. A little rain won't hurt and it might can help some."

Presently it was full night, full night with heavy clouds scudding up the sky.

Rain or no rain, wet or dry, it was all the same to Juba. That brown gal wasn't worried. She sat astride Araby's bare back, her fragmentary skirt curled about her waist, her naked thighs flashing above the riding boots, leaned forward till her face was almost touching the wild mane and felt the warm body of the colt straining between her clinched knees.

Out from behind the stable, across a field, down a shaded lane, over a low fence and across another field and she came to the big road. The gangling young horse, warming to the gait, beat a smooth rhythm with his small porcelain feet. Juba heard the footfalls now, heard the sweet muffled clatter on the hardened earth and her breathing became quick and excited. It occurred to her benumbed mind that she was giving the sign.

Those were not shadows running down to the roadside, pausing briefly and then darting back into the thickets. Those were not shadows, merely. Juba knew better. She understood.

Y'-all see me, every lasting one of you. And you knows what this here means. Gabriel said it plain. Dust around now, you old big-foot boys. Get a move on. Remember how Gabriel say it: you got to go on cat feet. You got to get around like the wind. Quick. On'erstand? Always big-talking about what booming bed-men you is. Always trying to turn the gals' heads like that. Well, let's see what you is good for sure 'nough. Let's see if you knows how to go free; let's see if you knows how to die, you big-footses, you.

There it was now – thunder. Yes, and rain too. There it was, a sudden spray in her face, a few big broken drops.

Araby tossed his head, nickered, caught his second wind and bounded forward like a creature drunk with pleasure. His heart was a leaf.

BOOK TWO

Hand me Down
my Silver Trumpet

1

They were going against Richmond with eleven hundred men and one woman. They were gathering like
shadows at the Brook Swamp. Through the relentless
downpour there went the motley rattle of their scythe-
swords and the thump of bludgeons hanging from their
belts.

The ghostly insurrectionaires raked wet leaves overhead with pikes that stood against their shoulders. They
splashed water ankle-deep in the honey-locust grove.

"A little rain won't hurt none," Gabriel said, his back
against a sapling.

"No, I reckon it won't," Martin whispered. "Yet and still, it might be a sign, mightn't it?"

"Sign of what?"

"I don't know. Bad hand or something like that, maybe."

"Humph! Whoever heard tell about rain being a sign of a bad hand against you?"

Martin's voice faded into the slosh of water, the swish and thrum in the treetops and the rattle of home-made side arms. Bare feet churned the mud. One of the Negroes with an extremely heavy voice had a barking cough on his chest. All of them were restless; they kept plop-plopping like cattle in a bog. Now and again a flash brightened their drenched bodies.

Near Gabriel, beneath the next tree, the thin-waisted girl sat like a statue on the black colt. Her wet hair had tightened into a savage bush. She still wore Marse Prosser's high riding boots, but above her knees her thighs were wet and gleaming. She sat rapt, only the things she had fastened to her ears moving.

"How many's here?" Gabriel asked.

"Near about fo'-hundred."

"Some of them's slow coming."

"The rain's holding them back, I reckon."

"They needs to get a move on. Time ain't waiting and the rain ain't fixing to let up. Leastwise, it don't seem like it is."

"It's getting worser. We going to have a time crossing the branches between here and town if we don't start soon."

"You better go on back with the other womens, gal; you's apt to catch yo' death out in all this water."

"Anybody what's studying about freedom is apt to catch his death, one way or another, ain't he?"

"But it's a men-folks' job just the same. It ain't a fitten way for womens to die."

Thunder broke and a fresh shower began before the old one had diminished. Presently another followed and again another, like waves succeeding waves on a tortured reef. The invisible Negroes milled more and more restlessly in the sloppy grove.

"I don't aim to go back, though."

Gabriel knew how to answer that. He decided to forget the matter.

"Ditcher and his crowd ain't here yet," he said.

"It's the rain, I reckon."

"We got to get started just the same. It ain't good to wait. Some of them'll start talking about signs and one thing and another. We got to keep on the move now we's here. Martin. You Martin!"

The older brother wasn't far away. He came near enough to whisper.

"You 'spect it's too much water tonight, Gabriel?"

"Too much water for what?"

"I's just thinking maybe Ditcher and the country crowd's hemmed in. Them creeks out that a-way might be too deep and swift to cross after all this."

"Well *we's* here. There's near about fo'-hundred of us, and we'll go without the others if they don't come soon. You and Solomon and Blue line them up. Find Criddle and send him here. We got to get a move on. There's creeks for us 'tween here and town, and I bound you there's high water in them too. Hush all the talking and make everyone stand still for orders. Hurry. Get Criddle first."

Martin was gone, splashing a lot of water.

"What line you want me in?" Juba said.

"You can take Ditcher's place till he come. Araby'll be something for the line to follow.

"That you, Criddle?"

"Yes, this here me."

"You know your first job?"

"H'm. That little old house this side of town."

"That's it. Just stay in the yard till the line pass by. There's a old po' white man there that's apt to jump on his horse and start waking up the town folks do he hear us passing. You stay in the yard till the line get by – on'er-stand?"

"H'm. I on'erstands."

"Well, light out then. You's going to wait there for us. If anything happen, you's got yo' blade and you oughta know by now what you got it for. Blue –"

"I'm right here."

"Get my crowd in line. We got to lead the way – hear?"

"They's ready."

"Well and good then. That you, Martin?"

"Yes, this me."

"Why in the nation don't you hurry and get yo' crowd in line?"

"Some of them's thinking maybe all this here thunder and lightning and rain's a sure 'nough bad sign."

"Listen. Listen, all y'-all." Gabriel raised his voice, turn-ing around in excitement. "They ain't a lasting man no-wheres ever heard tell of rain being a sign of a bad hand or nothing else. If any one of you's getting afeared, he can tuck his tail and go on back. I'm going to give the word directly, and them what's coming can come, and them what ain't can talk about signs. Thunder and lightning ain't nothing neither. If it is, I invites it to try me a barrel." He put out a massive chest, struck it a resounding smack. "Touch me if you's so bad, Big Man." A huge roar filled the sky. The lightning snapped bitterly. Gabriel roared with laughter, slapping his chest again und again. "Sign, hunh! Is y'-all ready to come with me?"

"We's ready," Blue said.

There was a strong murmur of assent. Then a pause, waiting for the orders. The colt whinneyed and the thin rider pulled him around so that his face was away from the force of the rain.

"Remember, we's falling on them like eagles. We's hush-ing up everything what opens its mouth – all but the French folks. We ain't aiming to miss, neither, but if anything *do* go wrong, there won't be no turning back. The mountains is the only place for us then." No one spoke. After a pause he turned to the girl. "Juba, I reckon you could hurry back and see for sure is Ditcher and his crowd coming. Tell them we's starting down the creek and they can meet us at the first crossing place."

Araby wheeled, sloshing water noisily, hastened away. Lightning played on the girl's wet garment. Solomon's voice came out of a pocket of darkness.

"We's waiting for the word," he said.

"Stay ready," Gabriel told him. "I'm going to give it directly."

2

Nothing like it had happened before in Virginia. The downpour came first in swirls; then followed diagonal blasts that bore down with withering strength. The thirsting earth sucked up as much water as it could but presently spewed little slobbery streams into the wrinkles of the ground. Small gullies took their fill with open mouths and let the rest run out. Rivulets wriggled in the wheel paths, cascaded over small embankments. The creeks grew fat. Water rose in the swamps and in the low fields, and gradually Henrico County became a sea with islands and bays, reefs and currents and atolls.

Cattle, knee-deep in their stalls, set up a vast lamentation. An old sow, nursing her young in a puddle of slime, let out a sudden prolonged wail and scampered into a hay mow with her eleven pigs. Down by a barn fence a lean and sullen mule stood with lowered head, his hinder parts lashed tender by the storm. A flock of speckled chickens went down screaming when the wind whipped off a peach bough.

General John Scott stood in a barn door with a lantern in his hand. He wore a frayed overcoat with sleeves that covered his hands and a wet, fallen-down hat with a brim that covered his eyes. His light hollowed out an orange hole in the blackness, and into it rain poured.

"Here I'm is," the old slave muttered. "'tween the earth and the sea and the sky, and how I'm going to get the rest of the way to Richmond to catch the stagecoach is mo'n a nachal man can tell."

The door flew open and a gust like a bucket of water slopped into his face.

Well, suh, if this here storm ain't the beatingest thing yet. Just when everybody was all fixed and fitten to go, here comes a plague of rain to put the whole country-side under water. Now how in the nation is folks going to get together? Lordy, Lordy. Listen, Lordy. You remember about the chillun of Israel, don't you? Well, this here is the very same thing perzactly... The Lord was on their side, sure as you're born, but some of his ways was mysterious plus.

Another bucket of water splashed in the General's face.

"Confound this tarnation door," he said aloud. "It keep on blowing open. This here rain don't let up directly, I'm going to light out walking again anyhow."

In a thicket on the edge of town wind raked the shingles of a small log house. The undersized cabin, hidden in a tangle of wild plum, columbine and honeysuckle, squatted like a hurt thing under a bush. A light burned inside one of the tiny rooms.

Grisselda stood at the window in an outing night-dress that covered her feet. She held a lamp so that it would throw a small beam into the yard. Presently the withered voice of her old father came out of the little dark chamber beyond the kitchen.

"You ain't scairt of the wind, air ye, Grisselda?"

"Oh, no. I don't mind the wind, papa."

"Well, why don't you blow the lamp out then?"

"I was just going to blow it out, papa."

She returned to the high bed. In a moment she was again

conscious of the old man's snoring. She lay very still, hearing beams groan after the gusts and squalls. Her face must have been flushed; it felt very warm. Suddenly she heard the thing again and the sound brought her bolt upright in the bed. It was a noise the rain could not make, a tearing of twigs that was unlike wind, and Grisselda knew that if it were not a living creature, it was the very beast of ill weather. She waited and heard it rubbing against the house, something heavier than a cat, something with softer feet than a yearling, a more elastic body than a dog. And the girl would have sprung from the bed and rushed into the kitchen screaming, but at that moment the breath was out of her and she could not move.

For many moments she was sitting there imagining the kind of things that might seek a tangled thicket off the big road on a night like this. A panther? A thug? Was the creature hiding or prowling? What would he seek in the cabin of a widowed old man and his young daughter, destitute white folks who were poorer than blacks slaves?

Grisselda remembered that she was sixteen now; she knew why a young farmer had noticed the color of her hair and why the middle-aged storekeeper had recently pinched her cheek. A lewd word dropped into her thought like a pebble falling into a well. She curled her feet uneasily, but in the next moment she was cold with fear again. The thing seemed to be setting its weight against the door. Grisselda sprang from the bed and ran into the kitchen.

"Papa!"

"Still prowling, air ye?"

"Didn't you hear nothing at all papa?"

"God bless me, who could help hearing a storm like this?"

"Not that – something in the yard, something against the door?"

"Against the door, hunh?"

She put a hand on the table and felt her own quaking for the first time. The old man murmured something. They waited.

3

It was going to be like hog-killing day. Criddle had a picture in his mind; he remembered the feel of warm blood. He knew how it gushed out after the cut. He remembered the stricken eyes. Then more blood, thicker and deeper in color. Criddle knew.

The only difference was that hogs were killed on a wintry day nearer the end of the year. Hog-killing required weather that was cold enough to chill the meat but not cold enough to freeze it. On such a morning three stakes were driven into the earth and bound at the top to form a tripod. From the apex a fat, corn-fed swine was suspended by his hind feet. After a very few moments, exhausted by struggle, the blood forced down into his head, he was ready for the blade.

Criddle knew how to hush their squeals: for a long time that had been his job. It was right funny too, the way Marse Prosser always called on him to use the knife. But it wasn't hard; you just stuck the knife in where that big vein comes down the throat; you gave the blade a turn and it was all over. Hog-killing wasn't a bad preparation for tonight's business.

"I'm going to start in right here, me."

He had lost the path, so it was necessary to tear a way through the undergrowth. Later there appeared a lighted window in the house and that helped. In his bare feet and naked chest Criddle felt as drenched and slick as a frog. When he reached the yellow patch of light, he squatted silently beneath a bush and paused to make up his mind about several small details. It was then that he noticed the face beside the lamp.

He passed a thumb meditatively down the edge of his scythe-sword and derived an unaccountable pleasure from the thought of thrusting it through the pale young female that stood looking into the darkness with such a disturbed face. Yet she looked flower-like and beautiful to him there, and Criddle, though he didn't know his own mind, was sure he meant the girl no harm. She reminded him of a certain indentured white girl in town, a girl who made free with the black slaves of the same master and woke up one morning with a chocolate baby. That wasn't the kind of cutting he was up against tonight, though. Yet and still, there *were* similarities. The domino spots brightened.

Listen here, church, y'-all white folks better stay in yo' seats and look nice. They ain't going to be no wringing and twisting this night. Anything what's equal to a gray squirrel want to be free. That's what kind of business this here is. Us ain't sparing nothing, nothing what raises its hand. The good and the bad goes together this night, the pretty and the ugly. We's going to be as hard as God his-self. That's right, gal; you just as well to blow out that lamp. It'll help you get used to the dark. That's about the very best thing for you now.

The rain was almost taking his breath there under the bush. Could he really hurt that girl? Could he make his hands do it? Well, they had nobody to blame but them-selves. Had no business buying and selling humans like hogs and mules. That rain! Criddle darted over to the house, crept along the rough, mud-plastered walls and came around to the door. There was a tiny ledge over-head; it offered a partial shelter. He wondered how long he would have to wait for the columns with Gabriel lead-ing them.

The road passed near the house. There was a rise just above the clump through which he had wormed his way, and over it the road passed. But there were other ways to town, and the old farmer, detecting the black rabble, could easily beat the lines into town by leaping on a horse. He would be sure to hear them on the road. Somebody would be sure to talk too loud. But the lucky thing about it all was that these possibilities had been provided for. Criddle could visualize a small, ineffectual old man squirming on the end of his sword. He leaned against the door, laughing. Then abruptly he became silent.

What was that sound? Voices inside?

The black stable boy stepped back a stride, faced the door coldly and waited. Don't you come out here, Mistah Man. If you does, you ain't going nowheres. On'erstand? You ain't carrying no news to town this night.

He held his sword arm tense; the scythe blade rose, stiffened, stiffened and remained erect.

"I'm going to start in right here, me."

4

Mr. Moseley Sheppard enjoyed a good rainstorm as much as anybody, but his enjoyment of this one was tempered by the thought that possibly it would prove more costly than he could afford. Then there was this cursed wind. Though the windows were closed, he noticed that Ben found it difficult to keep a flame on his wicks.

"Is it still in your head to make that trip you spoke to me about, Ben?"

"Yes, suh – please you, Marse Sheppard."

The old planter moved a window drape aside. Two fingers of the other hand went into the pocket of his satin waistcoat. Ben was laying kindling for a small fire. The night hadn't turned cold, but with such sloppy weather outside the house seemed damp and uncomfortable.

"You shouldn't do it, though. It's not a fit night for ducks, much less people."

"Niggers ain't people, Marse Sheppard."

"I won't argue that with you. They cost a lot of money just the same. If I did right, I wouldn't let you expose yourself like that."

"That's a fact for true," Ben agreed. "Yet and still, them grown gal young-uns of mine ain't seen me in I don't-know-

how-long. I done sent the word and they going to be hanging they head out the window, looking. Since you sold
them – "

"If they hang their heads out in this rain, they won't
have any heads left when you come, not if it's storming
there like it is here."

"You know how a nigger feel about his own chillun
what he don't see much. Since you sold them gals –"

"I'm not stopping you, remember," Marse Sheppard said
quickly.

Ben grinned. Now and again he could hear Drucilla and
Mousie moving about in the kitchen. Young Marse Robin
was in his room early for once, perhaps writing a careful
letter to a pretty cousin who lived in Roanoke. Ben's hand
trembled with the splinters and small wood. The fire was
catching on and the pink warmth of the great living room
reminded him that colossal things were supposed to happen
tonight, colossal things in which he was supposed to have a
part. Ben knew that by now the Negroes were gathering in
the grove by the creek, the place called the Brook Swamp,
that when they had gone against Richmond, God willing,
they would turn on the planters and their rich harvests,
their country homes. Oh, it was hard to love freedom. Of
course, it was the self-respecting thing to do. Everything
that was equal to a groundhog wanted to be free. But it
was so expensive, this love; it was such a disagreeable com-
pulsion, such a bondage.

Ben grieved with his thoughts. Here he was getting fixed
to call on his gal young-uns. Bless God, he'd never told
Marse Sheppard such a barefaced lie in all his days. And
God might take it on hisself to let a certain lying colored
man meet the devil the best way he could, since the fellow
was so careless with the truth. Come to think about it, all
this big rain just at this time was a caution in itself. How in
God's name was all them eleven hundred folks going to
cross the streams going into Richmond? There wasn't a
sign of a bridge across most of them.

But dying wasn't the only holdback. Everybody had to die some time. Another thing was leaving this house. Then there was the old frail man standing at the window. It had been so long, their association. They understood each other so well. They were both so well satisfied with their present status. It was a pretty thing to think about and a right sad one too. Ben began to wilt. Then suddenly another thought shouted in his head.

Licking his spit because he done fed you, hunh? Fine nigger you is. Good old Marse Sheppard, hunh? Is he ever said anything about setting you free? He wasn't too good to sell them two gal young-uns down the river soon's they's old enough to know the sight of a cotton-chopping hoe. How'd he treat yo' old woman befo' she died? And you love it, hunh? Anything what's equal –

"Get the toddy bowl, Ben."

"Yes, suh."

Rain poured against the tall windows, rattled the over-filled gutters. Ben went into the kitchen and found Drucilla and Mousie trying to shoo a frightened bird out of the house. Pharoah was standing near the stove, his coat and hat drying on a chair. The bird had evidently come in when he opened the door. It was a bad luck sign and had to be driven out at once. Drucilla and her daughter were shaking towels at it and giving the poor creature no rest. They were still swiping at it when Ben went into the living room with his bowl of toddy.

Marse Sheppard had taken a chair.

"This is good. Did you taste it, Ben?"

Ben, smiling, set the bowl at his master's elbow.

"No, suh," he said.

Then, rather nervously, he busied himself by needlessly touching the window hangings and adjusting chairs. Mr. Moseley Sheppard drank meditatively, his gaze on the small red fire. With the second glass he put out his feet and relaxed.

"What's going on in the kitchen, Ben?"

"They's shooing a bird."

"Shooing what kind of a bird?"

"Just a little old something or other like a field lark or a swift. It come in when Pharoah opened the do', I reckon."

"Pharoah?"

"H'm."

"What's Pharoah doing here?"

"Drying his coat."

"Oh. Well, maybe you'd better tell those gals to keep the door closed from now on."

"I done told them that, Marse Sheppard."

"And tell Pharoah that's a new wrinkle, him coming in the kitchen here to dry his coat by the stove."

"Yes, suh, I'm going to tell him too."

"If you change your mind about that trip, Ben, you can keep the lights burning till the rain lets up."

"Yes, suh."

"If you go, tell Drucilla to keep them."

The two black women stood wilted and panting in the middle of the floor when Ben returned to the kitchen. Fat, pumpkin-colored Pharoah was behind the stove, his back to the fire. The kitchen was in disorder, and a chair had been upset.

"The bird gone yet?" Ben said.

"Yes, thanks the Lord. Us got to start scrubbing now. All that there water slopped in whilst George was holding the door open for us to shoo it out."

Mousie got buckets and rags from a small closet. She tied her skirt above her knees and got down to dry the floor. Drucilla followed.

"If anything give me the allovers, it's to see a devilish bird get in the house," Mousie said.

"I ain't never seen it to fail," Drucilla said. "It's a sign, sure's you born."

"Sign of what?" Pharoah shot a glance over his right shoulder.

"Sign of death, that's what. Somebody's going to die."

"Peoples is dying all the time," Ben said.

"Well, this just mean one mo' gone," Drucilla told him. "And it's most apt to be somebody close by."

"Hush, gal."

She turned her head languidly, looked up at him from the floor with a strangely quizzical face.

"You don't believe it, hunh?"

"I ain't said I does and I ain't said I doesn't. I said hush up."

"Oh."

"Pharoah, you best throw something round you and get on out somewheres. Marse Sheppard's asking me how-come you in here drying yo' coat like as if you lived here."

"You reckon we can make it in all this rain, Ben?"

Ben went into the pantry without answering. When he returned, he said, "Maybe the rain'll let up soon."

"Better say you *reckon* it'll let up. There ain't no signs of good weather out there now."

"I said maybe."

"But what good it going to do us even do it stop raining after the water get chin-deep over everything?"

Ben put on a hat and a long cape that had been hanging on a nail behind the pantry door. He offered Pharoah a blanket.

"Marse Sheppard say keep the lights burning long's the storm keep up," he told Drucilla.

The two men stood in the doorway a few moments. They looked as solemn as ghosts. A gust of wind flickered the lights as the door opened. The tumult and agony of great trees filled the night. Ben uttered a small, audible groan. Pharoah walked behind him with fearful steps and a wrenched face.

5

The crackle of lightning ceased in the fields, but the sky still gave a pulsating blue light. Pharoah stood beneath a live oak holding the jack's bridle while Ben climbed into the buck wagon.

"It's a fool's doing," Ben admitted. "The Lord don't like it."

Pharoah lowered his head, his forehead touching the animal's hard face.

"Gabriel won't listen to sense. It ain't a fit night to break free."

"For a penny I'd stay home."

"Me too."

Pharoah made no move to follow Ben into the wagon. He stroked the jack a few times, and suddenly a palsied frenzy shook him. A moment later, when he heard Ben speaking again, he recovered partially, but his strength was gone so that he needed support to keep him on his feet.

"We can't get to no Caroline County tonight," Ben said. "That's all there is to it."

"H'm. That's what I been – "

"We couldn't make it way up there tonight in all this was we birds with wings. I didn't know it was this bad."

"Reckon we ought to tell Gabriel?"

"I bound you they's left already."

"It ain't late," Pharoah said. "They's most like to be at the Brook Swamp yet."

"We's going to be obliged to get this here jackass and wagon of Mingo's back to town anyhow. They ain't no place to keep it out here. Leastwise, we better get it back if we don't want to answer too many questions."

"That's a fact."

They reached the big road, jogging miserably in the slush. There was still the noisy lamentation of the trees and the downpour slopping against them by the bucketful. Pharoah held the driving lines sullenly.

"Hold on a minute," Ben said abruptly.

"Whop! Hold on for what?"

"Ain't that somebody yonder?"

They waited and presently a half-naked black boy slipped from the roadside shadows. He seemed, in the pitch darkness, as if he gave a strange light from his body, an unearthly luster such as the sky offered. Quickly, without waiting for him to speak, a curious animal-like sense of recognition passed between him and the Negroes on the wagon.

"Daniel?" Pharoah said.

"Yes, this me."

"What done happen – you lost?" Ben said.

"No. Me and Ditcher was going down to the Swamp to meet Gabriel."

"Well, howcome you going back?"

"We met Juba."

"Talk sense, boy. What's the trouble?"

Ben's voice showed excitement now. Daniel fumbled for words.

"The country crowd is hemmed in. They can't make it over here, and they is scairt stiff. Me and Ditcher swimmed and paddled and pulled till we got across, and we went to tell Gabriel. But we met Juba."

"Well, howcome you going back?"

"Juba and Ditcher say tell them to come what's coming and them to stay what's staying. They's going free tonight, them. They's hitting Richmond tonight, do they have to hit it by their lonesomes."

"The others wa'n't fixing to come, hunh?"

"No. They wants to put it off two-three days."

There was a pause. Ben struggled to keep his thoughts in order. He could hear his own heartbeats screaming in his ears.

"Where'bouts you seen Juba?"

"Up the road. She was coming on the colt to see what done happen to us – us taking so long to get there and all."

Ben turned his head. At his side he saw Pharoah faintly, a shadow ready to jump off the seat.

The wagon got started again, the wheels churning mud almost axle-deep, the jack behaving like the wild thing he was.

Daniel splashed away very excited. The tiny storm-ridden earth rocked like a great eye in a vast socket. There had been nothing to equal it among all the cloudbursts and tempests in Ben's long memory.

6

Romance won't mend the roof of your house," Midwick observed cautiously.

"No, but it's useless to fight against a thing like that when it's in your blood – don't you think so too?"

Fat and red and round of face, Ovid, who had just discovered that the seat of his pants was scorching, wheeled around, rubbing the spot briskly, and gave the other guard his face across the fire.

"Well, if you fail to grow out of it normally at the proper age, perhaps, God willing, it might be a hopeless fight."

There was a plenty of wood, the fire burned well, and the stable was a luxury on such a night. Midwick still relished a dark neglected hole where he could smell earth. That was the thing in his blood; it reminded him of Bunker Hill, Valley Forge and White Plains. The most vivid part of these campaigns, as he remembered them, was the smell of the earth. A thing could get in your blood all right. Midwick was pulling on his shoes. They were not thoroughly dry, but it was about time to go out again and take a stroll around the arsenal. The blasted muskets of the sovereign state might start popping off if a man in uniform failed to go around and try the doors every half-hour. And if an unimportant official should get drunk and run into the place by mistake, he'd end his natural life when he failed to see a guard immediately, even in such weather as this.

Ovid looked at the bats clinging overhead, his hands locked behind him.

"You don't really understand me, Midwick. It's a very adult sentiment – the thing I mentioned. I feel sort of like a caged thing that needs the open."

"Open country?"

"No, no. That's figurative. My blood requires adventure – delightful women, that sort of thing."

"Oh, God willing, it's a hankering after harlots. The town's got its share. And Norfolk – "

"Not ill-famed women. Lovely women. You know – young and dimpled. Can't you get the picture? One is standing on a white beach in threatening weather. Her hair is loose, her feet bare; white birds circle above her head."

"Yes, God bless me, I know. I know the kind that goes traipsing around barefoot when rain's coming up and she ought to be to home, but I can't see why a family man like you would worry his head about that kind."

"You don't understand." Ovid looked sorrowful. "Maybe you've wanted to put out with a good ship some time?"

"Not much. It was always soldiering for me when I was a lad, and now it's staying at home."

"I should have soldiered. It might have cured me," Ovid said. "Now, it's my luck to cry over what I've missed. But I'm still a good man. There might be a fling for me yet. Maybe a ship. A year in the Caribbees, taverns, orange trees, Spanish galleons anchored a mile or two out, pirate's daughters left at home."

"You should have soldiered. But here, give me the blanket. I'll make a turn around the place."

He went outside. A short while later Ovid heard him talking to someone in the rain, so he buttoned his own coat, snatched his musket and followed him around to the street side of the old penitentiary building. There were other men there, but he could not see them. They were talking to Midwick.

"Stand there," Ovid said boyishly.

"The night watch of Richmond, Ovid," Midwick answered.

"Oh. A nasty night, I'd say."

"Not even fit for ducks and geese. Good-night."

When they returned to the stable again, Midwick promptly removed his shoes once more.

"They won't turn water," he said.

Ovid sat on a heap of litter within reach of a jug. A little later he threw out his feet, leaned back and tilted the thing above his head.

7

That same blue brightness flickered over the line of stumbling shadows. Gabriel could hear a boisterous plop-plopping behind him, and he could see, when he turned his head, a parade of blurred silhouettes in the rain. Juba was back now, moving at his side on the fretful colt.

"We's got a crowd what can do the work. On'erstand?"

"I reckon so. They'll do the work if you's leading. But the country folks was many again as this. We's obliged to get along without them, and that's a care for sure."

"Too many is a trouble some time. A nigger ain't equal to a grasshopper when he scairt, and a scairt crowd is worser'n a scairt one."

The leader's immense shoulders slouched. He tramped in the heavy mud with a melodious swing of loose limbs. He had shed his coachman's frock-tailed coat, but the coachman's tall hat was still on his head; the front of his drenched shirt was open.

"Whoa, suh. Easy now, Araby," the girl said, pulling up the bridle and slapping the colt's face. "Easy, suh."

The rain was whipping him badly, but Araby decided to behave.

"We can do as good 'thout the others. Ditcher's here. It's bad to turn back."

"They's feeling mighty low-down now, I bound you – beingst they's left out."

"I reckon – maybe. The rain's bad and all, but I don't just know."

"You don't know what?"

"I don't know was it the deep water or was it something else that's holding them up."

"You talk funny. What you mean something else?"

Gabriel threw a glance over his shoulder. The line was coming down a rise. Here and there, in the blur and the downpour, a stray glint caught the point of a tall pike. Gabriel led them beneath a clump of willows and discovered an immense bough torn from one of the trees and hurled across the way. He went around it, churning mud up to his knees. Araby had a brief struggle before regaining firm ground.

"You ain't seen nothing, gal? You ain't noticed nothing funny?"

"I don't know what you means, boy."

Again Gabriel refrained from answering promptly. He walked a short way, swinging arms meditatively, then paused to wipe the water from his face with an open hand.

"The line's getting slimmer and slimmer," he said.

Juba took a sudden quick breath through her open mouth.

"No!"

"It's the God's truth. I can tell by the feet. They ain't as many back there now."

"Hush, boy. I ain't seen none leave."

"Some's left, though. But that ain't nothing. They'll all come back tomorrow, the country crowd too. There won't be nothing else for them to do after we gets in our lick. Nobody's going to want a black face around they place tomorrow. You mind what I say, it's going to be who shall and who sha'n't, do we get in a good lick tonight. Do we fall down, the niggers what's left'll be looking for us too. They going to find out that the safest place is with yo' own crowd, sticking together."

"What make you so sure they's leaving, though? What you think make them go way like that?"

"Afeared," Gabriel said.

"Afeared to fight?"

"No, not afeared to fight. Scairt of the signs. Scairt of the stars, as you call it. You heard them talking. 'The stars is against us,' they says. They says, 'All this here rain and storm ain't a nachal thing.'"

There was a light in a tiny house beyond the thicket to the left. The line didn't pause, however. Gabriel swung along beside the colt, his elbow now and again touching the naked thigh of the girl astride. He glanced at the light, but he knew that no stone had been left unturned. The thing for the present was to keep going. The rain was no lighter; the wind was not letting up, and somewhere ahead a branch could be heard roaring like a river.

A little later Gabriel whispered, "I'm tired of being a devilish slave."

"Me, too. I'm tired too, boy."

"There ain't nothing but hard times waiting when a man get to studying about freedom."

"H'm. Like a gal what love a no-'count man."

"He just as well to take the air right away. He can't get well."

"No, not lessen he got a pair of wings. They ain't no peace for him lessen he can fly."

"H'm. No peace."

"Didn't you used to loved a yellow woman, boy? A

yellow woman hanging her head out the window?"

"Hush, gal. I'm a bird in the air, but it's freedom I been dreaming about. Not no womens."

"You got good wings, I reckon."

"Good wings, gal. Us both two got good wings."

There was still the line of stumbling shadows behind. Suddenly they halted. They were at the crossing of the stream that lay between the plantations and the town. The colt whinnied and shivered, his front feet in the fast water.

"Wide," Juba said. "Deep, too."

Gabriel stood with his feet in it. Rain whipped his back. There was grief in the treetops, a tall wind bearing down. Gabriel could see the flash and sparkle of water through the blackness.

He bowed his head, heavy with thoughts, and waited a long moment without speaking.

Meanwhile the storm boomed. The small branch, swollen beyond reason, twisted and curled in its channel, hurled its length like a serpent, spewed water into the air and splashed with its tail.

8

Meanwhile, too, each in his place, the quaint confederates fought the storm, kept their posts or carried on as occasion demanded.

General John, his strength failing, crept into an abandoned pig sty and gave up the journey. He bent above his lantern, muttering aloud and trying to shield it from the wind.

'Twa'n't no use, nohow. Nothing outdoors this night but wind and water, God helping. Lord a-mercy, what I'm going to do with my old raw-boned self? Here I is halfway 'twixt town and home and as near played out as ever I been. They ain't no call to turn back, though. After Gabriel and

Ditcher and them gets done mopping up, it ain't going to be no place for we-all but right with the crowd. Gabriel said it and he said right. Do they get whupped, us going to have to hit for the mountains anyhow, so there ain't no cause to study about turning back. Yet and still, Richmond ain't for this here black man tonight, much less Petersburg. No, suh, not this night.

He squatted, his hands locked around his knees, and gave himself to meditation. Now and again a humorless grin altered his face, exposed the sparse brown fangs. The general's mood became first sluggish then mellow.

His head fell on his knees. A little later, his lantern gone out, he tumbled over on a heap of damp litter and slept.

The buck wagon came to a standstill midway the creek. The jack fretted and presently got himself at right angles with the cart.

"It's way yonder too deep for driving across," Ben said.

"Well, what I'm going to do now?" Pharoah asked.

"Turn round or stay here – one thing or t'other."

Pharoah moaned softly, sawing the reins back and forth while the animal danced in the fast current.

"These is bad doings," he said passionately. "I ain't never seen no sense in running a thing in the ground."

"Listen," Ben told him curtly. "Come to think about it, you was the nigger kneeling down side of me at old Bundy's burying."

"Maybe I was. What that got to do with all this here fool-headed mess?"

"Nothing. Only I remembers as to how you jugged yo' elbow in my belly that day and says, 'Don't you want to be free, fool?' Seem to me you was a big one on the rising then."

"Anybody gets mad some time. Freedom's all right, I reckon."

"But if you'd kept yo' elbow out of my belly, I'd of like as not been in my bed this very minute."

"You can't put it on me, Ben."

"No. Not trying to. Just getting you told. You making mo' fuss than me."

The jack whimpered and danced. Suddenly Pharoah rose to his feet in the cart, braced himself and put all his strength on the lines. The terrified, half-wild animal threw up his heels, bounded forward with a violent effort that jerked the shafts from the cart and sent the fat, pumpkin-colored Negro hurtling forward into the creek. The jack leaped again, and Pharoah felt the hot lines tear through his hands, heard the broken thills pounding the ground and the terrified animal galloping against the rain, fury against fury.

Ben climbed over the wheel and waded waist deep to the sloppy bank. He heard Pharoah slushing the mud on his hands and knees, heard him calling God feverishly.

"Lord Jesus, help. Lord a-mercy, do."

Ben felt a quick chill. He noticed that his good clothes were near ruined; and as he stood there trembling, he closed his eyes and tried to imagine himself tucked in a dry feather bed at home. But it was no good. He was wet to the bone, and that was a fact.

It was like hog-killing day to Criddle. He knew the feel of warm blood, and he knew his own mind. He knew, as well, that his scythe-sword was ready to drink. He could feel the thing getting stiffer and stiffer in his hand. Well, anyhow, he hadn't told anyone to snatch that door open and come legging it outside without looking where he was going.

Criddle had heard the columns in the road. They were not noisy, but there was something different in the sound they made. It was something like the rumble of the creek, nothing like the swish and whisper of poplars.

He heard them go by, and he felt as if he were free already.

He could just as well run and catch up with them now. Why not? But for some reason there wasn't much run left in his legs. They were, for the moment, scarcely strong enough to hold him up.

Cheap old white man, poorer'n a nigger. That's you, and it's just like you, hopping around like a devilish frog. You won't hop no mo' soon. Plague take yo' time, I didn't tell you to be so fidgety. You could of stayed in yonder and woke up in the morning. This here ain't no kind of night to be busting outdoors like something crazy.

And that there gal in the long night-gown and the lamp in her hand. Humph! She don't know nothing. Squeeling and a-hollering round here like something another on fire. She need a big buck nigger to – no, not that. Gabriel done say too many times don't touch no womens. This here is all business this night. What that they calls it? Freedom? Yes, that's the ticket, and I reckon it feel mighty good too.

Where the nation that gal go to? Don't reckon I ought to leave her running round here in that there nightgown like a three-year filly. Where she go?

Criddle knew what blood was like. He remembered hog-killing day.

9

Gabriel heard the murmur that passed down the line as he stood in the water. He turned slowly, put out his hand and touched the nearest shadow.

"You, Blue?"

"Yes, this me."

"Where'bouts Martin and Solomon?"

"Back in the line, I reckon."

"Call them here."

He was gone with the word, and the confused and frightened Negroes began circling like cattle in the soft mud. Now and again one groaned at the point of hysteria. Gabriel didn't doubt that the groaners presently vanished and that the others lapsed directly into their former animal-like desperation. Juba was on the ground now, twitching her wet skirt lasciviously and clinging to the colt's bridle.

"Tired, boy?"

He shook his head.

"Tired ain't the word," he said. "Low."

"Niggers won't do."

"They's still leaving, slipping away – scairt white. How we's going to get them across this high-water branch is mo'n I know."

"We could of been gone from here, was it just me and you. Biggest part of these others ain't got the first notion about freedom."

"Maybe. That wouldn't do me, though. I reckon it's a birthmark. Running away won't do me no good long's the others stays. The littlest I can think about is a thousand at a time when it come to freedom. I reckon it's a conjure or something like that on me. I'm got to do it the big way, do I do it all. And something been telling me this the night, the onliest night for us."

"It won't be the night if they keeps slipping away, though."

"I reckon it won't, gal. It won't be the night if we can't get them across this high-water branch."

"H'm. It's wasting time staying here if we can't cross. Just as well to be home pleasuring yo'self in a good sleeping place, dry, warm maybe, two together maybe."

"H'm."

They gathered quickly, Martin, Solomon, Blue and Ditcher with Gabriel and Juba. The others kept mulling in a sloppy low thicket beneath boughs that drooped under the relentless punishment.

"The branch is deep," Gabriel said. "And they's two mo' to cross like it further on. Y'-all reckon we can get this crowd in town tonight?"

Blue lost his breath.

"Quit the game now?"

"The weather's bad," Gabriel said. "It ain't too bad, but the niggers is leaving fast. They's scairt white, and they ain't more'n two hundred left, I reckon. We might could get them together again in two-three days."

"They's leaving for true," Ditcher said. "I heard some talk and I seen some go. They's afeared of the water and they's scairt to fight 'thout the whole eleven hundred. But they's most scairt of the signs. It look like bad luck, all this flood."

"It's bad to turn round and go back," Gabriel said. "Something keep telling me this here's the night, but you can't fight with mens what's scairt. What you say, Solomon?"

"You done said it all, Bubber. They ain't no mo'."

Gabriel turned first to one, then to the other, the question still open.

"You said it all," Blue echoed.

"They ain't no mo'." Juba murmured. "No mo' to say, boy."

"Well, then, it's pass the word along. Pass it fast and tell them all to get home soon's they can. On'erstand? If they don't mind out somebody'll catch up with them going back. Send somebody to tell Criddle ne'mind now and somebody to town to head off Ben and Gen'l John and tell Mingo and them that's with him. Somebody got to wade out to tell the country folks, too. We's got to turn round fast. It's bad to quit and go back. It's more dangerouser than going frontwise. These fools don't know it."

In a few moments the crowd left the low thicket, scurrying across fields by twos and threes. Gabriel walked in the slushy path, his shoulders slouched wistfully, his hand hooked in Araby's bridle. Rain blew in Juba's face. She sat erect, feeling the pure warmth of the colt's fine muscles gnawing back and forth between her naked thighs. There was something sadly pleasant about retreat under these circumstances. Hope was not gone.

"We's got tomorrow," she said.

"Not yet," Gabriel answered. "The sun ain't *obliged* to rise, you know."

"I hope it do."

"H'm."

The storm boomed weakly, flapping the shreds of a torn banner.

10

The cabins on the Prosser place were running a foot of water. Negroes sleeping in the haymow opened their eyes stupidly and tottered over to the loft window. A village of corn shocks in the low field was completely inundated. A scrawny red rooster, looking very tall and awkward on a small raft, drifted steadily downstream. He had not lost his strut, but his feathers were wet and he seemed, in his predicament, as dismayed as an old beau. The rain was over; there was a vague promise of sunshine in a sky that was lead-colored.

Mingo's frightened jack was still running, an arm of the broken thills dangling from his harness, sliding over the ground with a bump-bump-bump. Something had snapped in his head. He imagined the devil would pounce on him if he lost a single bound. He was running in circles sometimes and sometimes straightening out for a mile at a stretch. Leaping streams, plowing up flower beds, tearing through thickets and underbrush, it did not occur to him that the storm was over.

Ben and Pharoah stood in mud by the roadside, their heads together. They were still dripping wet and their clothes were mud-spattered from heel to crown. The wagon in the creek near by had been thrown on its side by the current; its wheels were lodged on the underside.

"It was a pure fool's doings, Ben."

"No need to stand here saying that all day. We best get gone."

"I reckon."

"That's all what's left to do. Come on."

Pharoah cried shamelessly.

Ben whispered beneath his breath.

Criddle was bewildered when he met the other two on the road.

"What done come of everybody?"

"Gone home. Ain't you heard?"

"I ain't heard nothing. Gone home for what?"

"Tell him, Pharoah."

The pumpkin-faced Negro tried to explain.

"They couldn't make it on account of the water and all. They's telling everybody to lay low two-three days and wait till the weather clear up. They didn't get across the first branch. Somebody was looking for you directly after the lines broke up."

"They broke up, hunh?"

"They *been* broke up. They been gone since before midnight, I reckon."

Criddle's domino spots got smaller and smaller. Finally they disappeared altogether.

"You ain't fixing to cry about it, is you?" Ben said. "It just going to be two-three mo' days."

"I ain't crying, but I don't see how they going to wait no two-three days with that white gal running loose in her nightgown. She'll let it out befo' you can spit."

"How she know?"

"Gabriel told me what to do, and I done it, me. I don't know what come of the gal?"

"I help you to say she going to tell it."

Ben thought of nothing but the broken wagon in the creek and Mingo's half-wild jack running furiously. He began to pray under his breath again, crying in his mind

111

like a child. Pharoah stood like a wooden man, his mouth hanging open, his swine-like eyes extremely bright. Suddenly he quaked violently. Then he covered his face and cried, cried absurdly loud and long for a grown man. When he recovered again and looked up, his eyes were quite empty. Some strange, inarticulate decision of his blood made a new man of him. It was evident on his face.

The three of them started walking. Ben led the dazed Pharoah by the hand a little way. Criddle followed, his shoulders rounded, his long arms hanging a bit in front of his short body as he walked. It was sloppy weather for a Sunday.

11

Mr. Moseley Sheppard was early to his counting room that Monday. A shaft of fine sunlight stood against the window. The silvered old man sat at a desk profuse with papers. He was carefully dressed; the small pink flower in his buttonhole was responsible for an appearance of almost springtime cheerfulness.

The planter was feeling fit again, and his spirits rose accordingly. His cares seemed small that morning. The fact that young Robin was strong for a yellow wench was nothing. That crops had undoubtedly suffered by the storm (such of them as remained in the fields) was only an incident. That he was growing old and lonesome in a great house, that his friends were few (those he could really count on) – these were no more than moods that good health dispelled.

Leaning far back in his chair, Mr. Moseley Sheppard took an inconsiderable pinch of snuff and looked out on a clean, fresh world tinted with pastel shades. And so pleased was he with the view he did not hear the door open. He was not astonished, however, when he saw a Negro standing timidly before him. The old fellow had been careful to close the door, but now, confronting his master, he was nervous and mute, He was neatly dressed, his face covered with salt-and-pepper whiskers, and he waited with bowed head. Plainly, there was something of moment that he wanted to say, but he was in no hurry whatever to say it.

"Well –"

The Negro's head went lower. His shoulders tightened and the flesh of his arms was suddenly pricked by innumerable needles. His fingernails hurt the palms of his hands.

"Marse Sheppard –"

"Yes." Then after a pause, "Go ahead, Ben."

Suddenly the aged Negro dropped to one knee, his hands resting on the arm of the planter's chair, and began weeping aloud.

12

Hush," Gabriel said. "Don't talk. A nigger done kilt a old white trash. That ain't telling nothing about the rising. That ain't so much as telling who done the killing. That ain't a thing to stop us. On'erstand?"

He was polishing the carriage with an oily cloth. Martin and Criddle and Juba were under the shed, Martin keeping watch in the doorway, Criddle leaning on a manure shovel, and Juba, sitting in the carriage like a great lady, twitching her foot and pulling on a corncob pipe.

"The Book said the stars in they courses fit against Sistra," Martin said.

"H'm. I reckon that Sistra must of been a rich old white man then," Gabriel said. "Them's the ones Jesus don't like. You mind my word. God's against them like a gold eagle is against a chipmunk. You heard Mingo read it."

None of them had rested well. Their faces were drawn and tired; Criddle's mouth snapped open with a tremendous yawn. He failed to follow the others when they alluded to Sistra or to the possible effect of the white man's death on the whole scheme.

"I could do with about two-three days' sleep, me."

"Us both too," Martin said. "All I can do to drag."

"Y'-all had yestiddy to sleep," Gabriel said.

"I laid down, Bubber, but sleep ain't been here yet."

"Tonight's another day," Gabriel told them. "The rain done played out. We's got to beat the drum and beat it hard this evening."

Juba got a sensuous pleasure out of the excitement. A little familiar shiver ran over her flesh. She could hardly wait to put on Marse Prosser's stolen riding boots again. She could still feel Araby twitching and fretting between her clinched knees. Lordy, that colt. He was pure joy itself. Almost as much fun as a man, that half-wild Araby.

Then very soon, as the day waxed and the puddles gradually diminished in the road, a half-crazed yellow Negro was streaking toward Richmond, his hat in his hand, his queue in the air. Before sundown he would reach the town if his wind lasted. In half-an-hour they would all know. Drums would beat. Bells would ring. Insurrection. Insurrection. Insurrection. The blacks were rising against their masters. The dogs had gone mad. They were in arms and organized to the number of eleven hundred. Richmond was threatened with fire and butchery. Other nearby cities were not safe. . . . His face wrenched, his eyes empty, the heavy Negro ran as if spurs were digging into his ribs.

Later Ditcher and General John came to the shed, and after them Mingo. Blue and Solomon joined the circle, and they lay on their bellies in a dying coppice as dusk came to the trees behind the stables.

"Ben and Pharoah ought to done been here," Gabriel said. "Us got to be turning round mighty fast two-three hours from now."

114

"Four-five hour," Martin said.

"Ne' mind. Some's going to be dusting befo' that even you hear?"

"H'm."

"Well, I'm telling you so. Listen. We wants them all to meet like how we planned it befo'. Onliest thing different is we's going down the line this time, and I don't mean I *reckon* so. On'erstand?"

Ditcher felt the flames in Gabriel's angry eyes. Blue ground his teeth.

"Hush a minute. What's that yonder?" General John said, straining his old cataracted eyes.

The others rose on their elbows or knees. A running fury inscribed an arc in the low field half-mile away. The thing was only a trifle more substantial than the twilight itself, but it gave the Negroes a breathless moment.

"Yo' jack, Mingo," Gabriel said. "He still running. Ne' mind that, though. Do we take Richmond, you going to have mo' horses and things than you can shake a stick at. Do we get whupped, us going to have to run so fast a lazy old jack like that couldn't keep up. Let me tell you the whole plan one mo' time."

"Everybody know the plan," Ditcher said. "Tell us what time."

Gabriel waited a moment, apparently irritated.

"Make sure you does then. Midnight is the time. We's meeting in the grove and marching double quick. And do anything go wrong, we ain't coming back here no mo'. Them hills off yonder was made special for niggers what's obliged to use they wings."

"It sound good," General John said. "It sound mighty good, Gabriel, and I like it a heap, I *tell* you. I been had my mind set on freedom a long time."

"H'm, but it ain't no good 'thout all the rest goes free too," Mingo said. "You ain't free for true till all yo' kin peoples is free with you. You ain't sure 'nough free till you gets treated like any other mens."

"That's good to talk about. We's got to start turning around now. Get yo' bellies off of these here leaves and start doing something now. Come on, y'-all."

Six miles never did seem so long before. But he'd get there if his wind lasted. By night there would be a troop in front of the courthouse. The local guard would be in the streets with long, out-of-date muskets. There would be drums. There would be bells. Pharoah tore through the dry hedges, splashed through muddy water. He had to tell it now. He was sure he would burst if he didn't tell it right away. Bloody insurrection. Bloody, bloody . . .

Little splinters of moonlight showered the dark hut. They fell in gusts as faint and fine as the spray of imaginary sparklers on an imaginary holiday. The tall Negro tossed his limbs boyishly on the floor. Beside him the thin-waisted girl tossed.

"It was right pretty how Toussaint writ that note. I'm going to get Mingo to write me some just like it. We can send them to all the black folks in all the States. Let me see now. How it going to read. 'My name is Gabriel – *Gen'l* Gabriel, I reckon – you's heard tell about me by now.' Ha-ha! How that sound, gal?"

"Right pretty, boy."

"Well, that's how it going to begin."

He couldn't lie still with the hour so near. He twitched his head, flipped an arm and threw one leg out. Juba stretched and drew up to a sitting position, her skirt in a tangle around her waist. Broken splinters of light still came through the chink holes overhead.

Presently there were a few Negroes outside, moving on cat feet, whispering.

"Some of them's ready, gal."

"Yes, I hears."

A pause – Gabriel's hands locked under his head, the girl's shoulders gleaming in the darkness.

116

"That was right pretty how Toussaint writ that note all right."

"What else he say?"

"*Come and unite with us, brothers, and combat with us for the same cause.*" He slapped his flank. "Sing it, church! Ain't that pretty?"

"Pretty 'nough, boy."

"*I have undertaken to avenge your wrongs.* You hear it, don't you?"

"H'm."

"*It is my desire that liberty and equality shall reign in-* well, when Mingo write mine, I'll have him say *shall reign in Virginia. – I am striving to this end. Come and unite with us, brothers.*"

"It do sound good a-plenty."

"Them folks is getting noisy outdoors."

"Maybe scairt."

"Sound like a big crowd now."

"They's mo' now than they was a few minutes ago."

"And they's scuffling round a *heap* mo'."

Gabriel lay on his elbow a moment, his brow furrowed. Then he sprang to his feet and rushed outside. Presently a thought halted him, the memory of a single word he had dictated into his imaginary letter to the black folks of the States. *Gen'l* Gabriel. He turned abruptly, went back into the hut and put on his shiny boots, his frock-tailed coat and his varnished coachman's hat. It was all very important when you really thought it over.

Scrawny black figures milled up and down the cabin row. They seemed unnecessarily jumpy. At first Gabriel got the impression they were running in circles. There was a great deal of whispering, all very rapid, very breathless. All the crochety old silhouettes had their corncob pipes in their hands. Humorous little tufts stood on their heads or stuck out behind for those who had enough hair to make queues. They were all gesturing with their pipes, throwing out excited arms.

Gabriel started toward a small group by a woodpile. A pale fragmentary moon was pushing up. There was no mistaking the alarm that had spread among the blacks. Their agitation was too plain. Solomon slipped from a shadow and met Gabriel on the path.

"It's something what'll burn yo' ears like fire to hear, Bubber."

"Tell me. Tell me!"

Gabriel forgot to whisper. His voice was a roar.

"The game's up, Bubber."

"What you mean? Tell me, I say!"

Solomon, fluttering like a bird, put his hand on his taller brother and tried to speak. Gradually the thought took shape. Pharoah had betrayed them. Volunteers were already being armed in Richmond to meet the attack. There was another tempest in the offing.

Every bell in the town was ringing. For nearly an hour drums had gone up and down the streets. Men and boys gathered in groups under the trees. They were being assigned to their leaders; they were listening prick-eared to the hasty instructions. Consternation, error, confusion increased with every bell toll, with every drum beat. All the available horses were being herded into an enclosure behind the courthouse.

And on a nearby street corner, empty-eyed, exhausted, alone, stood Pharoah, the pumpkin-colored mulatto. He was breathing hard. Now he could start home, he thought. Nobody would know who gave the alarm. The white folks would thank him. They wouldn't tell. They would protect him. Now he could start home in the heavy shadows.

"If Gabriel had of listened to me, he'd of fared a heap better. He wasn't fixing to do no good nohow, the way how he was going about it. I wanted to lead a line, me."

BOOK THREE

Mad Dogs

1

Get down, Criddle. Get down underneath of them sassafras switches, down amongst the dead leaves and all. Moon bright as day out yonder – get down low. You knows right well they ain't far away. They done nipped you once already. They nipped you like a man nips a grouse on the wing.

Killing a nachal man ain't nothing like hog-killing, boy. On'erstand?

You's got yo' chance now, maybe. You's free, I reckon. You's got a chance equal to the chance a gray squirrel's got – a gray squirrel what's been nipped. A gray squirrel bleeding with a chunk of lead in his belly. You's got a equal chance, Criddle. Get down; hush.

Marse Jesus, I knows you is a-listening. You's got yo' hand behind yo' ear. You is listening to hear me pray. But I don't know nothing about no praying, me. I's low-down as I-don't-know-what, but I ain't no moaning man, Jesus. I been working for Marse Prosser all the time. I ain't seen nothing but the hind parts of horses, me. I been shoveling up manure in the stable; I ain't had time for no praying. You know yo'self I ain't, Marse Jesus. Howcome you looking at me with yo' hand behind yo' ear? I don't know nothing about no praying. I been pitching manure all the time, me.

Get down, boy. You don't hear them horses yonder? Can't bend, hunh? Look across the hill. Ah, Gabriel is the one to entertain them biggity white mens. They better be studying about him, too – do they know what's good.

Them's them all right: soldiers. Scratch down underneath of the leaves and switches and things. No? Hurt too bad, hunh?

"Well, ne' mind. That there chunk of lead was mo'n a nip maybe. Feel bigger'n a watermellon now. Manure pitching in Marse Prosser's stable wasn't bad, was it? And the smell of the horses and the smell of the harness was right good, come to think about it. What you say, Criddle? What you say now? No mo' hog-killings, I reckon. No mo' Decembers, maybe. No mo' manure. Hush; get down, boy, low.

2

Meanwhile the young nation gasped and caught its breath, trembled with excitement. Fanned by newspaper tales and swift rumors, its amazement flared.

"For the week past," wrote the Virginia correspondent to the Philadelphia *United States Gazette,* "we have been under momentary expectation of a rising among the Negroes, who have assembled to the number of nine hundred or a thousand, and threatened to massacre all the whites. They are armed with desperate weapons and now secrete themselves in the woods. God only knows our fate: we have strong guards every night under arms . . ."

Another reported: "Their arms consist of muskets, bludgeons, pikes, knives and the frightful scythe-swords. These cutlasses are made of scythes cut in two and fitted with well-turned handles. I have never seen arms so murderous. One shudders with horror at the sight of these instruments of death."

A gentle letter writer remarked to a distant friend that "Last night twenty-five hundred of our citizens were under arms to guard our property and lives. But it is a subject *not to be mentioned;* and unless you hear of it elsewhere, say nothing about it."

A score of Federalist editorials, quick to make political use of the plot by applying it to the campaign between Thomas Jefferson and John Quincy Adams, hurled Mr. Jefferson's own words disrespectfully into his face with profuse capital letters, "The Spirit of the Master is abating, that of the Slave rising from the dust, his condition mollifying."

Elsewhere the disturbed country sawed at its morning bacon and read the story with bulging eyes –

"It is evident that the French principles of liberty and equality have been infused into the minds of the Negroes and that the incautious and intemperate use of the words by some whites among us have inspired them with confidence. . . .

"While the fiery Hotspurs of the State vociferate their *French babble* of the natural equality of man, the insulted Negro will be constantly stimulated to cast away his cords and to sharpen his pike. . . .

"It is, moreover, believed, though not yet confirmed, that a great many of our profligate and abandoned whites (who are disguised by the burlesque appellation of *Democrats)* are implicated with the blacks . . . Never was terror more strongly depicted in the countenances of men. . . ."

And as the nation read, it had the assurance that a strong detachment of United States cavalry was moving on to Richmond, the arrogant horses striking a brisk jog, splashing now and again in the little lingering puddles. . . .

A mellow golden morning arched the road. There was a pleasant rattle of side arms, a delicious squeak of new saddle leather, an immoderate splendor of buttons and chevrons. Captain Orian Des Mukes, straight, aristocratic, cavalier, gave his young orderly a profile on which was written a type of languid, moonlight bravery. He was talkative this morning, but for some reason he had insisted on such an immense chew of tobacco that he was obliged, periodically, to suspend a phrase long enough to avert his face and spit with a solemn gurgle.

"Well (splut), this, I bound you, is no exception. Men fight for just three things. The rest (hep) is all (splut) sham. There is no such thing as equality."

At Ash Lawn, Governor James Monroe slumped into a stuffed settee, festooning his arms on the high back. Beyond his window he could see gawdy autumn trees so heavy with color they seemed unreal. The tireless bluejays were still annoying the gray squirrels. On the gravel drive an inexpensive cariole waited at a respectful distance, a small Negro holding the bridle. The nearer bustle of surreys and coaches he could not see from his window, but their presence was disturbingly manifest. There was increasing excitement in the outer rooms. And presently, the Governor knew, the throng would be upon him. His attendants could delay but not withhold them.

A slender man at the writing desk tapped the inkpot with his quill.

"There's a strong impression that it comes of a too hasty

resumption of commercial relations with the revolutionary government in San Domingo," he said.

"I don't know. I don't know. But there is no need to deny the obvious. The blacks are in an uprising. Frustrated for the moment by betrayal, they have fled to the swamps and hills. Minimizing their powers will not help us quell the disturbance. By all means, let us have a price offered for the arrest of the chiefs. The cavalry has been dispatched. Let us have added guards here for our own safety and suggest that the night patrols be at least doubled in Petersburg, Norfolk, Roanoke and the other cities."

"But these evidences of serious concern on our part may hearten the blacks. They may imagine that they have a chance if they see us showing them attention."

"By the very nature of things in our state, the very number of blacks and the personal trust that is imposed in so many of them, we are left exceedingly vulnerable to this sort of hostility. I would like to feel that it could be disregarded. There is the political angle that I also regret, but who is going to tell us the extent of our *actual* danger? Who knows exactly how far-reaching this thing is? What Negro can you point to and say definitely he is not involved?"

The younger man curled his feet beneath his chair. The fine yellow sunlight, mocking former tempests, seemed to fairly burst upon them as the morning waxed. Outside on the lawn a uniformed guard strode across the view, a tall musket on his shoulder. The Governor let his arms fall, rose from the settee and paced the room with a faraway smile while the secretary busied himself with his pen.

3

A blue light sifted through the small barred window overhead. In his Richmond cell a man with agitated eyes paced the floor, folding and unfolding his hands with a transparent, remote air. He was a Scotsman, his queue tied with a black ribbon, his face furrowed beyond his years. Now and again his eye caught the flicker of a bright leaf falling past his window like a flake of gold, his ear caught the tiny golden clang as it touched the ground.

But the melancholy of Thomas Callender was compounded of more than autumn leaves and a blue window. Certainly there were brighter leaves than these in his memory, bluer skies. In his youth there had been wellheads clothed with growing vines and singing peasants with pitchers in their arms. But the shattering came so early, the broken wheel, the neglected watering place, the leaves falling sorrowfully, one by one – so early.

Perhaps, he thought, this was the end of his gawdy talents, the reward of his brilliance. Fate always chose the strangest turnings in his case. Once he had written poetry, and it had seemed then that a fire burned in his breast, a fire that would consume his life if he failed to put verses upon it. But the verses were second-rate and later the fire demanded prose. So prose it had been, pages and pages of it, the biting, acid prose of a man sick with the need of liberty.

It had seemed almost certain, a few years ago, that the bright fulfillment was at hand; but now, after all the blood, after the writhing, after the breathless flights, the dream was still a faraway thing. He had found it necessary to flee England to escape punishment for political writings. Then came Philadelphia and the job on the *Gazette,* that lasted till 1796 and again his own need proved his undoing. Hoping to escape again, perhaps for good and all this time, he became a teacher. But it was laughable, this notion that he could live without writing, and almost at once he was publishing the *American Annual Register* with the support of Thomas Jefferson and others. This brought no immediate disaster, so presently he was off to Richmond, at Jefferson's suggestion, to become a writer for the *Examiner.* But even then the gods were conspiring. The rest was too disgusting to recall. That foul medievalism, the *Sedition Act.* A sharply barbed pamphlet entitled *The Prospect Before Us.* And then the gaol.

Good men had come to grief before, Callender reflected wistfully, but the thought failed to cure his own melancholy. In fact, it was more agreeable to consider the slow golden rain of autumn leaves outside his high blue window. He was sick to his belly from the offal stench of political wrangling. Far better the red leaves. Far better. But now there were voices at the door. A guard was turning a key in the lock.

A tired young man followed the uniformed attendant into the cell. There was urgency on his face but he seemed almost too worn to speak.

"They are saying you caused it, sir."

"I don't know what you're talking about."

"The insurrection of the blacks. One hears no name so often as Callender."

"Cant. Federalist cant. The nincompoops of John Quincy Adams are braying again. Where is the insurrection?"

The young man told him briefly what had happened.

"Everyone knows that Mr. Jefferson has been your friend. It hasn't taken them a day to make a campaign use of the disturbance."

Callender slumped into a chair, folding and unfolding his hands. His gaze strayed upward to the small indigo window.

"An asinine lie. No Democrat would have been fool enough to encourage a thing that could only help the opposition."

"What do you suggest?"

"I'll write a piece to the *Epitome.*"

"Thanks. That may help."

4

All that afternoon they gathered in rum shops and taverns and in the public square. Excited and nervous, the men of the town wanted eagerly to be doing something but couldn't make up their minds where to start. There were so many things to be considered. At dusk somebody lit a flambeau in an apple grove and a crowd of gangling boys began to mill under the small trees.

"They'll thank us for doing it," a thick-chested boy said.

"Sure – Jacobins. That's what they are. They're Jacobins," whispered a boy with a harelip.

"Lots of times I've heard the old man say they're dangerous." The third speaker was lank; his face was small, lorn and doll-like.

The thick-chested boy twitched impatiently.

"Fits, yes. Let's get together. They're next things to – to – why they're almost heathen when it comes to being low."

They were all of a class accustomed to running the streets after dark, when they could elude the watch, and there were among them boys with holes in their stockings and some who were emphatically unwashed. But they were all intoxicated by the bold light of their flambeau and by the delicious whisper of loose leaves underfoot. There was also a holiday feeling of license based on the general bewilderment of their elders and the continuous parade of soldiers and volunteers through the streets.

"They're against religion, too," the whisperer said with an effort. "Infidels. The cursed Africans practice devil-worship and nakedness, but these are next thing to them."

There were bugles in another part of town and occasionally the sound of drums. The streets were far from empty, and it was hard to imagine that night had come. The boys with their little minuteman hats, their loose hair falling on their shoulders, clustered nearer the leaders shouting their readiness to undertake anything, relevant or absurd, so long as it was immediate. Above all things they wanted to move. Waiting was the one torture they couldn't endure.

The lean, doll-faced boy deposited a slingshot in his pocket.

"Why, I've even heard the old man say – "

"Never mind," the heavy fellow said. "Let's start. Everybody'll need two big stones. We can get a crowbar behind the blacksmith shop."

They followed the torch and rallied like any other troopers under its glow, but the light was unnecessary. A moon rose and brightened the footpath so that they could even see the color of the trees. Heaven, perhaps, the lorn, small-faced boy imagined, had spilled its paint pots on the leaves too soon. Autumn was early this year, bright and early.

There were farmers in the streets, delaying their ox carts after dark, still exchanging impressions in high-pitched voices and trembling at the prospect of long journeys into the infested country. Their cheeks were bulged, but the incredible spouts they sent splashing into the road were now invisible. Yet the farmers kept drawing the backs of their hands across their mouths and talking very rapidly.

"I've heard the old man say some pretty hard things about some of them foreign radicals."

"Never mind, we'll show them something."

The crowd delayed noisily while two or three of the larger boys plundered the blacksmith's back yard for irons that would serve as crowbars. They returned promptly and again the crowd moved. Presently they came to a final halt. That portion of town was as dark and tree-shaded as any and as quiet, but overhead across the street there were lights and fiddles sawing on little childish gavots. Apparently there were no pupils in the dancing school.

"Save your stones, boys."

"Stand back a minute. Let Hamlin and Willowby at

the door. There; get the bar under the lock. Both together. Now push. Good, she's coming."

A terrified black child went by on a mule. Shadows were darting under the trees now and again, shadows deeply preoccupied with their own errands. Presently a wild beast shout went up from the crowd, a shout at once joyful, fiendish, playful and victorious, and the young animals swept into the print shop. M. Baptiste hastened to his window and tried futilely to see through the leaves.

Then the real storm broke. Cases went over with a clash and boom. Some boys began at once to tug on the presses with their wild, intoxicated strength, having the debauch of their young lives. The composing table was upturned, smashed to splinters. The stools instantly got the same medicine. Then followed a hideous dismemberment of the small pieces; one by one, the last clinging joints were separated.

Meanwhile, by some miracle of happy exuberance, the presses were drawn outside. There, by dint of stones and crowbars, they were wantonly leveled. Then the boys remembered the windows and let their remaining stones fly.

M. Baptiste started across the street but retreated promptly when a stone careered near his feet. Others ran out into the darkness and started turning round and round in a hopeless bewilderment. What, in God's name, was happening?

"Dash the light," the harelipped youngster whispered. "Run for it."

Inside somebody stumbled over the wreckage, scrambled to his feet and came thundering out with the horde.

"Cut across the fields. Over that fence and back to the grove from behind. Scatter when you get out there. You can't tell – "

5

M.Creuzot's first thought ran to his musket; he was now quite certain that his mind had warned him against lending it to Mingo. It was a tall weapon of a French make and easily recognizable. No need to weep now, though, now with the town full of drums, militiamen and men and boys who had volunteered. The situation, where M. Creuzot and his family were concerned, was beyond tears. The wan printer blessed himself at the draped window of his front room and tried to extricate himself, mentally, from the desperate snare. Would he bow down and face the music, or would he attempt flight with a stout wife and two small boys? And Laurent. He would have to be considered one of them now; their problem was the same.

A few moments later, eating supper around a rude kitchen table, M. Creuzot looked at his meat and wine without desire. André and Jean were ravenous as usual. Their mother stood over the stove like one unaccustomed to a table and moistened a morsel of bread in the gravy left in a pot.

"They're everywhere," André said. "Listen, I hear drums over by the river."

"Can't we go out tonight, papa?" Jean said. "We've been in the house all day."

"Maybe. If your mama wants to walk with you."

"You come too," André said.

"Not tonight."

"Are you sick, papa?"

"No, not sick."

"Well, why don't you eat?"

"Why, oh, yes, I'm going to begin now, son."

His wife rattled a kettle self-consciously. Her heavy black hair seemed almost sinister without a direct view of her large smiling face, but when she turned there was reassurance enough.

"Never mind your papa. Eat, Jean. Don't sit staring," she said.

"It's an awful confusion,"M. Creuzot said. "Maybe we'll be going away from Richmond soon."

"Why?" Jean said.

"Well, lots of things. All this noise – these soldiers."

"Will they hurt us?"

"No. Business is not so good here, you know. Mr. Biddenhurst says Philadelphia is a finer place."

The boys still looked bewildered. M. Creuzot drank his wine, nibbled at his meat and pretended to disregard their rigid attention. Soon someone was at the front door and M. Creuzot sprang up with a suddenness that frightened the others. Taking one of the candles, he went through the door and into the adjoining room. M. Baptiste materialized from the empty blackness of the doorway. His face, apart from his pointed whiskers, was chalk-white, and there was a ghostly distress on his features.

"Mon Dieu," the printer said, looking at him.

"Have you heard it?"

"We haven't heard anything. But your face –"

"Hell's loose, my friend."

"I know that, but what's happened?"

"Vandals. They've broken in your shop."

"Broken in?"

"They've annihilated everything. 'Jacobin' is the word they used. We're all involved somehow in the uprising of the blacks."

"The blacks? What are the blacks doing?"

"Who knows?"

They went into the next room and stood facing each other over a round table. Mme. Creuzot came in, wiping her hands on her apron, and the youngsters followed as far as the door. There they stood, gazing in wonder. The white-paste buckles of M. Baptiste, the dancing master, twinkled nervously.

M. Creuzot's face suddenly went haggard.

130

"Mingo borrowed my musket," he whispered. "Is he among the blacks who have made trouble?"

"A leader of some sort, I daresay."

"The musket *could* be offered as evidence against me, but I am innocent. What can one do?"

"The stages are running. Had you thought of that?"

"I'd like to find Laurent."

"I'll send him. I'll go by his room from here."

"Thanks. Tell him to hurry."

"I've been thinking about Charleston for myself. I have friends there."

There were a few more words, a few more details and M. Baptiste was outside again, facing the candle with that same woebegone countenance. Then he turned and was gone, and the door closed. Mme. Creuzot was back at the kitchen door, entreating the youngsters to finish their supper, while her husband kept blessing himself in the shadows of the front door.

6

And you acknowledge complicity?"

"Don't know as I does *that,* yo' honor."

"But you were one of them? You plotted with the others to massacre the people of Richmond?"

"No, suh. Befo' God, I ain't done that."

The court of *Oyer and Terminer,* composed of Henrico County justices, had no occasion to nod. Crowded into a clerk's small office, the wigged justices wearing hats and street clothes had taken seats on tables, stools and desks. Three or four newspaper reporters had wormed in with guards and spectators; they had promptly appropriated the writing places. The wheels of customary court justice were too sluggish for a crisis such as this one. The fastidious old slave, the salt-and-pepper whiskers quivering on his face, stood before the circle of men twisting a pair of faun colored driving gloves in his hands. Presently, for no apparent reason, the tone of inquisition changed. The questioner paused abstractedly. When he opened his mouth again, his voice took a new note.

"You Ben Woodfolk?"

"Yes, suh."

"You the property of Mr. Moseley Sheppard?"

"I is, suh."

"How long?"

"Fifty year, I reckon. Near about that long, leastwise."

"Well, how did you become associated with the plot?"

The Negro's eyes roved. There was a bough sweeping against the blue window at his shoulder. Ben became aware of perspiration on his face and of the new Sunday hat crushed under his arm. He recalled an ugly grinning thing squatted beside a burying hole in Marse Prosser's low field. Suddenly the experiences of the past weeks seemed far away.

Ben moistened his lips and began telling the impromptu court how it had been that old Bundy's invitation to become a "mason" had led to his reluctant interview with Gabriel and Blue and how the long net, against his will, had seemed to involve him more and more without actually taking him in.

The newspaper men began writing rapidly.

"Who were the leaders?"

"Too many to talk about, suh. Gabriel's the head man. Him and Ditcher."

"Ditcher?"

"Yes, suh. He is named Jack Bowler. They calls him Ditcher."

"Oh. And who else that you know?"

"Gabriel's two brothers, Solomon and Martin. Marse Prosser's Blue. Gen'l John Scott –"

"Who is he?"

"Gen'l John belong to Marse Greenhow. He work for Marse McCrea some time."

"Well, what was his part in the plan?"

"Gen'l John? He carried the biggest end of the money, him. He was going to lead a rising in Petersburg, too."

"Yes, yes. Possibly he is the one somebody saw take ten dollars from his ragged jeans recently."

"H'm. I reckon so."

"Were there any free Negroes? Any white people?"

"Well, suh, Mingo was one. He kept the names. I don't know was there any white folks, yo' honor."

"But how were they going about it, Ben? What weapons do they have, and how did they hope to take the city?"

"They's got plenty scythe-swords and pikes and like of that."

"Any muskets?"

"About a dozen flintlocks, I reckon."

"Um hunh. How many bullets?"

"A peck," Ben said soberly.

"That's pretty slim ammunition, isn't it?"

"I don't know. They figured how they wasn't many guards at the arsenal or the powder house. I reckon they figured on starting in there."

At this disclosure the justices all became sober and ceased to smile.

Mr. Moseley Sheppard twitched fretfully in his seat. He had noted the scarlet bough outside the tall window, but his eyes were now on the perplexed old Negro trembling before the circle of inquisitors. The justices sat with their hats on, and some of them rested gloved hands on the knobs of canes that stood between their feet. Now and again a quick sniffle came from the dour circle, a short catch of the breath attending the intake of snuff. Mr. Moseley Sheppard could almost have wept for Ben's distress. In fact, his eyes were watery when the presiding justice abruptly turned to him with a question.

"Mr. Sheppard –"

"Yes."

"Is that substantially the same confession that the defendant made to you?"

"Yes, sir. Quite the same."

"How long ago was it made?"

"Monday morning last."

"And you'd be disposed to vouch for the credibility of the testimony?"

"Quite."

"Well, now, a few more questions to the defendant –"

The voices continued, purged of emotion, repressed, cold, unmoved, yet quavering faintly with a guarded, hidden excitement that amounted to terror. The sky darkened, and a great shadowy leaf fell from the bough.

Thus it befell that Mr. Moseley Sheppard produced his astonishing testimony in a Richmond court. How could any Virginian sleep? How could he be sure from now on that the black slave who trimmed his lamps was not waiting to put a knife in his heart while he slept? How could he know his cook was not brewing belladonna with his tea? This sickness called the desire for liberty, equality, was plainly among the pack.

Where would the madness end?

7

A blanket had been thrown over the seat to protect the cariole's upholstery from early dew. Ben threw it aside nervously, climbed to his place and twitched the driving lines. The old Negro felt like a child new-born. His heart was a leaf.

He say I's clear, that's what he say. He say, You's a good boy, Ben. Don't you let none of these evil niggers tangle you up in nara another such mess, though. Hear? He sure was scairt a heap, I know that. Him and the rest of them white mens was scairt *plenty*. I reckon they won't feel right good again long's Gabriel and Ditcher and the others is on the wing neither.

Ben's heart quickened at the thought of the big crowd at large on the countryside and perhaps in the hills. For some reason it *did* tickle him to see a mighty powerful black fellow acting right sassy, scampering and cutting up like a devilish pant'er or a lion. It did him more good than a pint of rum. But it was bad doings and dangerous this time. Ben wasn't ready to die. He was past that reckless age. He wasn't even studying about freedom any more. At first, of course, he had been drawn along, but he was glad to be out of it now — now that he was clear and didn't have Gabriel's eyes to face. It was a burden lifted; yes, it was like a new day for Ben.

New-borned, Lordy. New-borned, new-borned, thanks Jesus. I heard tell about a woman come walking up out of the ocean, a brand-new woman come up dripping clean out of that there green water and them white waves and all. I heard tell about such a woman plenty times, but I just now knows how she felt. The man say I's clear's the day I's borned. Marse Sheppard he say —

Suddenly in the midst of his rejoicing a kind of nausea commenced rising from Ben's stomach. Nothing from his head, mind you, nothing in his thought telling him he was a no-'count swine and lower than any dog, just something from his stomach making him so sick he wanted to vomit. He pictured his ruffled shirt-front soiled by his sickness, smeared loathsomely, and with a shiver of revulsion, he found his hand across his breast.

Lordy, Jesus, I ain't being no dog. I ain't being low-down. I's just being like you made me, Marse Jesus. This here freedom and all ain't nothing to me. There's blood in it, Lordy, and the sight of blood make me sick as I-don't-know-what.

The little mare had a pleasant gait. For a while the cariole rattled over cobblestones, then came the gritty dirt path with tiny lanes for the wheels. There was a flambeau burning in front of the *Dirty Spoon;* the river, with a burnished metallic brightness, gave an indigo flash. There were shadows creeping along the waterfront, and in the light of the rum shop a ragged Negro sleeping face downward on the ground. Ben heard only the whir of wheels, a small legendary whir resounding against the dim wall of sound that was the river.

On it rolled, the night darkening steadily, the feet of the small alert animal showing like upturned teacups on the black road. In less than an hour Ben observed that the mare had turned without his direction and that the little hooves were twinkling on Marse Sheppard's own gravel drive.

"Well, suh, bless me if you don't know the way home, little Miss. Was I blind I wouldn't need no better guiding. You is all eyes and footses once you get yo' head turned this way."

For once there was no lantern hanging in the carriage shed. Ben drew up the reins and stepped to the ground. The broken, fragmentary moon sprang up beyond the stable. The place was frightfully quiet. But Ben knew better than to expect a stable boy now with half the black men on the wing and the other half quaking in their huts. He began unhitching the little mare. Presently a heavy figure tumbled out of the haymow and crept down beside the cariole.

"Listen – "

"That you, Pharoah?"

"Yes, this me. You heard anything?"

"Anything like what?"

"Somebody say Criddle is long gone."

"Long gone, hunh?"

"H'm. He dead out yonder 'neath of a palma Christe tree."

"Bullets?"

"Yes, I reckon. Soldiers. That ain't the beginning neither."

"It ain't?"

136

"No."

Ben carried an armful of harness into the stable. He was inside several minutes, feeling his way along the wall and putting things on the proper hooks. When he returned he did not speak at once but began passing a dry cloth over the neck and flanks of the horse. Pharoah stood with a petrified stare, hunched at the shoulders and breathing audibly. His arms hung loose.

"Well, what in the nation was you doing in that there devilish haymow?"

"I tell you things is a-popping round here."

"I reckon," Ben said. "They is a-popping in town too. But you – *you* ain't obliged to hide from nobody, is you?"

Pharoah chose to ignore the question. He put his hands together and began twisting an old hat. His queue was untied and his hair had risen on his head like a porcupine's bristles.

"They went by just now with two-three of Marse Bowler's slaves."

"Which ones?"

"Don't know which ones. Mousie say they pulled them out a pigsty. Them pudden-head boys crawled in there in such a big hurry they left they feet sticking out."

"Nobody's hunting *you*, is they?"

"The niggers is saying I'm the one what told – "

Pharoah lost his voice. His eyes kept darting across the yard.

"Saying you's the one what told, hunh?"

"Somebody was hiding in the bushes, and when I passed, they throwed this here out at me."

He held a knife in his hand.

"You should of stayed in town."

"Did somebody tell you it was me that told?"

Ben became uncommonly grave. He walked the little mare around to the barnyard. When he returned, he was shivering. He backed the cariole into the shed by hand and raised the thills.

"Everybody know you told."

"I ain't named no names."

"Naming names ain't nothing. You just as well to named names. You told plenty. White folks can look and see for theyselves who's gone. Naming names ain't a thing."

"Where you been? Ain't *you* told nothing?"

"Me told?"

Ben coughed. Then he became silent for a space.

"I been in court. They was trying me."

"Is you clear?"

"H'm."

"Well, ain't you had to tell nothing?"

"Nothing much. Nothing amounting to nothing."

"I wish I's locked up in jail."

Pharoah disappeared beneath some fruit trees, and Ben started up the path to the great house. There were candles in the kitchen and in the front a porch lamp flickered in its sconce. Ben's feet seemed heavy on the gravel path. Somewhere, in some dying thicket, a brown thrasher called. Shadows of leaves made a charcoal lacework on the ground. A nervous little cough escaped Ben and he raised a thin palsied hand to muffle it. At the same instant something whistled through the shrubbery; something as damp and cold as an icicle brushed his coat sleeve and slipped through his hand. The old slave swayed back on his heels, tottered a moment and then went down on his knees.

It was as Ben imagined. There was at once a scuffling and scampering on the dead leaves beneath the hedge, followed by running feet on the slope beyond. Ben waited to reassure himself, then rose, his hand sopped by unaccountable mud, and started toward the house again. In the light before the window he saw the cut in his palm and was about to go back and look for the knife when a sudden panic took him. The first thing, he decided, was to staunch the blood. Furthermore, daylight would be safer time for prowling in the leaves. He cupped his wounded hand to hold the blood and let himself into the kitchen.

138

8

Alexander Biddenhurst got the story from newspapers and the accounts he read, like those read by the country at large, were marked by hinted implications more serious than were indicated in the testimony of Ben and the report of Pharoah. It is true that the Salem *Gazette,* with other papers, resented this campaign of reticence and suggestion, but the same veiled reports continued. "The minutiae of the conspiracy have not been detailed to the public," this journal remarked, "and perhaps, through a mistaken notion of prudence and policy, will not be detailed in the Richmond papers."

New York's *Commercial Advertiser* had been informed that a conditional amnesty was to be sought, since the plot, it was felt, involved immense numbers and would demand that nearly all the Africans in that part of the country be apprehended and punished. Later that paper expected the whole procedure to wait on a special secret session of the Virginia legislature, scheduled to meet as soon as the men could be gathered.

Yet reports came through and, straight or warped, the newspapers printed and reprinted them. They told of Gabriel's sober, thoughtful face, his obsession for the same romantic dream that was the lasting creed of the poor, the unwanted, the world over. An immense fellow, amazingly young to exercise such influence, was conjured into the imaginations of thousands; he was a black of vast abilities and life-long preparations. Since the age of twenty-one (he was twenty-four now) he had traveled about, with apparent innocence, recruiting confederates and accumulating stores of arms. He was now at large with hundreds of followers, and his shadowy figure standing on the summit of a twilight hill recalled the savage uprisings in San Domingo that put the slaves in the masters' saddles. The possibility of such a wide conspiracy, when one considered the desperate and fatalistic temper of the serfs, was hard to overestimate.

Mr. Alexander Biddenhurst polished the thick lenses of his spectacles with a silk handkerchief. In his upstairs rooms at the corner of Coats Alley and Budd Street he had drawn away from the writing desk and reclined in a low chair surrounded by frayed Ottomans, shabby cushions and books turned face downward on the floor. His lamp was spitting feebly, and it occurred to him that there was no more oil in the house. He decided to dash the flame and conserve his little remaining fuel for a possible need during the night. One never knew, when he tucked his coverlet over his shoulders, who would knock on his door before morning. That, at least, had been Mr. Biddenhurst's experience in Philadelphia, at the corner of Coats and Budd. He went into the bedroom, feeling the way by hand, and began undressing.

He awakened to a crisp morning and a shaft of golden light against his window. Mrs. Chubbs had already let herself into the small apartment and was busy with the coffee pot. Mr. Biddenhurst pulled on his shirt and tied his curly black hair indifferently. A moment later, one arm in his coat, he was flying to the door in answer to urgent raps.

Alexander Biddenhurst felt singularly exuberant this morning, and the noise of his own heels gave him an immense pleasure.

"Hail, goddess," he shouted to the fat housekeeper as he whisked past the door without giving her a chance to reply. But an instant later, his hand on the knob, the sound of voices downstairs gave him pause. They were nervous, covered voices, and Mr. Biddenhurst's speculation ran at once to the fugitive blacks who were stopping at his door more and more frequently these recent days, seeking brief succor and guidance to the next imaginary post on their shadowy flight to the town of St. Catherine, across the Canadian border. Why it would come to be a business soon – these runaways would develop a regular transit line if they continued this system, he reflected. And always it was like this too; just after daybreak, following a night of travel, they would call on him and he would give them directions to one of the addresses on his list. At the homes of freed Negroes or gracious whites they would find pallets in attic or cellar and warm porridge for their bones sometimes. An unimportant young lawyer, a foreign-born citizen of a great city that knew him hardly at all, Mr. Biddenhurst felt this small contribution to the cause of freedom and equality in the large, cheerfully rendered, justified in some part a life that otherwise meant but little to anyone now. And there was melancholy in the thought, too, though indeed it gave him no hurt at this exuberant hour of the morning. The door swung open.

Gasps and shrieks of astonishment.

The roly-poly red-haired fellow stood with arms dangling, his face rent with an embarrassed smile, his ill-fitting hat clinging to his head by a strand, but Mr. Biddenhurst threw his own arms into the air, embraced the boy and began presently to slap him on the back.

"Laurent!"

"It's me. I'm sorry to take you like this, so sudden-like."

"But I don't believe it. That's *not* you."

"Did you ever see a Frenchman you could mistake for me?"

Mr. Biddenhurst laughed heartily and made a motion to close the door behind the excited boy.

"Hardly," he said. "But you could be an apparition. Let me touch the wounds."

"Fortunately I have none, no serious ones at any rate. But you have another surprise in store."

"Let me get near the sofa. Now. You can tell me now."

"There are others downstairs," Laurent said. "Shall I call them?"

"Of course. I heard the voices but seeing you made me forget. Who is it?"

"I'll go. I had the feeling you were spying me through the keyhole – your hand was on the knob so long."

"The incurable dreamer, you know. Who's down there?"

"I'll get them."

In a moment the little group was on the stair, their hesitant, disciplined steps scarcely audible in the rooms above. Mr. Biddenhurst stood in the door and recognized with a jolt the top of M. Creuzot's hat. The printer was followed by his wife and small sons, and behind them all came Laurent, a heavy traveling bag in each hand this time. There were warm embraces all around.

"But I'm speechless, M. Creuzot."

"It's the season of blowing leaves," the printer said mirthlessly. "You know how leaves behave."

"Sudden, delightful swirls – I know, but still –"

"There's a tempest in Richmond," the other murmured. "A crowd of boys, shouting 'Jacobin' at the top of their lungs, demolished my shop."

"And you suspected they'd demolish you?"

"That's one way of saying it."

Mr. Biddenhurst managed to be silent for a spell. His eyes ran to the small boys peeping into the kitchen, to their mother busy with the folds of her shawl and to the lugubrious red-haired Laurent holding a drape aside as he peered out on the street.

"We cannot escape it," he said at length. "There is a struggle that takes us in. It takes us in against our wills. There is no escape for men of conscience."

"It is unjust."

"Of course, just as poverty is unjust. Just as slavery and class distinctions are unjust. The consequences of these evils fall back on us indirectly. We're marked."

André and Jean had inched their way into the kitchen. They were making friends with Mrs. Chubbs. Suddenly they were laughing. Mr. Biddenhurst, hearing them, threw out his feet and laughed too. M. Creuzot's blue eyes were still downcast.

142

"We'll want to get settled somewhere today," he said. "Let's think about coffee now. That other will follow in its time."

Meanwhile the sun went higher. A beam fell across the shelves of inexpensive books, and Laurent turned and began scanning the titles along the wall, his eye obviously running to typographical features rather than subject matter. Mme. Creuzot, wearied of fussing with folds, finally decided to remove her shawl completely. A fresh burst of laughter came from the kitchen, and Mr. Biddenhurst threw out his feet again.

9

Still the blurred rattle of kettle drums was unbroken, and swarms of uniformed guardsmen gave the streets of Richmond no rest. A hysterical woman wearing a night shift ran out of her house in the early dawn with screams and declarations that she had heard voices in her cellar. A crochety old man leading a cow by a tether carried an immense stone in his right hand. He was followed by a linty old hag who walked with a gnarled corkscrew cane. In the public square a jittery morning crowd was slowly dispersing. Half a dozen obscure blacks had just been hanged following a summary hearing before the wigged justices who composed the *Oyer and Terminer* tribunal for the emergency. This stern show of retribution, as had been expected, was proving itself a useful sedative, but the city was still mad, still frothing at the mouth; and now that the real slave chiefs were known, it was not likely to be long pacified by the blood of a nameless rabble. An immense dog, imprisoned in an outhouse, scratched at the wall and howled bitterly. A fine, silvery mist stretched over the city, over the trees and lawns and finally broke like a cobweb.

A pippin-cheeked man wearing a brown suit and brown shoes with buckles came out of a notary's office and tacked a full-page leaflet on the announcement board. A moment later, leaving a circle of gawking peasants around the bulletin, he spat gingerly into the gutter and walked away. Carriages were on the streets early, rumbling on the cobblestones. And just the night before, the man reflected, there had been such a crowd of them wedged and jammed at the square, it had seemed they would never be disentangled; yet here they were again coming back as eagerly as they had gone. And so much the better, too; why, here was an announcement from Governor Monroe that would raise their hair. The brown-clad man selected a lamp post near the waiting rooms of the stagecoach line and again put up a copy of his bulletin. There was still a small sheaf of the papers in his hand, so he slipped away again as a new crowd began to gawk over his shoulders.

In the courtyard stood the yellow woman with the black enameled hair. She was swinging a scarlet parasol with a vacuous air. There were two horses at the hitching bar and a swarm of pigeons near the water trough and on the ground. Melody's heavy bracelets jangled softly but her furbelows were still. She was watching a troop of guards haul a cowed Negro through the streets. They were flogging him freely and making a scene that drew a medley of spectators.

She began walking again, the lacey parasol twirling, and passed through the crowd with quiet self-conscious hauteur. Suddenly she saw the face of Mingo the freed Negro flickering between the other heads like a drowned moon in a bog. He had lost his hat, and his queue was untied so that he had momentarily the look of a savage. Melody thought: It's ugly doings for true. This here town is going to the dogs, and the peoples is getting meaner'n apes. I wonder how Philadelphia is.

A moment later she turned her face on the sight and began walking once more. Down the empty blue street she passed half a dozen squares. Shops were opening to the soft morning and there was a string of carts beneath the cottonwoods on a noisy side street. Farmers in filthy home-spuns were holding up yams, cabbages, rutabagas and ears of corn and vying noisily for the small indifferent trade. Melody passed them and turned into a neatly arranged shop where she was known.

"He was putting up a fight, that Mingo."

"I wasn't looking. A dozen bananas, please. Some grapes."

"Grapes, bananas – yes. He was the third this morning."

"Third?"

"Yes, the others I didn't know."

"These quinces –"

"A penny for two. We've got the Democrats to thank – plague take them."

"I reckon we has. Four, please."

A little later she stopped before the announcement board outside the notary's office. Two farmers in leather jackets had put their heads together and were reading the small type laboriously. Melody, glancing over their shoulders, between their heads, paused long enough to spell out in part the bold headline of the governor's offer. REWARDS FOR CAPTURE... SLAVE CHIEFS... PLOT TO MASSACRE... GABRIEL PROSSER $300.00... Jack Bowler... The lines were broken up and confused by the two heads that bobbed and shifted before her line of vision; and presently such letters as she saw clearly, wrinkled and curled and danced in her excited eyes. Suddenly she became aware of coarse remarks coming from a crowd of men withdrawn to the edge of the road. Melody gave them a slow, bitter, sidewise glance and started walking again. She twirled her parasol lightly, but there was perspiration in the palm of her hand and she was not gay.

10

Thomas Callender put down his heels hopelessly. Even now, though a prisoner by reason of the Sedition Act, he seemed as actively involved as ever in the political snares of his day. It didn't seem right. He was a sensitive writing man, a poet at heart. Those conscienceless men who were trying to bring about the re-election of John Quincy Adams would halt at no lying inference, no false interpretation to befuddle the voters. Everyone knew, for example, where he (Callender) stood on the question of slavery and on the question of wealth and private property and the equality of men; everyone knew where Thomas Jefferson stood. Yet these Federalist swine now sought to identify both of them with hated atheistic propaganda and with the French *Amis des Noirs* and their encouragement to the slaves to free themselves by armed insurrection. It was fairly obvious guile, Callender thought. He curled his feet beneath the writing table and added another paragraph to the piece he was writing.

> *... An insurrection at this critical moment by the Negroes of the Southern States would have thrown everything into confusion, and consequently it was to have prevented the choice of electors in the whole or the greater part of the states south of the Potomac. Such a disaster must have tended to injure the interests of Mr. Jefferson, and to promote the slender possibility of a second election of Mr. Adams.*

Such a statement should not be necessary, he told himself, but dishonesty was so rife in the opposing party one had to say something to spare the innocents. Callender leaned back, festooning his writing arm on the back of his chair, and waited for the approach of a guard whose heels were at the moment clicking in the aisle outside.

"A young man wants to know if the letter to the Norfolk *Epitome of the Times* is ready?"

"Tell him to wait. He can take it presently."

"Could you say how long?"

"Half an hour, possibly."

Callender dipped his pen in the inkpot and set to work again, more hastily this time.

The sun was pushing up rapidly. An overgrown boy with large feet and a slow wit dashed out of a house and came plop-plopping through the yard carrying an antique matchlock. He shot wild glances in both directions then fled down the street to an open shop at the corner.

"Will this do?" he asked the shoemaker, handing the musket across the counter.

"It's powerfully old."

"Grampa shot turkeys with it, turkeys and Indians."

"I reckon it'll need some tending to."

"There ain't time to fiddle around, is there?" He failed to get an answer from the tiny wizened man with the pipe in his mouth, so he went on talking. "With a lot of wild Africans fixing to scalp us, somebody's got to do something, they're a lot of mad dogs let loose, them niggers. It's true – I heard it from one of the volunteers."

"This won't do. Too much rust. You might scare them with it, though. If somebody seen this looking out of your window, he might change his mind about coming inside."

The boy's eyes rounded; his mouth became a circle. For a moment he could not utter a word. Then his voice returned in a whisper, a whisper that grew with each word.

"Yes, yes. That's topping. I know how: poke it out at them. Like this. Sure, that's it. I know. Thanks. This is it. See? Like this."

He was pointing the thing venomously, driving the unseen savage into a corner. The shoemaker took his pipe in his hand, nodded agreement. The boy bounded out of the store so blindly he ran into a squad of militiamen. But he

147

was up like a cat, hastening to the small inconspicuous house down the road.

The men with Captain Orian Des Mukes were in and out of town at intervals of less than an hour. By turn they followed every road into the country; returning periodically, they offered the townsfolk the pleasant reassurance of squeaky new saddles, burnished sabers and the tock-tock of metal horseshoes on the cobblestones.

This had continued nearly a week now, but still there had been no clash with insurgents, and the impression was going out that maybe there would be none, that perhaps the blacks were scattered and would have to be ferreted from their holes by searching detachments.

"This parading," Captain Des Mukes said. "It's cursed tomfoolery, Sergeant."

"I reckon it is for a fact, Cap'n. What's your idea?"

"We'd just as well be hunting rabbits with this outfit. Somebody's got to get out and comb the hills and thickets. Nothing against stationing the cavalry in town, understand? They could be ready for an eventuality."

"That's sense, suh."

"But them ringleaders are like as not out of the state by now. Mark my word, when them black sons hit the bush, they went down on all fours like they been wanting to do for years. They dusted, that's what they did, every blasted one of them. This is nonsense, drilling around here like we were waiting for an attack by an artillery division."

"You're talking sense, Cap'n."

At nightfall Mingo lay face downward on a wooden floor. The room might have been a cave or a den, so far as he could tell; nothing was distinguishable in the blackness. Yet they had taken pains to bind his wrists to the flooring so that he lay on his belly with arms flung out. He wriggled helplessly, his nose pressed agains the boards.

No mo' little buck wagon, Mistah Mingo, no mo' saddle

shop, no mo' nothing now. Reading's bad for a nigger. You just reads and you reads and pretty soon you sees where it say, Brothers, come and unite with us and let us combat for a common good; then you is plum done for. You ain't no mo' count for bowing and scraping and licking boots. Oh, it's bad when niggers get to holding out they arms, touching hands, saying Brother this, Brother that, they is about to meet the whirlwind then.

The stars in they courses fought against Sistra, and that's a fact for true. That's howcome all the rain and wind that night. We was fixed to wear them out that night; dog it, we was *ready*. Black folks was as sure to go free Saddy night week ago as God is sure to judge the wicked. We was ready to fall on this here town so fast they wouldn't had time to whistle.

The stars was against us, though.

Mingo knew that night had come to the streets and that the night watch had been doubled; he knew too how many times the hangman's trap had been sprung since morning. The sounds came to him distinctly. But he couldn't tell exactly where he was, and he failed at first to understand the strategy that delayed his hanging while others were being rushed to the gallows so breathlessly. Now at last a possible reason was dawning. He had just heard a strange voice talking outside.

"Keep that one," it had said. "There were hands in this plot that haven't been suspected yet. Why, Lord, man, the thing could hardly have failed of success. A surprise blow like this – you mark my word, such audacity and diabolical invention came from a trained mind, possibly a professional revolutionary. Search carefully for papers that might point to Callender, Duane, United Irishmen or to France by way of San Domingo. And by all means hold this Mingo; *he knows how to read*. He was free and in open communication with radical elements. He carried the lists."

Mingo groaned and fretted and twitched till he rubbed

the skin off the tip of his nose. His nerves blunted by the torturous anxiety of the past days, he felt that he would sooner take his punishment at once and have it over with than to writhe longer on the floor clutching at a hope too slender for any comfort at all.

Now among the townspeople, however, the first paralyzing consternation was past. The attack, depending entirely upon surprise and audacity for success, had been delayed by the severest tempest in the memory of any living Virginian. The band of drenched savages, with their chiefs, were scattered. It was not likely that they would reunite, their numbers having dwindled greatly and their design having been betrayed. Many of the rebelling slaves were back at their places, protesting their innocence and laying all blame on the leaders who inveigled them; more than a score had been punished publicly.

Now the town was gathering its wits, but the ringleaders were still at large. That wizened and sinister old sack of rags they called General John Scott – what had become of him and his grinning brown fangs? That giant stud called Ditcher, the one with the immense shock of hair, where was he? And the incredible Gabriel, twenty-four, massive, dour-visaged and undisputed leader of them all, had he given up the game?

There was a woman too, they said, a thin-waisted brown gal with a penchant for wearing her master's riding boots, twisting her skirt around her hips and galloping a fiery black colt in the big road. There were lots of stories about her. Not much was known definitely.

Richmond was armed to the teeth now, and men could sleep. Ovid, night guard at the arsenal, stood long at his picket gate as night darkened. The sky was too heavy with stars. Leaves were falling like shadows on the gabled roof of his small house, and through the door he could see the numerous faces of his children in the circle of light around a lamp. Ovid filled his pipe leisurely.

"No more cause to fret yourself, Birdie." He stroked a small hand.

The woman's voice came out of the shadows.

"Not fretting, Ovid, thanking God. Think how it might have been with you and Mr. Midwick there alone."

He could toss his head about it now.

"I don't know. There's always something in a brave man that rises to the occasion. My taste for adventure and danger –"

"Oh, it's fine to think about it like that."

"I must trot now, Birdie."

11

Alexander Biddenhurst read Governor Monroe's proclamation in the newspapers, and the thing that struck him was the smallness of the price placed on the rebel heads as compared with the gravity and earnestness of the governor's statement and the obvious concern of the state manifest in their calling of the United States cavalry and the doubling of patrols and guards in every city of consequence. Possibly, he concluded, the very gravity of the situation made a larger money offer unnecessary.

He was standing beneath a tree, his elbows resting on a cobblestone fence. Before him and beyond this wall crisp fields tumbled away into knolls and broken declivities. Small bright pumpkins were scattered across dun acres of reaped cornstalks. Mr. Biddenhurst folded his paper, shoved it into a coat pocket and resumed his morning walk.

Would the frustration of this bold plot delay or hasten the great emancipation of all serfs and bondmen? Surely it was becoming increasingly plain that liberty and equality for any poor class could not prevail so long as the system of chattel slavery continued to mock them. But this thwarted attempt by Gabriel – this colossal advertisement of wild discontent and desperate hope, would it not put the planter class on its guard, give them a chance to fortify their inequitable position?

Certainly no one could be blamed, especially since it was everywhere conceded that, barring the storm, the blacks could hardly have failed to duplicate the recent success (within certain bounds) of their brothers in San Domingo. But life was like that: beauty beats a frail wing and the scales of fate are shaken by a bubble. Now the hope of freeing the slaves was more remote than ever in the United States and would have to wait for the slow drip of spring to cut a way through stone. And eventually the stone *would* fail; there could be no doubt of that. Only now, at this moment, Alexander Biddenhurst felt his own efforts so futile and unnecessary.

The only thing left for him was to continue his same endeavors. There were many tender old people (with time and money to burn) who longed to see justice triumph, though it reduce their own fortunes. More and more these would be willing to support the small, semi-secret groups working for the deliverance of bondsmen here and there, singly, as the occasion arose. Romantically excited, they would continue to aid those who were trying to establish a secret highway to the Canadian city of St. Catherine. And young men like Alexander Biddenhurst, lawyers, scholars, poets, would receive their support in the discharge of this work while neglecting the saner courses of business. They would keep the spark alive by agitating, agitating, agitating. They would work into the schools, winning the youngsters and the teachers; they would go among the blacks, flaunt the old taboos, slap the hands of the wretches, tell them there was deliverance ahead and to be ready for the revolution at any hour. Comforted by the philosophers and writers, they would carry on their near-hopeless mission; they would be the drip of spring on the determined rock.

An ox cart trudged slovenly in the fine sunlight. A

handsome young fellow wearing a red jacket and shiny boots came jauntily out of town with a falcon on his wrist.

On Budd Street, before he reached his own doorstep, Mr. Biddenhurst met the Creuzots coming in from a narrow lane. The tall printer was swinging a cane, but his wife's hands were twisted into the folds of her shawl, her covered head bowed slightly. The boys trotted ahead.

"I think we've found the house we want," Mme. Creuzot said with her usual calm cheerfulness. "But Philadelphia's not as pretty as Richmond."

"No, not as pretty. But you'll grow to like it better. There's something about the place that takes hold on you after a time."

"People are straight-laced down there," M. Creuzot said.

"It's something like that – the real difference is. It's a matter of temperament, viewpoint. There's a false, crêpe-paper grandeur down there, a hollowness. How near is the house you're looking at?"

"Only a few squares. Look – I don't know the streets yet – two houses around the second turn there, just beyond the lamp post."

The plump woman, smiling eagerly now, did her best to point.

"People walk faster here," M. Creuzot observed. "We'll have to get adjusted. I don't imagine there'll be time for much chess. Or music."

The younger man laughed.

"You'll manage to squeeze them in."

They were walking again, nearing the doorway where Jean and André waited. Mrs. Chubbs, looking very linty and fluffed in her bonnet and shawl, came down the steps with a basket on her arm. She hurried up the street as if she feared the greengrocer would presently close shop; in a moment or two she turned a corner. Mr. Biddenhurst led his guests upstairs and stood against the door while they entered.

153

"If you're not going to be reading your newspaper right away –"

"Of course not, it's yours, M. Creuzot."

"Thanks."

"Not at all. You know, it offends me just a trifle to see you all so jubilant about leaving my humble –"

"Listen to him," Mme. Creuzot laughed. "He's just a boy. As if we could stay here always."

"Why not?"

"He loves to play, that boy. Laurent is still out."

"He's inspecting the town, no doubt."

Jean's eyes were round.

"Are you really a boy, Mr. Biddenhurst?"

"Well, not quite yet, but I soon shall be. You see I used to be an old bent man – like this. I walked with a crooked stick and my back wouldn't straighten up, but now I'm getting younger and younger, and I've just begun getting *smaller,* too. Soon I shall be a little boy, then perhaps a baby."

"Aw, mama, that isn't true, is it?"

"Well –" She threw off her shawl and ran to the window. "Look down there – a man with a monkey."

"But is it true, mama. Is Mr. Biddenhurst –"

She had to face him.

"Well, we'll have to wait and see."

They all laughed, but the smaller boy's eyes were still round.

12

Ben slept fretfully on chairs behind the great cookstove. Then after daybreak, when he had let Drucilla and Mousie into the kitchen, he went out to the stable and hitched the cariole. There was no hurry, of course; Marse Sheppard was still asleep behind his mosquito nets, and Drucilla's griddle couldn't be heated in a minute. Ben drove the little mare around the gravel path and fastened her reins to a hitching post.

The old Negro had rested poorly, his bones had an aching stiffness, but he was not drowsy. He delayed on the piazza, adjusting a cluster of wooden outdoor chairs around a small table, then walked around to the back and took two wooden water buckets from a stand on the back porch. These were not empty, but Ben poured their remaining contents on the ground and carried them out to the well shed. A moment later he was busy with the sweep, amused by the delightful splash and spatter of water down under the earth.

The two buckets were considerably more than a load for Ben at his age, but there was something about carrying only one at a time that made him unhappy – he had carried two for so many years – and he was more willing to strain his back than to make a second trip. Drucilla opened the door.

"Here you come again, trying to outdo yo'self like some half-grown boy. You ain't fooling nobody but yo'self."

"I ain't old as you might reckon, Miss."

"You done spilt half that water on yo' feet just the same. Now look a-there."

Ben went upstairs and began arranging the old planter's washstand. The great bed on which Marse Sheppard lay looked as feathery and fluffed as a sitting hen. Under one wing and only partly revealed was the white bedroom crock, a shell of a hatched egg. After a while Mousie brought fresh water for the pitcher, and the silvered old man rolled over on the side of the bed so that Ben could untie his nightcap.

Ben sipped a second saucer of coffee behind the stove; and when Marse Sheppard was nearly finished with his meal, he hurried around to the cariole and stood holding the mare's bridle. Marse Sheppard came down the wide

white steps, the ruffles of his shirt-front falling like a cas-
cade on his bosom, and took the place beside Ben in the
small carriage. A moment later they were in the big road
headed for town.

"I reckon they haven't seen hide or hair of them yet?
Nothing of Gabriel or of Bowler's big stud either?"

"No, suh, nothing."

"At any rate, nobody that could bring them in has seen
them yet."

"I reckon they ain't."

"There was that General John, as they call him, too.
How about him?"

"They ain't found him neither."

"Those boys must have meant business."

"H'm. Must of did."

There was a crowd at the courthouse when they reached
town. In the midst of them stood Ditcher, surrounded by
officers and soldiers. He seemed incredibly large as he
stood there. Ben pulled up the little mare. One of the officers had just spoken to the giant Negro. Then a hush fell
on the entire group.

"*Nobody* ain't brung me in, suh. I walked down that
street yonder on my own two feets. On'erstand?"

"Well, you're under arrest *now*, by –"

"H'm. That's howcome I'm here. I heard tell that the
Governor wanted me, and it look like nobody wasn't ever
coming to get me."

The swarm of men and boys buzzed around him like
hornets. In a moment he walked meekly through a double
door, following an officer, followed by dozens of others.

"Well, that accounts for one of them," Marse Sheppard
said.

"Gabriel's apt to give them mo' trouble than that,"
Ben said.

BOOK FOUR

A Breathing
of the
Common Wind

1

They slipped out of one thicket, ran across a lane and plunged into another. Darkness came down hurriedly like a curtain. Gabriel stroked the girl's long wiry fingers.

"This here's the fork of the road, gal, and yonder's the way back."

"Yonder's the way back, but I ain't a-mind to go, boy. On'erstand?"

The coachman's boots that had suited him so well as a general were far from comfortable now. They squeaked and pinched his toes. The purple coat, the coachman's varnished hat and the ruffles on his shirt bosom were all a care to Gabriel now that the ranks of his crowd were broken, now that every man had his own skin to save.

"Which way Blue go?"

"Through the swamps, I reckon. Trying to catch up with Solomon and Martin."

"He should of gone with them what crossed the river."

"Which way you going, boy?"

His eyes darted, but his face did not alter, and he waited long enough to let her know that some of his thoughts were his own.

"I ain't got a heap of rabbit blood in me," he said. "I ain't got no mind to go scratching through the woods. You better start back now. They ain't studying much about womens in this rising. Maybe Marse Prosser don't know you's in it even."

"Maybe he don't. Maybe he do. I ain't studying Marse Prosser."

"What you studying about, gal?"

"About not leaving you."

He pressed the tenuous fingers again and felt a quick suggestion of their real strength.

"Ne' mind that. No need to hold back. What's going to be is bound to be. On'erstand?"

She shook her head.

"I ain't got no mind for nothing like that. All I knows is I feel bad as all-out-doors and I'd heap sooner take a pure killing 'n go the other way."

"I knows. H'm. Some birds is like that too," he said. "That ain't the thing now, though. You might can help me some time if you go back. See? You might could draw me a drink at the well some morning befo' day. You might could help me out some time when I'm near 'bout give out. You could bring me a jug or a chunk of meat some night, maybe. Down in the low field I might be squatting side of a corn shock some night."

There was nothing she could say to that. Nothing she *would* say, at any rate. They began walking, threading a

158

way through the switches of undergrowth. Presently the carcass of a dead animal was under their feet. Buzzards and possums had already cleaned the bones, but shreds of harness were still on the skeleton and the arm of a broken thill lay under the heap. They looked at it briefly, and Gabriel thought of Mingo and of Pharoah and of Ben. He had a fleeting impression that now Juba would surely speak. But there was nothing she could say.

"See, gal, it's going to be me and them from now till the rope snaps. On'erstand? I ain't fixing to go way and hide in the Dismal Swamp. I ain't got no head to fly across the line or nothing like that. I'm after getting up a crowd of don't-care niggers and punishing them white folks till they hollers calf-rope, me. I'm out to plague them like a hornet. God's against them what oppresses the po'. I ain't fixing to quit now."

"They is all scattered now – Ditcher and Solomon and Mingo and all. You going to be one man by yo' lonesome, boy."

"One man. That's a fact and a caution; but just the same I ain't running away nowheres. I'm laying low but I'm staying here, gal. It ain't the same with me like it is with them. I been the gen'l, I reckon."

"Listen there –"

"Nothing but cottontails."

"You reckon so?"

"You better go back now. Keep one eye on the edge of them trees yonder and the other'n on that little dumpy hill – you know how."

She wasn't paying attention.

"It ain't no trouble to keep the way."

"Well –"

"Well what?"

"Howcome you don't get going?"

"I ain't going now," she said. Then after a pause, "You's right nigh played out, boy. Lay down and rest yo'self."

"Who played out?"

159

"Stop puffing out yo' chest. You going to pop open one these times. You's tired a plenty."

"Not me, gal. I ain't tired."

"Lay down anyhow. Here, side of me."

"When you going then?"

"Just befo' day, maybe. I want you to sleep some first."

She twisted and turned like an animal on the switches and leaves. Finally, working down to a place of comfort, she stretched tremulously then curled beside the big solemn-faced male. Gabriel threw out his feet but did not lie down at once. He sat with hands behind him on the ground, his face upraised, his varnished hat gleaming bright black in a clump of dull shadows.

2

Whoever piled light wood against this here fence must of knowed what he was doing, but I'd lay a pretty he didn't know about this here hole he was leaving underneath of the bottom. I bound you he didn't know it was just my size neither. Onliest thing about it is I can't straighten out good and I can't sit up none. Good place to sleep, though. Martin or some of them other lazy niggers is the ones what ought to found this. Yes, suh, sweet as you please for somebody what's studying sleep. I should of put my feet in first. Better crawl out and do that *now*. I'm got to put a knot front of that hole too. Back on out, gen'l; let's go and come again, suh.

Heap better this a-way. I'll be so I can see out some, soon's day come. Who's'n'ever's woodpile this is sure ain't been bothering it much. Weeds about to cover the devilish thing from top to bottom. Don't look like nobody's touched it in a year or mo'. Humph! Just laying out here begging for somebody to crawl under it. . . .

Nothing for a general to crow about, though. Crawling down underneath of a woodpile on his belly. Lordy. I counted on a heap of things, but I sure ain't never counted on this. I heard tell about generals getting kilt and hanged and one thing and another, but I is got my first time to hear tell about one scratching around like a dog under a woodpile. It don't suit a general, this here hole; and it don't suit me a *little* bit. Laying on this sword don't feel good neither. Swords belong to hang down. This here hole ain't going to do me – I see that sticking way out. A general, do he lay down at all, supposes to hang up his sword. Lordy, this ain't me, this sure ain't Gabriel down under here. Gabriel ain't scairt of the living devil; and do he lay down at all for a nachal man, he lay down dead. That's Gen'l Gabriel, Lord, not this here crawling thing.

Yet and still, a good general might would get down low to win; he might would eat some dirt, when his time ain't come, waiting till he can get in his licks good. But that don't look like me. I don't look good to myself eating dirt no kind of way. I'm going to get out of here and hang up my sword, me. Yes, suh, I invites whoever can to come and take the general.

'Member this, though: you takes him standing up, do you take him at all. On'erstand?

The low morning sky was streaked like marble. The peak of a roof here, the silhouette of a grove there, the shape of a hill beyond, each gradually, one by one, took its form from the blackness and assumed its place on the horizon. Cows came to life on a dim slope and a broken-down rail fence suddenly appeared.

The immense Negro, distraught and sleepless, crawled from beneath the light wood and staggered along the fence. The cumbersome sword whipped his left leg. There was a noticeable dent in the top of his two-foot hat. His shirt-front was as smeared and colorless as a gunny sack. He wavered weakly a few steps then leaned against the fence, crossing his legs proudly and festooning his arms on

161

the shoulder-high boards. There, without smiling, he faced the east and soberly invited the sun to rise.

Humble – yes – *humble* – I reckon – *humble yo'self, the bell done rung.* Yes, suh, I hears what you say, and I knows what you means. I heard you say see God, too; *see God 'n see God 'n see God.* That's well and good; *see* God then. You say *He'll come riding down the line of time.* Talk about it if you's a-mind to; I reckon He *will* come riding down the line of time; I reckon you's right. You ain't said nothing to the general, though. On'erstand? I know right well you don't mean Gabriel. Humble – humph!

Ring all the bells you please, peoples. The general ain't scratching down underneath of no mo' lightwood pile. This here general is crossing his legs, spitting through his two fingers and calling the turns. Come on up, Mr. Sun. Let's have some daylight. This here is my own neck and I'll keep it if I can, but I ain't wallering in no dirt to keep it. This here country is mo' fulled up with soldiers and mens with guns than it is fulled up with ground hogs. And that's mighty well and good too. I'm going to run them till they tongues hang out, run them till they start going round and round in one place. But I ain't crawling in no hole, peoples. They takes the general standing up, do they take him at all. They takes him with his sword in the air, do he have one then. On'erstand?

3

The village of shocks in the field of slain hay was, at that hour, peopled by sparrows. Along the boundary of the acres someone had been building a new stone fence. A drag, neglected in the field, had a dozen egg-shaped boulders still on it, and there was a mortar trough an a sand heap near the spot where work had last ceased. A pair of stolid plow oxen grazed beyond a narrow draw. A lantern blossomed like a yellow flower in the stable door, but already the sky was pale and streaks of light stood ready to show the day.

Gabriel, more the general than ever, followed an obscure lane between hedges of dying spiraea; then, strolling easily with a hand on his steel, he swung into the open, crossed a knoll and came down into a poplar clump.

When they tongues is hanging out and they's running round and round in the same place, that's the time to hit back fast. Me and Ditcher could mash up near about a hundred of them by our lonesomes. But plenty mo' niggers'll come; they'll drop out of the sky when they hears sticks a-cracking together and drums a-beating. They'll come shouting like jackals and hyenas. Something'll happen. Something'll happen for good. Can't say as to how. Maybe all of them get kilt. Good'll come, though. I bound you that, peoples.

It's hitting fast what counts, hitting fast at the right time. Them soldiers and all is feeling mighty spry now, killing off niggers by the dozen – I know about them. Ain't nothing to dying. Humph; you's got to die to find out things, I reckon. You's got to die to find out what you don't know. I ain't moaning about them what dies. Good'll come. I'm worried about getting in hard licks when my time come.

His hand was still on his steel when he came to the stubble field and passed between the tall well-made haycocks. A dewy sweetness rose from the field, and Gabriel was suddenly constrained to loiter. Now and again the muscles tightened on his shoulders, quivered and ran. Then without warning something ripped the air; a musket reported near at hand, and Gabriel, off with the crack, plunged forward with raised hands, his hat tumbling before him. Only one knee touched the ground, however, and his stride was scarcely broken by the business of snatching the jittery headgear from between his feet. Running low, cutting arcs and curlicues between the stacks, dashing, changing pace, the big Negro faded like a mist in the hay field. There was a sort of superiority in his flight, an air not mingled with fear or distress or urgency. It was easy, calculated, catch-me-if-you-can running, and Gabriel pulled up proudly where the haystacks ended. He examined his hat and found that nearly a score of buckshot holes dotted its high crown. "H'm. Close," he said.

Then, a little self-consciously and with a lordly lassitude, he turned, feet apart, and watched the excitement five hundred yards away. The farmer who had fired the shot was still in the field fiddling with his flintlock. Another armed man had materialized from the blue slope behind the barns and was skirting the field by way of the stone fence. There was a vague commotion around the houses too, doors banging and a blur of voices audible half a mile on the unruffled morning.

Gabriel considered the question of striking out again. Should he wait until they were within musket range and then outdistance them once more, or should he go at once, allowing himself the sweet luxury of walking insolently into the thicket while they tore the dust? A horse and rider left the barn, galloped down toward the big road. Gabriel fancied the spread of alarm on the countryside, perhaps the coming of a squad to comb the woods behind him. He decided to walk nevertheless. So the pursuers, if they saw him at all before he vanished into the thicket, saw him with hat cocked, a hand resting easily on his steel, his shoulders rocking arrogantly.

Safely out of view, he hastened again. Switches whipped his legs. He went through puddles of crisp airy leaves and felt them foam up around his knees and settle down again with a tiny golden splash. Somewhere, incredibly sweet, there was the voice of a brown thrasher. Gabriel recalled a marsh of shallow water, a marsh dense with trees and vines. And now, without his taking thought, something was drawing him toward it.

164

4

Juba moped. She stood outside the circle of savage gossiping hags and settled her weight on one leg. She had given them her left shoulder and an arm set akimbo on her hip, and now, running nervous fingers through her wild shock of hair, she cut her eyes at them spitefully.

At intervals the others leaned forward confidentially, their heads coming together near the ground, their blunt posteriors rising and broadening simultaneously. At the center of the circle, beside the outdoor fire, squatted a woman with a baby. She was moistening a rag in a cup of gruel and offering it to the infant. Her teeth jutted between sagging lips; lean wrinkled breasts hung against her belly.

"The way that gal is putting on you'd think he's the last man in the state what's got a seed to give."

An older woman, wrinkled and witchlike, clasping a clay pipe in her mouth, picked at the toenails of a scaly foot.

"Gabriel's all right. He a mighty fine boy, even if he is got a face longer'n a mule's. But all this Jesus talk I hears ain't helping him none."

The sleeves were torn from Juba's garment, and the rag that remained of the upper half was drawn tight around her breasts. It had parted from the skirt, too, and there was a streak of nakedness at her waist. Now that she knew what they were getting at, she gave her hips a twitch and moved a few steps.

"You ain't never heard Gabriel moaning and praying. What you talking about?"

The others looked a little surprised, but they were far from displeased with their success in piquing her interest. She had ignored them so long they had begun to imagine that she failed to hear them, even when they talked in her presence. The woman with the baby leaned forward and spat into the fire.

"No sense of you trying to get yo'self hanged, though. You's a fool; that's what you is."

"Ne' mind about that. If I don't care do I get hanged, that's me. If I's a plum fool, that's me too. On'erstand?"

The shadows gathered quickly, almost hastily, and now, in no time at all, it was night at the cooking place. Juba walked completely around the circle of slave women. Somewhere among the folds of her butternut garment she found a pipe and a moment later she was kneeling at the fire. But she was not one of the crowd on the ground; even when she brushed against them while holding her pipe to the flame, she was as haughty and aloof as a harlot. The old woman scraping at her crusted toenails did not look up.

"A man, do he 'spect to win, is obliged to fight the way he know. That's what's ailing Gabriel and all them. He is obliged to go at it with something he can manage."

Juba looked perplexed, but she did not speak till she was on her feet again.

"What you mean, woman?"

"They talks about Toussaint over yonder in San Domingo. They done forget something."

Her face grew more hideous in the firelight. A frayed stick that she had been chewing hung on her lip.

"Go on. What Gabriel forget?"

"I don't know about all that reading in the Book. All that what say God is going to fight against them what oppresses the po'. That might be well and good – I don't know. Toussaint and them kilt a hog in the woods. Drank the blood."

"He did, hunh?"

"H'm. Gabriel done forget to take something to protect hisself. The stars wasn't right. See? All that rain. Too much listening to Mingo read a white man's book. They ain't paid attention to the signs."

"Gabriel don't know a heap of conjure and signs and charms. He ain't never had no head for nothing like that."

The old female drew up the other foot. Suddenly she seemed faraway and cruelly unconcerned.

"Nah, I reckon he ain't," she said.

"Well, he ain't done for yet. He going to be a peck of trouble to them yet, I bound you."

"Maybe. I tell you there's a heap of them what *is* done for, though. Criddle, Ditcher, Mingo and I don't know how many mo'. Then they's a lot mo' what nobody's seen hide or hair of and what's just as apt to be dead as they is apt to be live."

Juba shrugged.

"Plenty niggers died with Toussaint too, didn't they?"

"It didn't work out the same. You'll see. Toussaint kilt a hog. There's plenty things Gabriel could of done."

"Listen, woman. Maybe some time I might see Gabriel *now* – some night maybe. Has you got a good hand I can give him to put in his pocket?"

The infant, not satisfied with its rag, whimpered and presently set up a faint, croaking lamentation. The four or five women who were not smoking had snuff-smeared mouths; periodically they leaned forward and spat into the fire. Juba squatted down beside the old creature who was still preoccupied with her scaly black feet and waited for an answer.

"Maybe."

"Listen, woman," Juba said. "I don't know nothing about *maybe*. Is you going to make me a hand for Gabriel, one what'll keep him safe whilst he's running?"

"He ought to come hisself. That's the most surest way. I could make you one for him that might help some, though."

"Come on." Juba pulled at the other's rags. "Come on now. Some time I might can bring him to you, some night late, but that ain't now. Come on, woman."

"Take yo' hands off'n me, gal. See there, you done pulled it off. I can't be sitting out here buck naked, old as I'm getting."

Juba put the garment under her arm. The old female gave up her toes reluctantly, struggled to her feet.

"Come on now," Juba said. "Here's yo' rag."

"Gabriel should of come hisself. Matter of fact, he should of come long time ago, did he have any sense."

Night had come with emphasis, but bats were still leaving the peaked gable of the barn. They wavered upward, shadowy and fabulous, like legendary birds. When Juba and the old crone reached the door, a foul stench came out of the hut and assailed them like a plague. Juba halted and heard the women they had left cackling around the fire. Then, puffing fast to keep the smoke in her nostrils, she followed the older woman into the hovel.

5

The town of Richmond breathed a bitter murderous resentment, but much of the original excitement had now abated. Militiamen still mulled the streets, however, periodically dragging anonymous Negroes before the justices. For the most part, the first-fruits of this messy harvest were inconspicuous nobodies, but the leaders were marked now and grimly promised to the noose.

Meanwhile the trap was not idle. A crowd swarmed in the open yard. Among them was the dazed, vacuous girl whose parent got himself impaled on Criddle's scythe-sword. All were restless and touchy during the intervals, but the arrival of a fresh victim gave them a moment of pause that permitted the trap to fall during a hush. Then, blinking hard after the jolt, one by one they regained their wits and sought to show a casual air. But the girl, waiting hungrily for each new kill, neither blinked nor recovered. She stared, leaning a little forward, tearing her homespuns absently. There seemed to be an impression among those who had ceased to regard her presence that she was entitled to whatever compensation she could wring from the sights, but she got little attention now.

Somewhere near by, bound face downward to the floor, Mingo caught a change in the voices he heard, discerned the pause and waited for the trap. He could feel gooseflesh rising, and he kicked the floor wildly, imagining that he could not bear the gruesome horror another time. But there it was, a bungling clap-clap, and he wilted again, cold and tremulous and with tears in his eyes. What was it Toussaint said? *Brothers, come and unite with me.* Suddenly Mingo awakened to a meaning he had not previously seen in the words. Toussaint was in jail now, maybe dead. *Brothers, come and unite with me.* Mingo felt momentarily stronger. Do the dead combat for a common cause? Well, he thought, it was possible that they did, yes, quite possible.

Near by old Ben, clean and well-favored, wearing new driving gloves and a hat in neat trim, stood at the curbstone, his arm hooked in the horse's bridle. His satin breeches were fresh and glossy, but they were also a bit too loose around his scrawny old knees. He scarcely filled his coat. A mournful dignity bowed his head, though his shoulders stood back fairly strong; and as he waited, his lips parted now and again and his tongue slipped between them, but they were never moistened. They remained as white as if they had been painted. Hearing the blurred bustle in the yard and finally the rattle of the sprung trap, he put a hand over his eyes and groaned aloud.

At the same moment two men came out of a shop door.

"They're at it again."

"H'm. Lot of live stock they're wasting, too."

"Can't be helped: They've gone mad, the black dogs. Some kind of disease, I reckon. It's got to be stamped out."

Ben opened his eyes and saw their backs against the clear afternoon sky. A barefoot rustic, standing on his horse to see above the crowd, got down and kicked the animal's ribs.

Gabriel heard nothing that he could distinguish, but he saw a crowd breaking at the head of the alley and he could imagine the rest. Presently he threw himself over a back fence and slipped into an abandoned stable. Frayed and perplexed and desperate for food, he could at the moment see no special danger in his position. Matter of fact, the woods had become unsafe; they were not seeking him in town. Lordy, where was old Ditcher? What had befell Solomon and Martin? How about Blue – had he caught up with the others? And General John – where, where? A good many had swung. Were any of these among the number? They could swing as many as they were a-mind to, plague take their time, but the nigger they really wanted was Gabriel, the general. And it just happened that there was a plenty fight left in that individual, if they only knew it. Of course, he couldn't whip a whole squad single-handed, but he could well-nigh worry them to death if his luck held out, if he managed to keep his hide free of buckshots.

His hat was battered beyond recognition, and the purple coat had begun to show its hard use. His shirt was gone. A strip of bright black nakedness flashed between his buttons. Gabriel rested his hand on an overhead beam and leaned forward, his long insidious gaze fixed rigidly on nothing. A little later he sat on a heap of filthy straw, rested his back against the wall; presently his chin fell against his chest, his eyes closed. His exhaustion was so profound he did not awaken when he finally toppled over on his side.

Then the hours were lost until at length he sprang up fiercely and began hacking at the shadows that crowded the stable. In the midst of this vastly satisfying set-to he awakened, his nerves tingling pleasantly, his feet no heavier than feathers, and replaced his blade. Sleep was gone now. He went out, threw himself over the fence and started up the alleyway. His mind became splendidly active.

Well, now, ain't this a pretty. We-all could of been doing a heap better'n we is doing. Somebody need to be going round and round this town at night; every now and then he need to stop and beat a drum and holler like the devil. Folks would think there was near about a million man-eating Africans in the woods; they wouldn't get no sleep, and that's how we could wear them out. Me and Ditcher and Blue and Solomon and Martin and a few mo' could do that. I'm got to find them. If we can't make no drums, we can sure pop up underneath of a bush every now and then and holler like devils. The others'll hear us, too; they'll come. I'm got to find my crowd, me.

"Stop." The word had been on the surprised man's lips and it leaped out involuntarily and without meaning, for Gabriel was facing him like a beast and in the same instant he sprang at the soldier's face. "Bloody swine – my musket – get your hands off – I'll kill you. Damn black – help, help! No, don't shoot – Oh, God please, no, no. Don't, don't, don' –"

"Here, take yo' musket, suh. Generals don't use 'em. Anyhow a sword'll do the work mo' quiet-like. Got to leave you now. Wa'n't no cause for you to make all that fuss, hollering for help. You wasted yo' breath, Mistah. You could of breathed two-three mo' times, did you keep yo' mouth shut."

There were running feet on the walk. Somebody opened an upstairs window and held a candle out. Presently a horse clattered on the cobblestones. Gabriel charted his directions deliberately. Then, pulling himself together, he slipped between two buildings, leaped a fence, ran a few paces in a lane, scaled another fence and presently faded in a clump of fruit trees.

6

Norfolk was unruffled. News filtered through from Richmond, of course, and the papers had much to say about the disclosed plot, but there was less to worry about here. It was true, if one accepted the rumors, that Norfolk had been included by the blacks in their dream of empire, and there had been reports of unexplained slave gatherings outside the town, but nothing had come of these thus far, and, aside from doubling the night patrol, nothing thus far had been done.

The waterfront was the same. Sailing boats tugged at the wharf, rocked sleeplessly as the seas came in. Barefoot deck Negroes shambled along the landing, twisting little useless hats in their hands and kicking up dust along the landing. Without the hats to occupy their hands, they let their arms fly back and forth with an air of important hustle. The fact that it was all mockery and that they were usually bent on a sleeping nook struck them as being apparent, yet their faces disclosed nothing but innocence and industry.

The streets in that part of town were forever cluttered with ox carts, carriages, wains and saddle horses. The air had a flavor. Heaping cargoes of indigo, tobacco and hides waited on the landings. Incoming boats brought sugar, tea, coffee, dates, cinnamon, bananas, cocoanuts, rum and fragrant woods. Some of the argosies were unloaded by black rousters in loin cloths, some by brown men in turbans, emissaries of legendary worlds. A medley of languages was heard.

General John was intoxicated by the aroma of things. He stood behind a crude shed and watched the labor of tiny fishing craft out near the rim of the sky. His long oversized coat was in strings, but he had caught it together at the throat in an effort to cover his naked belly. The coat was a blessing, too. It had pockets, which his jeans had not, and just now pockets were powerfully useful to General John; he had something to put in them.

These here Norfolk people ain't studying me. They ain't paying me no mo' mind than if I wasn't here. Dog take my time, though, they is apt to think something do they see me slipping round here behind this old shed. Yes, suh, bless Jesus, I'm going to walk out yonder big as life, I'm is; I'm going to go over there to the stagecoach station like as if I owned the devilish place. Peoples ain't paying me no mind. This here diving and ducking'll make them think something's rotten. Here go me, peoples.

There now, see? Didn't know me from Adam. Nice down here, all the spice and things, the barrels of rum and the sweet-smelling wood and all, mighty nice. I'd catch me a boat, too, was there one fixing to sail directly. But I can't be waiting around now. Even if they ain't studying me, I can't wait all week. That there stagecoach is the thing. Looka there – see that? This tarnation town is busting wide open with niggers, and every lasting one of them look just alike to the white folks. These peoples don't know me no better'n I knows them, and that suits both two of us mighty fine. Looka there – see?

Go on there, brother, don't *you* start turning round and looking me up and down now. You neither, Mistah Man. Go on about yo' business – on'erstand? H'm. Now, tnat's a little mo' better. Y'-all don't know me from bullfrog, and if you did, it wouldn't do you a speck of good. The Governor ain't said he's going to pay you for catching anybody excepty Gabriel and Ditcher. Go catch them if you's big enough. Next town I hits, leastwise the first one across the line, I'm going to buy me some clothes to wear. These rags ain't fitten for a hog. Look a-them shoes: nothing but tops. And my pants, Lord a'mighty, they don't even hide my privates. This old coat is a caution to look at, but it sure do do a heap of good. They wouldn't let a nigger walk through town with pants like this, showing all his – Lordy, no they sure wouldn't.

Well, now, I'm here, ain't I? Soon's that there stage-driving man get his horses out in the yard I'm going to get in and set down too. I sure is tired a plenty; peoples, that ain't no tale, neither. For a fact, I believes I could sleep two-three days 'thout waking up or turning over.

Well, suh, what in the name of lands is them folks doing? Oh, buying tickets, hunh? That's something I can do whilst I'm waiting, I reckon.

"Howdy, Mistah Man. Yes, suh, I'm aiming to travel some, I sure am."

The stranger was promptly joined by another, and it occurred to General John that the two looked very little like stagecoach officials. Their eyes were uncommonly stern. And their interest in the wizened old Negro was, to say the least, not a casual curiosity.

"Your papers," General John heard one of them say in the course of a long period, the remainder of which escaped him.

"Papers, hunh? Papers for what, suh?"

Out of a tiny waiting room, curiously, came a uniformed guard. He was armed. Suddenly the three men dropped the veil.

"Where the hell you come from, old nigger? Who you belong to anyhow?"

General John became tense; his old withered lips went white. He shot quick glances at first one man and then another. His head fell forward, but under his rags his shoulders tightened and the quaking old fellow rose on the balls of his feet. His anguished smile revealed the horrid dark fangs that were his teeth, but there was now a shadow of cunning in his eyes that suggested an ancient fox.

"I's a free nigger, suh. I ain't *no*body's, me."

He bowed lower, thinking fast, still poised on his toes, as ready and elastic as a cat. Then his mind fastened on something.

One way was hopeless, to be sure, but there were other things that he needed to consider. He snatched a paper from his pockets. It was too large; it should have been only half the size. Yet in a flash he crammed more than half of it into his mouth and began swallowing hard as the guards laid hands on him. They snatched a crimped fragment from between his lips, boxed his head severely and bent him double in a frantic attempt to make him cough up what he had swallowed.

"Just what I thought. Search his pockets, rip the insides out of that old coat. Money, too. H'm, I thought so. Calm yourself there, you old dog's vomit, or I'll run you through now. He's one of them. By God, he looked *too* harmless; I thought something was rotten. Here, look –"

General John's courage began to melt. His thought, racing like a squirrel in a cage, slowed down to a walk. The men's hands were on him, clasping viciously. His face smarted from the blows, his head ached. He grinned at them weakly. He was a weird sight.

On the portion of the note that he had saved, the guard read: *Alexander Biddenhurst, corner Coats Alley and Budd Street, Philad* – The writing was a clear, though illiterate, scrawl. The man's eyes danced. Suddenly, harking back to General John's last remark, he added, "You're not going anywhere, old dog." The armed guard almost had to chop a way through the circle of spectators.

7

And in Richmond, bound to the floor of his cell, Mingo could still hear the hangman's trap falling periodically. Obscure Negroes were dragged before the justices in the morning and hanged the same day. The known leaders, as they were taken, were not punished immediately, however. There was still that question of Jacobin hands turning the spoon in the kettle: Gallatin, Duane, Callender, Fries and certain United Irishmen had not been cleared of suspicion, either. Their French babble about the natural equality of man had taken root like dragons' teeth. The black chiefs would have to be held for questioning. So Mingo, who knew how to read, who kept the lists, lay with his face to the floor. Ditcher, chained like a bear, sat on a stool in a dungeon. Rats romped about his bare feet.

Meanwhile Ben brought the cariole into town alone. The afternoon was fine, and the autumn trees were growing brighter and brighter. God's upturned paint pots had indeed spattered them all with red. At the edge of town he saw a familiar young man standing beneath a balcony, his arm hooked in a horse's bridle, his hat off, his wig exceedingly white, but Ben had to look twice before he fully recognized young Marse Robin. Leaves were falling. The face above had a taunting way of vanishing and reappearing every moment or two. It was wonderful, Ben thought, how oblivious young folks could be to death and woe. Maybe it was being white that enabled them to be unconcerned. What did a few niggers more or less mean to them? God bless them, they weren't studying any evil; they were just thinking about their own problems. And right now, seeing that young Robin was just getting himself cured of a honey-colored woman with hoops in her ears, he must have had his hands full. Ben twitched his lines, and the little mare's porcelain-clean feet twinkled again.

You're a good boy, Ben.

Yes, suh, young Marse Robin; thank you, suh. It do pleasure me a heap to hear you talk that a-way. I's aiming to be good, befo' God I is. You and yo' pappy is two mo' sure 'nough quality white mens. God bless me, I was about ready to turn my back on y'-alls once, but I bound you I won't do it nara 'nother time. That old dead Bundy – him squatting side of that hole in the low field. Jesus! He the one what was cause of it – him and Gabriel. But God beingst my helper, I'm standing by you from here on, suh. I ain't strong for no such cutting up as Gabriel and them was talking. I been a good nigger, suh, and I's too old to change now.

Pharoah, the pumpkin-colored one, came out of a shop carrying a full basket. Seeing Ben, he threw up his hand pleasantly and stepped down on the street.

"Well, now, what time you make it, old man?"

Ben looked at the sky.

"Two-three hours befo' dark, I reckon. Where you's bound?"

"Home."

"Well, howcome you can't wait and ride piece-ways back with me?"

"I ain't aiming for dark to catch me on the road, Ben."

"Scairt?"

"Nah, just careful-like, I reckon." He shuddered a moment. "The niggers is just nachal-born tired of seeing me live."

Ben didn't answer.

"Listen, Ben, ain't you told it, too?"

"Seem like somebody think I has. Tried to hit me with a knife."

"No?"

"Yes, they did. Leastwise, they throwed it at me. Look at this hand. I ain't saying whether they was trying to kill me or whether they wasn't. It sure look like somebody don't love me much, though."

"Lordy, I can't stand it, Ben. Seem like I'm all the time about half-sleep and half-wake. You reckon they's poisoned me?"

"Conjure poisoning? Well, ain't you carrying nothing against it?"

"String round my neck. That's all."

"I don't know, Pharoah. Some time I feels mighty peculiar myself."

"Got to hurry along now. Don't want night to catch me on the road."

"You can just as well ride piece-ways with me."

"Ne' mind, Ben. I can't wait."

Ben clucked to the mare.

An hour later he was back at the same spot, driving out of town. He had tucked the lap rug around his knees and sat gravely erect in the small carriage. A North African sailor passed him in the road, a turbaned Negro, bright black, barefoot and without a shirt. He looked up, giving his pendants a toss, then promptly averted his face. Suddenly a host of swifts flecked the sky above an old chimney. They kept rising, gushing up like blown-out cinders. Ben set his eyes on the road again. Between the small ears of the small horse he discovered a distant spot near the bend of the road where the bushes were troubled.

Ben took a quick breath, stiffened in his seat and tried to prepare himself for danger. The bushes rustled again, then became still. There was the steady tock-tock of little porcelain feet on the firm road, and the eager animal never slackened pace a moment. In another moment they were at the bend. Ben pulled up the reins and at the same instant the bushes parted. Pharoah sprang out and ran down to the cariole.

"Let me ride some, Ben."

"You ain't home yet?"

"Somebody's after me. Let me ride piece-ways."

"Nobody ain't studying you – not here in the broad daylight, nohow. That's 'magination."

"'Magination nothing. Let me ride some now. Marse Sheppard won't care none."

"I tried to get you to wait in the first place."

"It's getting dark heap quicker'n I reckoned. Somebody done spied me, too. I heard them amongst the trees. You know I done already had one knife throwed at me."

"Climb on up."

"Much obliged, Ben."

"Maybe you shouldn't of been so burning up to run tell everything you knows. Leastwise, not if you's aiming to live a long time. Get up, Miss."

"It wasn't me what give them the names and all. Ain't you told nothing, Ben?"

"Ne' mind me. It ain't helped *you* none to talk yo'self near about crazy."

"You said they picked you up once, then let you go?"

"Now if you hadn't gone busting to town like you did –"

"Somebody say the white folks let you go cause you told, cause you told them plenty."

"I told them about me. They come and got me. They was aiming to hang me with the rest, I reckon."

The blood left Ben's lips. Pharoah shivered. Again there was a brisk tock-tock on the firm road.

"Some's catching the rope what ain't done nothing, Ben. Howcome they let you go – seeingst you told them about yo'self?"

Ben turned his face.

8

The small chest-like trunk had been dragged into the middle of the floor, and the young mulattress stood above it in a billowing leaf-green dress. The window hangings were down now, and the room was flooded with yellow light. Melody passed a bright velvet garment through her hands, inspected it lovingly from top to bottom, then knelt to pack the garment away as neatly as possible. There were other articles, too: petticoats hanging on the backs of chairs, capes thrown across the table, pieces of china worth saving, a silver vase, a decanter, a medley of footgear strewn around the gilded box.

Melody felt a certain sadness, but she knew her own mind and she had made her decision. Richmond had suddenly become too small for her. She had a *feeling*. Something told her that she couldn't stay there, enjoying so many conflicting confidences, without becoming entangled. Her imagination was at work, too. Why, for example, was young Marse Robin losing interest? Not that she cared, but might it not have a meaning, coming as it did at this turbulent time? Oh, there were so many angles, so many things involved. Was it suspicion that she saw on his face these last few times?

Well, let it be; she was leaving town. Philadelphia, according to Alexander Biddenhurst, would be a more wholesome place for a young freed woman, particularly an alert and handsome one, despite, in this case, her obvious inclination toward easy virtue. Why, it was a hateful thing, he thought, to sell one's graces to the sons of aristocratic planters. Being the favorite of such men would never help her to serve the cause of liberty and equality. She was selling out her own class, the masses of black folks, the poor, the enslaved. Of course, her sympathies were all right, but of what good was sympathy for the unwanted coming from the darling of their oppressors? No, it was leaving time now. Good-by, peoples. Good-by, church. These zebra-striped stockings – well, toss them into the trunk too. They wouldn't take up much space.

There were, in fact, very definite and substantial things that could bring her trouble if she delayed her departure. There was the flight of General John with the address she had given him in his pockets. Lordy, what had come of him? How was he getting along – him and his raggety self? Do tell, Lordy – po' old General John. Yes, and there were heaps of people who remembered that Biddenhurst himself had – maybe it was infatuation and maybe it was something very different – at least, he had known her. And it was funny about him, very funny. Not very ardent, to be sure, not warm or sensuous, but a curiously exciting person. All on fire. Liberty, equality, book learning. . . . He was a case, that Philadelphia man. Looked as if he might have been part Jew, but he hobnobbed with the French.

Presently shadows streaked the bright room, and Melody, rising from her knees, saw clouds in the sky. The storm was less than a month past, but here was a promise of rain again. No matter about that, though; old Benbow Bowler understood that he was to come for her trunk before day in the morning and deposit it on the schooner *Mary*, scheduled to leave Richmond at dawn. Melody untied her headcloth, went into the front room and swung the shutters out. She couldn't let folks see her through the front windows with her hair tied, but by now she was bored with packing and curious to see who might be passing.

The street was empty. A mist was gathering down toward the river. In the other direction two oxen were tied to a tree in a field where they had been pulled off the road with their cart. The clouds mounted. Melody leaned across the sill on her elbows, her feet off the floor and swinging childishly. After a while she closed the shutters and lit a candle. It was time to prepare supper.

Her mind told her to dash the light. If anyone knocked at the door, she would lie still and make no sound till the person was gone. Her house was upset from front to back. She wanted no visitors, and she wanted no one to carry out the news that she was leaving town. She wanted to answer no questions. Melody lay across the bed in a rumpled dress and listened to the drip of water in the roof drains. The shower itself was so fine and veil-like it made no sound. Three times she heard the rattle of broughams on the road. Not one stopped. Melody drew the coverlet above her shoulders and slept.

She awakened to a violent banging downstairs at her back door. And when she snatched on her cape and ran to the window that overlooked the yard, she saw a magical glow over the wet earth. Sheet lightning played like a blue fairy light, seemed to emanate from the very earth. In it she could see a burnished black figure, naked above the waist, wearing a badly battered hat, tottering like a man in a daze: an uncommonly large Negro, sorrowful yet dignified, undismayed, unafraid, turning a slow insidious eye up to her. And suddenly, with a burst of recognition, she put her hand on the sill and felt her own quaking.

"You, Gabriel."

"H'm. Me."

"Lord, boy, howcome you knock at my door this time of night?"

"Ain't nobody here but you," he told her.

"You right sure about that?"

"Right sure, yellow woman."

"Well –" She went to a shelf for the key. He hadn't moved when she returned. "– here then."

It struck the ground at his feet. She went into the next room and waited for him to let himself in. No, better not make a light. She drew the remaining curtains, pushed back the shutters. That was a help. One wouldn't have to stumble over the table with this blue brightness playing on things. Presently Gabriel came through the kitchen, handed her the key.

"Thank you, gal."

"What's that rag in yo' hand?"

"My coat. It's sopping wet."

"Here – let me have it. There's still some coals in the grate."

"I ain't got long."

" I know. Just as well to hang it here, though."

"Thanks a heap." He raised his head. "Mm-mm. Lordy!"

"Lordy what?"

"The perfume and sweetness and all. It's fit to kill and cripple in here."

He was luminous like the earth, giving the same blue light in the murky darkness. The muscles quivered and ran on his arms and back. When Melody came out of the next room, there was a blanket in her arms.

"Put this round you, boy. Take that old broken-up hat off yo' head, too. Sit down. Rest yo'self some, beingst you's here."

He obeyed. His sword fell against the floor with a clank. If he had only been dry, he would have felt like some*body*. But a general can't feel like somebody as long as he's wearing a pair of sopping wet pants, as long as he can hear water slushing in his shoes. Gabriel's chin fell against his chest. After a long while he looked up slowly.

"Is you seen anybody, gal? Is you heard any talk?"

"Some, I reckon. Why don't you fly, though. Howcome you keep hanging round town, beingst everything's like it is?"

"I don't feels like running. I just feels like figthing, me."

She stared at him for a moment and decided to let that point rest.

"Has you et a plenty?"

"Little bit. Don't feel much like eating here of late."

"No, I reckon you don't. Just the same you need to keep something in yo' stomach if you aims to keep moving."

"Some time I picks up a apple, some time a ear of dry corn, some time nuts or berries or eggs. I ain't plum empty."

"You could do with mo', though; I bound you that."

"Maybe so. What is you heard? Who is you seen?"

"Wait. Let me see what's left in my kettle."

"Tell me now. Has you set eyes on Ditcher or Mingo or Blue? Has you heard tell of Gen'l John or my brothers?"

She reached the door.

"Some of them," she said "Wait."

9

Gabriel, warmed by the food, relaxing in his chair, threw out one foot majestically, leaned back, his elbows on the arms of the chair, his chin in the palm of his right hand. There, almost lost in shadows, his dark insidious gaze ran from an uncertain point on the floor to the woman on the couch. She had a lazy, indolent air, that Melody, but her presence was so soft and delicate, so charged with fragrant odors, that Gabriel began to feel himself dirtier even than he was, a befouled thing and sorely out of place. His flesh tingled, but there was a drowsiness on his eyes. He could have slept. His head began to rock.

"There, rest yo'self if you's a-mind to, boy. Sleep some. Want to lay down?"

Gabriel remembered his wet pants, his grimy, unclean person. It embarrassed him.

"No," he said, "ne' mind that. Just got to nodding here. What was that about Ditcher?"

"Ditcher give himself up directly after the Governor put up the reward for you and him."

Only Gabriel's eyes showed surprise. His voice came back deep, troubled, but unastonished.

"He in the lock-up, hunh?"

"Been there two-three weeks."

"Not two-three weeks."

"Well, maybe one-two."

"Where'bouts Gen'l John?"

"Philadelphia – if they ain't headed him off."

Gabriel spent several moments with his thoughts. Then suddenly he twitched his feet, stirred in his chair.

"Well, here's one what ain't going to give hisself up. No, suh. And here's one that ain't aiming to fly away neither."

Melody rose on her elbow, tossing one foot indifferently.

"Was you right smart, you'd fly, though."

"I reckon I ain't smart. Not smart 'nough to run."

"Whose house you going to knock at tomorrow night?"

"I don't know. Howcome you say that?"

"See that thing yonder?"

"That there box? Yes."

"That's my trunk. It's all packed up and locked. Benbow be here for it any time now. I'm leaving befo' day on the *Mary*, boy."

"You?"

"Nobody else. It's leaving time, if you ask me."

"Somebody got to stay and fight. It's well and good for you, kicking up yo' heels; you's free. You don't know how it feels."

"'Pears to me, you's free too. Who been telling *you*

where to go and what to do these here last two-three weeks?"

"Well, now, I reckon so, me. But a plenty mo' niggers ain't free."

"You can help them mo' better if you's live than if you's dead."

"I might could get up another crowd here."

"You might couldn't, too. Who you think's going to fight now, after seeing all them black mens get kilt — hanged? You can't do a heap by yo'self."

"There ain't nothing else for me, though. I just as well to get kilt. Maybe I can get in two-three mo' good licks befo' my time come. That might would help some others what ain't free."

"It ain't sense. You's big and strong and mighty fine, boy. Was you away somewhere, way away and live, well then, maybe —"

Gabriel pulled himself together in the chair. His hands gripped the arm-rests, and he let the blanket slip down from one shoulder.

"Listen —"

"I hear. A wagon or cart or something."

"It done stop now."

"Benbow, maybe."

She ran to the front window and looked down. The shadowy cart had halted, but no one was apparently getting to the ground. It was a cart, too, a crude two-wheeled affair and not a carriage or brougham or cariole. If it was Benbow, why didn't he come in? He knew where she lived; he knew all the details. Surely he didn't expect to see a light in the window.... Come on up, Benbow, stupid nigger; you can't be wasting time. The *Mary* ain't fixing to wait on nobody.

Not getting down, hunh? Moving along. Well, maybe it wasn't Benbow. Funny, though, stopping out yonder like that. Funny as the devil. What's that, now? Sound like something scuffling up leaves across in the field. Some-

thing scuffling underneath of them trees all right. Somebody's hogs or something.

"H'm," Gabriel said.

He could not see her across the room, but a shadow was
shaking its head.

"Gone now," she said. "Whoever it was. Nobody didn't
even get down from the thing."

She waited at the window. Down at the river landing
things had begun to stir. There were flares. Now and again
a voice identified itself. There was no doubt that they were
making ready the *Mary*.

Gabriel rested his chin in his palm again, and his eyes
promptly closed. They did not open till Melody returned
from the window some time later.

"That's him for sure now. He's coming round to the
back," she said, excited.

Gabriel sprang up, confused.

"Coming, hunh?"

"Benbow. Coming to take my trunk."

"Oh. I was about to go to sleep. I couldn't make out
who you meant was coming."

"*About* sleep?"

"Maybe I *was* sleep – just that one minute."

"You need to rest, I bound you, but it's near about leaving time now." She ran from window to window, drawing
the shutters and pulling together such hangings as were
still up. Then she ran into the kitchen and made a small
light. "Come on up, Benbow. That's you, ain't it?"

"H'm. This me, Miss Melody."

He came in directly and stood in the door: a short pudgy
black with masses of woolly hair pulled together ruthlessly
and tied in a queue. Gabriel rose, dropped the blanket,
slapped on his hat and stood looking down, his hands on
his hips. His air, unintentionally lofty, seemed to disturb
the smaller fellow. Benbow's lips went white with surprise.

"Didn't you pass by few minutes ago?" Melody said.

"Mm – yes. Seem like I seed somebody, though; seem

like they was police or something – so I kept on moving. Maybe, though, they was looking for Gabriel. Maybe they know he's here."

"No cause for them to stand down there," Gabriel said indifferently. "They got they guns."

Benbow trembled a little.

"You' trunk ready now?"

"That's it there. You better hurry, too, Benbow. Look like they's getting things ready down there at the landing."

"Here," Gabriel said. He raised the small, solidly packed box and waited for Benbow to get under it. "Take it that a-way. See? No trouble to it. Did you see the boys working on the *Mary*, Benbow?"

"Two or three of them was a-stirring."

"That's a good-size schooner, Gabriel. You just as well to be down in it when she pull away. These police and all here waiting to see you come out the front door –"

"Well, maybe I ain't going out the front door."

Benbow was creeping down the steps. Then he was on the path, going around to the front.

"I got to dress in a hurry," Melody said. "Believe I'll ride on the cart with Benbow. It's powerfully dark out yonder."

Gabriel got his coat from the kitchen chair, tossed it across his arm.

"What time you say the *Mary*'s aiming to pull out?"

"Just about day. You better get on it if you can."

"There's a heap of things to think about when you's a general. Right now I don't know my mind."

"You better forget some of them things on yo' mind – hot as they is on yo' track. Thing you need to do is see how fast a good general can run when push come to shove." Gabriel was walking away absently, hardly hearing what she said. "Here, wait a minute," she said. She wrote something on a sheet of paper. "Here's somewheres you can go in Philadelphia, do you get away."

Gabriel took it, started down the rear stairs. At the bottom he tore the note up, tossed the pieces on the ground.

10

He said he might be squatting side of a corn shock some night. Down in the low field, maybe. That's how I heard him say it, and I sure do wish he'd come right now. He allowed how I might could help him some. A jug of water, maybe, when he's near played out, some meat or bread or like of that. It's all here, boy. Howcome you don't come get it? Everything I can tote, tall boy, everything you talk about I got. It all come out of the big-house kitchen, too, right off of Marse Prosser's table. See here – yams, meat, corn bread, collards, a jug of rum, everything. Me, too; I'm here, boy. What else mo' you want?

Yes, and I got this here charm, too. I know you ain't got no mind for such doings, but it's what you needs. On'er-stand? That big rain and all – that was the stars against you, boy. Toussaint and them, they kilt a live hog, drunk the nachal blood underneath of a tree. It made a big difference. You never did hear tell of nobody hunting him like a dog. Martin and all his Jesus; Mingo reading out the Book – nothing to that. Come on back, boy, and get this charm. Come lay down, rest. Nobody's studying you down here this time of night, nobody in the low field but me. Come pleasure yo'self with a blue-gummed gal, boy. Might change yo' luck.

He said he might be squatting side of some corn shock. I heard him say it like that, and I been here time and time again since he said it. But, peoples, it's a heart-sickening thing to keep on waiting when he don't show up.

Nasty night this evening. This little slow misty-like rain. Fit to give a body his death of dampness. Mighty dark, too. Funny how you can see things though. Everything look like it got its own light. Everything got a purple-like shine. Me, too, my hands and legs, this old rag, all shining. I reckon it's the sheet lightning on things.

He'd be shining too, did he come. He'd be something tall, something with a purple shine slipping through the

188

high bushes, wriggling, coming this way. Lordy! He'd slip down side of me. I know how. I know how. I'll see him easy, do he come. He'll be shining.

Better be stirring now. Freeze yo' round yonder, sitting on this damp ground all night. Need to stir about some.

There were cattle splashing in the bog. Now and again a coon barked in a black clump of trees. The thin-waisted brown girl wriggled out of her rags and stood for a moment rejoicing beside the creek. Lightning played around her. She stood with feet apart, arms thrust overhead. Then, splash! And she was slipping through the water like a moonbeam, a slim, transparent thing that disturbed the stream hardly at all.

Why didn't he come some time? When he was nearly played out, thirsty, hungry, lonesome, why didn't he look for her in the low field? She might be able to help him. It was just like he said. But she couldn't help him if he stayed away. Here was this charm, for one thing. It would be a protection to him. It was a thing he had neglected, an important thing. Was he right safe? Could he possibly be unable to come, or afraid? Had he changed his mind and made a dash for safer ground?

She pulled herself out of the creek, shook the water from her matted hair. The air was cold. Lordy, it was colder than she could endure. She snatched up her rags and ran to the row of huts.

"There's plenty to eat and drink out there, do he come now," she told herself. "But the charm is here in my hand. He wouldn't know what to do with that 'less'n I told him, nohow. Maybe he'll come tomorrow when it ain't so rainy and wet."

11

It was a rat, sure as you're born, back behind the rum kegs, down in the hold of the schooner *Mary*. The devilish thing was as big as a cottontail and as full of fight as a porcupine.

Down on his hands and knees, eyes starting from his head and nostrils dilating, Gabriel saw the thing vaguely like a shadow. A moment later, when a scrap of light broke through, he drew his steel and held out a challenge. The rat, desperate in his corner, quickly showed a set of willing teeth. Gabriel came a trifle nearer, put the sword point practically in the varmint's face.

Bad, hunh? Wants something to set yo' teeth into, do you? Try this here blade one time. See how this taste in yo' mouth, suh. Back on up if you's a-mind to. You can't go nowhere but in that corner. You's got to fight now. Showing me them teeth so big – you got to use them now. There: bite that. There, suh. Just as well to die fighting. I'm got you where I can say what's what now. Oop-oo-oop! No, you don't neither. You ain't getting by me that slick. There now, see what you done? Kilt yo'self. Jumped right straddle across my blade. Well, suh, that's you all right. Look just as nachal as can be. You got on yo' last clean shirt, too.

The schooner was moving along pleasantly. Now and again the kegs jostled. Cries of the men on deck rent the air at intervals. A peculiar lassitude settled on Gabriel. His eyes kept closing involuntarily. None of the usual feelings of sleepiness accompanied it, but periodically his eyes closed and things went black for a few moments.

Just as well be sleep as wake here now. No way to break and run, back behind here with the rats. Just as well to sleep from here to Norfolk. Yes, suh, just as well – ho-hum, just as well to stretch out – just as well – ho-hum.

His body was still asleep when his mind went to work again. He couldn't follow a train of thought, but he was aware of a parched throat. He was thirsty, near perishing for a drink. Water, rum, anythink. Lordy –

His eyes opened. He raised himself on an elbow. Were they in Norfolk yet? How long had they been there? Now if he could only get Mott's ear. Lucky for Gabriel, he had seen that young cousin of his as he came on. Otherwise he might not have been so neatly stored. He might not have enjoyed such a long sleep. It was plainly dark outside. Things were quiet aboard. If he could only get Mott's ear about now. He went down on his belly and slept again. Later Mott came and Gabriel put two coins in his hand.

"Norfolk, hunh? Well, I'm staying down here a spell anyhow. I ain't getting off yet a while. That yellow woman –"

"Gone."

"H'm. Well, you can fill me a jug somewheres, if you's a-mind to."

"Stay long is you wants. The *Mary* going to be here a mont', I reckon. Maybe mo'."

"Where it going then?"

"To some them islands."

"Well, I feels like sailing awhile. I ain't getting off just yet."

"I'll bring you the jug directly."

Eleven days had passed. Gabriel had sent Mott to have the jug refilled. Then as he lay on his elbow, he heard stern voices on the deck. He caught a few words. Men were questioning Mott.

"You don't know? We'll take *you* then. Maybe you'll find out before it's too late."

They were fixing to arrest Mott, hunh? Well, suh, nothing like that. They was suspicioning Mott because he kept going and coming with that jug, with bread and meat in a basket, was they? They was aiming to lock him up, hunh? Nothing like that. Mott was powerfully afeard, and that was plain.

"No, suh, I ain't been in no Richmond, me. Leastwise, suh, I ain't been off'n the boat there. No, suh. No, suh, not me."

Gabriel slipped between the stacks of cargo. Then he remembered a bludgeon that had lain beside him and returned for it. Now he was doubly armed. Sunlight was like transparent gold on the deck. He came up, staggered in the intense light and started toward the four policemen who were at the moment haranguing the frightened Mott. The boy clung to his jug, but his knees were smiting.

Gabriel, towering like a giant, reeling noticeably, his clothes in outlandish shape, his eyes vacuous, was upon the group when they first noticed him.

"No, suh," Mott was protesting. "Not me — I ain't seen —"

"I'm the one," Gabriel said in a trance.

They all wheeled in confusion and excitement. For an instant a shadow of fear hung over the entire circle. The men stuttered. He was so obviously the wanted chief, that even Gabriel could see that they were parrying when the first one got a few words out.

"You? You, Gabriel?"

They had been too astonished to draw their muskets. Gabriel had been too absorbed in his own daydream to take advantage of their delay. Now they all stepped back, leveled nervously. Gabriel dropped his club.

"I'm Gabriel. You oughta could see that boy ain't —"

"You — you giving up?"

"I ain't running. I wants a drink of water. I'm perishing for something to drink."

They got his blade. Suddenly a thought struck one of the policemen.

"Papers. Letters. Search him."

In a few seconds his clothes were ribbons. He looked at them with calm, detached eyes. His gaze, commonly dark and insidious, became indifferent, faraway.

"Is y'-all through?"

"Funny. Nothing but his money. No letters at all. Mighty funny –"

"You think he could have conceived it all himself?"

"Hard to tell."

"Through now?" Gabriel said.

Mott was slouched against the rain barrel, moaning audibly.

"He does have the look of one that –"

"I ain't got much rabbit in me," Gabriel said. "I ain't much hand at running. I was in for fighting, me."

He was very tired.

BOOK FIVE

Pale Evening . . .
a Tall Slim Tree

1

Now for the second time Virginia was paralyzed with excitement. Benjamin Lundy, living in Richmond, but wisely contemplating a move to Tennessee, wrote letters.

"So well had they matured their plot, and so completely had they organized their system of operation, that nothing but a miraculous intervention of the arm of Providence was supposed to have been capable of saving the city from pillage and flames, and the inhabitants thereof from butchery."

So dreadful was the alarm, so great the consternation, that Congressman John Randolph of Roanoke, speaking with hand on heart, exclaimed, "The night bell is nevermore heard to toll in the city of Richmond, but the anxious mother presses her infant more closely to her bosom."

In Norfolk, meanwhile, crowds surged around the old jail. Bayonets bristled before the gates. In the mulling rabble were dozens of incurably curious blacks. Someone had reported that the dusky chief was about to be moved to Richmond. They had all come to catch a glimpse.

Yes, apparently something was going to happen. Police officers kept going and coming, passing the guards at will, exercising to the limit their prideful prerogative. Each time a lock turned, each time the gate cracked to admit an officer, a ripple of anticipation swept the crowd. Everyone went up on tiptoes, bobbed his head.

Where? Where? Is he coming now?

A sullen black sailor from a San Domingo boat stood with the others. He did not rise on his toes as the rest did; he did not bob his head. He had seen Dessalines ride a horse. He knew the sight of Christophe. He understood now that words like *freedom* and *liberty* drip blood – always, everywhere, there is blood on such words. Still he'd like to see this Gabriel. Was he as tall as Christophe, as broad as Dessalines? Was he as stern-faced as Toussaint, the tiger? They were saying now that the stars were against this Gabriel, that he had neglected the signs.

Yes, something *was* going to happen. They were about ready. Curse those long-necked white people. Couldn't they keep still a single minute? The officers were clearing a way. Evidently they were going to return the prisoner by river boat. There was the coach. Plague take those skinny white people; there they went crowding like swine.

Gabriel stood a moment, seen of all, then walked to the waiting coach. Mounted guards swirled around the conveyance. The crowd broke. The miserable young sailor stood alone, his thick lips hanging wretchedly.

196

It was an unsatisfactory glimpse. In twenty-four days the legend had become too great; the crowd wanted to know more. They were obliged to get it from the newspapers. In Norfolk they read the *Epitome* story.

"When he was apprehended, he manifested the greatest marks of firmness and confidence, showing not the least disposition to equivocate or screen himself from justice — but making no confession that would implicate any one else ... The behavior of Gabriel under his misfortunes was such as might be expected from a mind capable of forming the daring project which he had conceived."

Excitement spread like a fire catching up barn after barn. Wherever there was a black population, slave or free, there was consternation. The Negro became suddenly a dangerous man. In Philadelphia fear was rife. It was proposed there that the use of sky-rockets be forbidden, because in San Domingo they had been employed by the blacks as signals. And Alexander Biddenhurst, hearing the argument, went home and made a note in his journal.

"I can well understand how men's startled consciences make cowards of them. They recognize in the Negro a dangerous man, because they recognize in him an injured one. Injured men like injured beasts are always dangerous. By the same token extremely poor men are dangerous."

Then, pleased with his own words, he went out again, walked beneath the maples and took in the fresh air.

The *Daily Advertiser* pointed out that "even in Boston fears are expressed and measures of prevention adopted." This reference, of course, was to the advertisement then appearing in Boston newspapers. The police, it seemed, were taking this occasion to enforce an old ordinance for suppressing rogues, vagabonds and the like, an Act which forbade all persons of African descent, with stated exceptions, from remaining more than two months within the Commonwealth. Above a list of about three hundred names the advertisement read:

NOTICE TO BLACKS

The officers of the police having made returns to the subscriber of the names of the following persons who are Africans or Negroes, not subjects of the Emperor of Morocco nor citizens of any of the United States, the same are hereby warned and directed to depart out of this Commonwealth before the tenth day of October next, as they would avoid the pains and penalties of the law in that case provided, which was passed by the Legislature March 26, 1788.

Charles Bulfinch, Superintendent.

By order and direction of the Selectmen.

Virginians, for their part, could look forward with hope to the next meeting of the state legislature. With gossips estimating a larger and larger number of Negroes involved, with the reporter for the *Epitome* discovering a meeting of one hundred and fifty blacks near Whitlock's Mills in Suffolk County and getting the assurance that some of these were from Norfolk, with the story of a similar gathering appearing in Petersburg newspapers, with a real insurrection being suppressed near Edinton, N. C., and with all these things being linked more and more closely to the one large design of Gabriel, the opinions of legislators became increasingly necessary. People couldn't sleep as things stood.

2

Well, suh, I done sung my song, I reckon. It wasn't much, though. Nothing like Toussaint. The rain was against us. That Pharoah and his mouth wa'n't no mo'n I looked for. Something told me we was done when we turned back the first time. It was a bad night for such doings as we was counting on. A nachal man can't beat the weather, though. Nothing to do but take the medicine.

The black boys there, working the boat and all – faces longer'n a mule's, every lasting one of them. They'd a-come with us once we got our hand in. They been powerfully polite to me. They know. They know I'm the gen'l. The weather turned out bad, that's all. There's a heap of things what could of been by now. Heap of black mens could of been free in this state, only that big rain come up. Befo' God, it looked to me like the sky was emptying plum bottomside up. Excusing that, niggers would of gone free as rabbits. These black boys know. They know I been a gen'l, me. They been polite, too.

Trees and all, all along the river there, little old houses in the thickets, red leaves a-blowing – mighty pretty. H'm. Didn't see none of this when I was going down two weeks ago. Lordy, me and that old rat was too busy having it out back behind them kegs and things. Yes, suh, worth seeing, too. I shouldn't of come, though. My mind ain't never told me to fly away. There ain't nothing good for Gabriel nowhere but right here where I was borned. Right here with my kinfolks and all. If I can't be free here, I don't want to be free nowheres else, me.

Bless me if I ain't had my time last three-four weeks, though. Ain't seen old Marse Prosser's face since I-don't-know-when. I been free. And, Lordy, I's free from now on, too. Plenty things they might can do to me now, but there ain't but one I'm looking for. Look at them here, lined up round me like the petals round a sunflower. All of them with they guns and everything – they knows what's what. They all know right good and well that they's riding with the gen'l. They know I'm a free man, me.

They kept going downstairs. Then, when he could see nothing at all, they opened a door and led him inside.

"Down there – understand?"

He bowed on his knees.

"Flat on yo' belly, nigger. There's points on these muskets if you need a little help."

He put his face on the floor.

"Stretch your arms out. Wide. There now."

They locked the heavy bands around his wrists. Then for the first time he seemed to perceive, without seeing, that there was some one else in the cell, bound to the floor beside him. He couldn't imagine who it was. He wasn't even concerned.

Some of the guards went out. Two remained, and some other men came a moment later. Someone walked over and slapped Gabriel's back with a sword.

"Say, who were some of the foreigners that put it in your head?"

No answer. Then a prick of the pointed blade.

"You – where'd you get the sweet notion to butcher the people of Richmond?"

Gabriel heard the other prisoner squirm. Neither spoke.

"You had money. White men gave it to you, didn't they?"

There was an end of patience.

A boot thudded – not against Gabriel's ribs but against the ribs of his companion.

"Talk, dog. You had the lists and the records. Who gave you those pamphlets?"

Then, with a jolt of surprise, Gabriel heard Mingo's voice.

"We didn't read no pamphlets. Them pamphlets didn't have nothing to do with us. We was started long before –"

"How many names did you have listed? Why did you plan to spare the French residents? Why were *you* so active in the thing? You were free."

"We was –"

Gabriel raised his head abruptly.

"Die like a free man, Mingo."

His voice, as he said it, had a savage quaver that suggested a lion. Mingo felt the air suddenly chilled. Trembling, he put his face against the rough boards again. Presently the other men left the two with their guards.

3

The wrinkled black crones made a half circle before the cabin door. Near by, within easy eyeshot, a host of naked youngsters scampered like little midnight trolls. The old birdlike women sat with scaly bare feet curled beneath them, heads tied in rags, and smoked their pipes in a dreamy haze. Now and again a heavy lip curled, disclosed the want of teeth.

"Ain't that gal young-un of yo's getting heavy, Tisha?"

"Lordy, she *been* getting heavy, chile."

"I thought so all the time. Well, that's good. Two-three days rest from the field'll do her good."

"Yes, she do need a rest. Beulah works so hard. Having a baby'll give her two-three days to kind of catch her breath."

"H'm."

"Hagar, what's that you was saying a little while ago?"

"Oh, about when I was a gal on Marse Bowler's place?"

"Yes, what about it?"

"Well, it look for a long time like I wasn't going to have no chilluns. Marse Bowler, the old one what's dead now, commenced to get worried-like and started talking about selling me down the river whilst I's young. One day I heard him tell some strange white man he didn't believe I could make a baby. That stranger he just turned down the corners of his mouth and say, Bullfrogs! I'm got a stud nigger on my place that'll –"

"Hush that foolishment, Hagar."

"It's truth, gal. And, well-suh, when me and that roaring bull –"

"Hush, gal. You's fixing to say that right away you commenced to spitting out all them ten-twelve babies of yo's. You need to get religion and hush lying. Ain't that Juba coming yonder?"

"She need to be in the field working, do she know what's good for her roundyonder."

"That Juba don't care nothing about her skin."

"She would, did she know what I knows."

"What you doing round here, gal?"

Juba came nearer, her hands on her hips.

"What it look like I'm doing?"

"Snappy, hunh?"

"No, not snappy. Just telling what you ask me."

"You ain't sound to me like you was telling. Sound to me like you was asking me something back."

"Well, I'm doing just what it look like I'm doing. On'erstand?"

"Oh. Give him that charm yet?"

"I ain't seen him."

"Well, I heard somebody say it's too late now."

Juba put her nose in the air, gave her shoulders a toss.

"I heard that."

"It's true, hunh?"

"I reckon so. Mott say they brung him back this morning."

"Well, now, that's howcome you put down yo' hoe and come back here?"

Juba shrugged. A moment later she slid down beside the others, took a pipe out of her bosom.

It was evening when Marse Prosser called her from her cabin.

"You, Juba."

"Yes, suh, Marse Prosser."

She came out into the twilight, her eyes wild, bloodshot. His scowl seized her at once, but she avoided the burning pin-points of his stare. For some reason she had

202

a feeling of being undressed. It was nothing, of course. She waited sullenly.

"How much tobacco you cut this afternoon, gal?"

She rolled her eyes, her gaze rising to meet his attention, then straying off into the darkness. It was an insolent maneuver, but she refrained from speaking.

"I'll teach you, sow."

"You talking to me, Marse Prosser?"

A deep purple red flushed his cheeks.

"You – you varmint. Get on down to the stake. Trot along – trot, I tell you." He prodded her with the butt of his lash.

She halted, planted her feet every time he poked her, and eventually he was obliged to use the lash end on her bare legs.

At the stake she snarled and tossed her hips as she took the place indicated beneath the yard lantern. A crowd of frightened blacks materialized in the dusk. They followed at a safe distance, the whites of their eyes, the palms of their hands, their rounded white mouths distinct in the shadows.

Later they set up a soft dove-like lamentation.

"Pray, massa, pray. Oh, pray, massa."

"H'ist them clothes."

She understood and obeyed, snatching the old tattered skirt up over her naked buttocks.

The white palms, uplifted, fluttered in the darkness. The mouths, as round as O's, grew large, then small again.

"Lord a-mercy."

"Here's something else to toss up your petticoats for, ma'm. Here's something worth fluttering your hips *about*. Understand?"

She didn't speak, didn't even flinch. Presently her thighs were raw like cut beef and bloody. Once or twice she turned her head and threw a swift, hateful glance at the powerful man pouring the hot melted lead on her flesh, but she didn't cry out or shrink away. The end of the lash became wet and began making words like *sa-lack, sa-lack, sa-lack* as it twined around her thin hips. *Sa-lack, sa- lack, sa-lack.*

"Oh, pray, massa; pray."

Something shook the lantern overhead, and the near shadows began to tremble and bounce back and forth like dervishes. When would Marse Prosser get tired? Maybe he was waiting for that Juba to break down. Maybe he was aiming to take the starch out of her hide. Well, he was certainly a powerful hand at laying it on, anyhow. The voices increased in the thicket, the quaking hands multiplied.

"Another such caper from you, and I'll fix you so you *can't* cut tobacco – then sell you down the river for good measure – sell you down to one of them Georgia cotton raisers – where you'll eat hog slop and sleep in a stable with mules."

She said nothing. She wouldn't even let herself cry. Lordy, she was just so full of meanness, she could almost taste it. Cry? Humph!

Sa-lack, sa-lack –

"Pray, massa. Oh, pray, massa."

4

The plight of Mrs. Cassandra Rainwater was that she was now too old to accomplish the things she dreamed. In her taffeta and lace she was even too wan and fragile to get around Philadelphia in her own carriage as she wished, and more and more she was obliged to leave with young Biddenhurst errands and contacts that might well have profited by her own attention. This in no wise inferred that the young man's talents were at all short of remarkable or his understanding, his sympathies, less than splendid; but her years, her feminine discernment, her lightness of touch must have offered advantages. Yet her plight was a common one; the sword was outwearing its sheath.

And indeed, over and over again, she had reason to be

thankful that she had discovered Alexander Biddenhurst, discovered in him a romantic love of liberty like her own and a rather special burden for abused minority groups. At first there had been their mutual resentment against those who stole the Indians' hunting grounds. And now they were together convinced that liberty, equality and fraternity should prevail in the American States as well as in France. Each had read Rousseau and Voltaire with conviction, and each had been intrigued by the *Amis des Noirs*. Each hoped that somehow slavery would end promptly, even if the end had to come with blood as in San Domingo. The spirit of the master was abating, that of the slave rising from the dust. Jefferson was right; though, of course, he failed to go far enough. They themselves were not afraid to say (to each other, at least) that they approved the Jacobin ideal of utter equality for all men, everywhere. They enjoyed working for it as best they could. But Mrs. Rainwater, widowed and old, could do little of herself now, very little.

Yet she could still contribute her vision – her vision, her insight and, of course, her money. Fortunately she had a plenty of that, and scarcely any dependents. She rested the needlework that had occupied her fingers and adjusted her cushions. The young man rose to go, the afternoon sunlight making grotesque blurs behind his thick-lensed spectacles.

"I don't think you told me you were in a hurry, Alec."

"It's only the stagecoach that I was expecting to meet."

"Oh, yes. You did say – but about your moving. You didn't finish."

"I thought it would be well if they found my lodgings at Coats Alley and Budd Street empty. Of course, it proves nothing that that slave had my name and address when he was captured, but moving will save me the necessity of talking. They may want to make something of my being in Richmond at the beginning of the summer."

"Oh, that. Possibly."

"I couldn't have gone at a more suspicious time, had I actually been inciting the slaves to insurrection."

"You think those with axes to grind would be slow to believe that I sent you merely to look around, to study sentiment and get a cross-section view?"

"They'd never be satisfied with the facts. Being unsuspecting, I *did* say a good many strong things. Mostly I said them to draw out their thoughts, but you see how it's all coming to appear to an outsider."

"Possibly you're right, but they'll find you if they want you badly enough. Be sure to leave your new number anyhow. And come to think about it, why don't you use my carriage to meet the stage?"

"Well, if you say —"

"Of course. Didn't you say she's a young woman?"

"Yes. You and I are becoming a sort of bureau for the aid of fugitives — if nothing more."

"That's something. I hope we're getting at something far deeper, however. Whenever we succor a fleeing creature, I hope we make a soldier for liberty."

"No doubt we do."

"How about the Creuzots and Laurent?"

"Doing well. Their home is simpler than the one they left, but I have no doubt they'll become the kind of influences we want."

"I must have a talk with M. Creuzot. Is he coughing more than usual?"

"Not more."

"That's good. I'm especially eager to get some Negroes, some escaped slaves. They'll bring such an emotional fervor to the work."

"If I may go now —"

"Yes, of course, Alec. Take the carriage."

"Thank you."

Twilight had fallen. There was a cheerful confusion and bustle beneath the elms where the stagecoach unloaded.

Mrs. Rainwater's amber coachman held his horses in a soft rain of leaves, while Alexander Biddenhurst ran across the road to meet the veiled woman traveling alone.

A little later, as the horses jogged along indolently, Biddenhurst realized that the carriage was too heavily scented. A dreamy lassitude had settled upon the tired, excited woman. Ah, he thought, it's a strange free masonry, this love of freedom, a strange free masonry. Of course, any man might be drawn to a fragrant, faintly tinted creature like this one, but that he should be a partner with her, sharing a secret, working for other ends, was strange. Yet all that did not forestall the joy of living, the pride of the eye.

"Melody – that's the name for you all right."

"You think so, Mist' Alec?"

"Listen. I'm not a rich planter's son, and you're not in Virginia now. *Mist' Alec!*"

She smiled in a drowsy haze. She was very tired.

5

And you are the one they call the General?"

"I'm name Gabriel."

"I've heard slaves refer to a General something or other."

"Gen'l John, maybe."

"Didn't they call you General?"

"Some time – not so much."

"Then old John there was the leader, not you?"

"No. I been the leader, *me*. I'm the one. Gen'l John is just named that. I'm the one."

"You *are* the General?"

"I reckon so. Leastwise, I'm the leader. I ain't never turned my back to a nachal man. I don't know if I'm a sure 'nough general or if I ain't."

Gabriel, still in the frayed coachman's clothes, sank back into a lordly slouch. Now, suh, curse they ugly hides, they could make up they own minds about the gen'l part. Is I, or ain't I? One hand clasped the arm of the witness chair; the other hung idly across his knee. His eye kept its penetrating gaze, but now there was a vague sadness on his face. It was as if shadows passed before him now and again. It may have been woe or remorse rising in him, but the look was more like the dark, uncertain torment one sees in the countenance of a crushed beast whose spirit remains unbroken.

Only that morning there had been another execution, a small herd of anonymous field Negroes. The townsfolk were hardened to the spectacle now. Even the customary eyewitnesses were missing. The word had gotten about that these were not the ringleaders, and the mere sight of slaughter for its own sake was no longer attractive or stimulating. So many little groups like this had come to the scaffold since mid-September – five, ten, fifteen at a time – so many. It was a routine. These blacks had contracted a malady, a sort of hydrophobia; they were mad. It was necessary to check the spread of the thing. It was a common-sense matter. Only this morning there had been a difference.

At first no one had seen or heard the wiry old man with the turndown mouth. He had seen the first of the executions, and he had raised his voice then.

"You idiots. You're putting them through too fast, I tell you. No sense in killing off a man's live stock in herds like that unless you know for sure what you're doing."

He scrambled in the crowd and tried to fight his way through. But they thought he was talking about the blacks being idiots. A chorus of approval rose around him. No one saw him as an individual, only as a part of a snarling crowd.

Today, with things much quieter, they had heard, for he succeeded in delaying the hangings half-an-hour.

"See that long yellow boy there. Well, that's John Thomas. That boy's been to Norfolk for me. He just got back last week. And, by God, if you hang him without proof, you'll pay me his worth. Bloody apes, what's wrong with you? Have you gone stone crazy for life?"

John Thomas did not swing. There was a rumor that several other planters had also been to the justices since morning. And already a statement had been issued – some "mistakes" had been made, admittedly. But Gabriel, lying on his face beside Mingo, knew only what the swinging trap indicated. Yet it occurred to him that all this pause, this unhurried questioning, could not possibly have been in keeping with the trials that had preceded his. He concluded at length that the "General" was simply receiving his due recognition, this in spite of the prosecutor's whining, sarcastic voice.

"Here, now, you mean to say you were the one that thought up the whole idea?"

"I was the one. Me."

"Yes, but not all alone, surely –"

"Maybe not all alone."

"Well, then, who were your accomplices? Who helped you think it up?"

Gabriel shrugged.

"You got Ditcher and Mingo and Gen'l John. You done hanged a plenty mo'. I talked to some of them. I told them to come on."

"It's plain that you do not intend to implicate anyone not already in custody. You're not telling all you know."

Gabriel looked at the man long and directly.

"I ain't got cause to talk a heap, suh."

"You haven't?"

"H'm."

Then the prosecutor spun quickly on his heel, barked.

"What do you mean by that, you –"

Gabriel's eyes strayed indolently to the window, to the golden leaves of an oak bough. The court was oppressively rigid, the justice in their wigs and robes, the spectators gaping, straining their necks.

"A man what's booked to hang anyhow –" he mused.

"Oh. So you think –" Then a diplomatic change of tone. "You know, Gabriel, it is not impossible to alter the complexion of things even yet. A – I mean, you have a fine chance to let the court know if you have been made the tool of foreign agitators. If there were white men who talked to you, encouraged –"

That sounded foolish to Gabriel.

"White mens?"

"Yes, men talking about equality, setting the poor against the rich, the blacks against their masters, things like that."

Gabriel was now convinced that the man was resorting to some sort of guile. He fixed his eyes earnestly.

"I tell you. I been studying about freedom a heap, me. I heard a plenty folks talk and I listened a heap. And everything I heard made me feel like I wanted to be free. It was on my mind hard, and it's right there the same way yet. On'erstand? That's all. Something keep telling me that anything what's equal to a gray squirrel wants to be free. That's how it all come about."

"Well, was it necessary to plot such a savage butchery? Couldn't you have contrived an easier way?"

Gabriel shook his head slowly. After a long pause he spoke.

"I ain't got no head for flying away. A man is got a right to have his freedom in the place where he's born. He is got cause to want all his kinfolks free like hisself."

"Oh, why don't you come clean? Don't you realize you're on the verge of hanging? The court wants to know who planted the damnable seeds, what Jacobins worked on you. Were you not treated well by your master?"

Gabriel ignored most of what he said.

"Might just as well to hang."

"That's bravado. You want to live. And the best way for you –"

"A lion what's tasted man's blood is a caution to keep around after that."

"Don't strut, nigger."

"No, suh, no strutting. But I been free this last four-five weeks. On'erstand? I been a gen'l, and I been ready to die since first time I hooked on a sword. The others too – they been ready. We all knowed it was one thing or the other. The stars was against us, though; that's all."

It was astonishing how the thing dragged on, astonishing how they worried and cajoled, threatened and flattered the captive. "Mistakes" *had* been made, due to haste and excitement, but there was no possibility of a mistake here. Gabriel seemed, if anything, anxious to have them get the thing straight, to have them place responsibility where responsibility belonged.

In another room, under heavy guard and awaiting their call, the last of the accused Negroes sulked. Ditcher's massive head was bowed, his wiry queue curled like a pig's tail. It had never been more apparent that he was a giant. His legs suggested tree stumps. The depth of his chest, the spread of his shoulders seemed unreal. His skin was amber. Now, delaying in the guarded room, he was perfectly relaxed. Indeed, he might have nodded had it not been for the jittery, nervous activity of the armed men around him. They annoyed him.

"We could had them on they knees long ago," he was saying in his mind. "Only that devilish big rain. That's what stopped us. We could all been free as squirrels by now. It wasn't the time to hit. We should had a sign."

Mingo's clothes were better, but his hair had been torn from its braid. He had lost his spectacles. His eyes had an uncertain, watery stare. He was not merely downcast; he looked definitely disappointed. Words were going through his mind too, but they made a briefer strain.

"Toussaint's crowd was luckier. Toussaint's crowd was luckier."

There were others, a dozen or more, unimportant fellows. Then near the door the withered old dead-leaf clad in a rag that had once been an overcoat. He kept licking his white, shriveled lips, kept showing the brown fangs. He was trembling now.

"Somebody's obliged to foot the bill," his mind was saying. "Ne' mind, though. Near about everybody dies *one* time. And there ain't many niggers what gets to cross the river free – not many."

Any one of them would have sped the business along had it been his to do it. No cause for a heap of aggravating questions. Them white mens ought to could see that Gabriel didn't care nothing about them; he was going to tell them just what it was good for them to know, and precious little more. But there was nothing they could do, nothing but wait.

". . . and how did you imagine you'd take the city?"

"We was ready to hit fast. We had three lines, and the one in the middle was going to split in two. They was coming in town from both ends at once. They wasn't going to spare nothing what helt up its hand against us."

"How about the other two?"

"Them's the ones what was ready to take the arsenal and the powder house."

"Which line were you to lead?"

"The one what went against the arsenal."

"What arms had you?"

"We didn't need no guns – us what went against the arsenal there. All we needed was to slip by in the dark with good stout sticks. We could manage the guards."

"Mad dogs – that's what you are. The audacity! It's inconceivable that well-treated servants like –"

"We was tired being slaves. We never heard tell about no other way."

"You'd take the arsenal and powder house by surprise;

then with ample arms, with the city in ashes, with the countryside and crops for your food, you thought you'd be able to stand your ground?"

"H'm."

"How many bullets had you to start with?"

"About a peck."

"And powder?"

"'Nough for that many bullets."

"Any other arms?"

"Pikes, scythe-swords, knives, clubs, all like of that – 'nough to do the work."

"How'd you know it would do the work?"

"There wa'n't but twenty-three muskets in town outside the arsenal."

"You knew that!"

Gabriel felt that it was unnecessary to answer.

There was a hush; a shiver passed over the courtroom.

"It was a diabolical thing. Gentlemen –"

He talked for a time with his back to Gabriel. Later he turned to the prisoner again, but this time he spoke like a changed man, an awakened man who had had an evil dream.

"Did you imagine other well-fed, well-kept slaves would join you?"

"Wouldn't you j'ine us, was you a slave, suh?"

"Don't be impudent. You're still a black –"

"I been a free man – and a gen'l, I reckon."

"And stop saying general, too. Ringleader of mad dogs. That's what you've been. I call on this court of justice –"

Gabriel felt the scene withdrawing. It was almost like a dream, almost mystic. Further and further away it receded. Again there was that insulting mockery of words he could not understand, that babble of legal language and political innuendo. It was all moving away from him, leaving him clinging to an arm of his chair, slouched on one elbow. A lordly insolence rose in him. Suddenly he was vaguely aware of that whiney voice again.

"The only question yet raised, sir, was whether or not the wretch was capable of conceiving such a masterpiece of deviltry, such a demon-inspired –"

It was far away. Gabriel's eyes strayed again. The window – blue. The crisp oak leaves – like gold. Demons. Freedom. Deviltry. Justice. Funny words. All of them sounded like conjure now.

"Maybe we should paid attention to the signs. Maybe we should done that," Gabriel thought.

6

Ben stood in the kitchen door and watched the fellow sitting on a chopping block beside the woodpile. Early-morning sunlight flooded the yard, and the pumpkin-colored slave sat beneath a bright arch of transparent gold. His elbows rested on his sprawled knees, his brown ham-like hands dangled between. Trouble had dogged old Pharoah since the day he carried the news to Richmond, and now his thoughts were in a whirl.

Lordy, me, I couldn't help telling. I just couldn't live and know all them peoples was fixing to meet they master 'thout knowing it. Seemed like I'd go hog-crazy if I didn't tell it. I *had* to; I didn't mean Gabriel and them no hurt. Just the same, they wants my meat. They wants a piece of my skin, Lord.

Ben watched him and saw the daydream play on his face, saw his lips curl, his eyes flicker. He saw, too, a crisp golden shower of oak leaves on the sorrowful mulatto and on the woodpile. Ben turned to Drucilla who was stirring something in a kettle, her immobile, mask-like face glowing in the heat.

"They's wearing Pharoah down all right, following him around like they do, throwing knives at him every chance they gets."

"What else he 'spect?"

"I don't know."

"H'm. I reckon you don't."

"But it's a powerful bad thing to sit around waiting for yo' medicine when you know you's sure to get it."

"*You* ought to know."

"What you mean, gal?"

"Nothing – just you ought know."

"Howcome *I* ought know mo'n anybody else."

"I didn't say you ought to know mo'n anybody else."

"It sounded like you meant that."

"Did it?"

He leaned against the doorpost again. She shifted a few pots, stirred a while longer. Ben kept watching Pharoah's bowed head. A few moments later, when he had decided to say nothing more to Drucilla, he heard her speaking to his back.

"Just like that yellow varmint. Least thing he could do, was he equal to a hound dog, was keep his mouth shut. But, no, he wanted to lead one line; and when they wouldn't let him, nothing would do but he must go tell everything. You and him –"

"Me and him what?"

"Nothing."

"What you keep on hinting at me, gal?"

"Nothing. Call him and see do he want a cup of coffee to ease his mind. You can put a drop of Marse Sheppard's rum in it."

Such fall weather... Lordy! Ben preferred not to raise his voice. He strolled down the gravel walk, went over to the woodpile. He spoke to Pharoah; but the latter, shaking his head woefully, showed no immediate interest in Ben's suggestion. Later, however, he rose reluctantly and followed the other to the kitchen door.

"No need moping yo'self sick, though."

"I ain't so scairt. That ain't it."

"Howcome you do it, then?"

"I'm sick, Ben. Sure's you borned, I been poisoned."

"Hush. Ain't nothing wrong with you."

"Don't tell me. I been finding frogs' toes and like of that in my pipe. They keeps my bed sprinkled with conjure dust. I been doing everything I know how to fight it, but it don't amount to nothing. I'm got slow poisoning sure's I'm a foot tall."

"Hush. A cup of coffee'll do you good. Then walk around till work time. You can make *yo'self* sick just studying like that."

Drucilla had placed a cup on the stove and poured an inch of rum in it. When they reached the door, she poured the boiling coffee.

"Wait there," she ordered Pharoah.

"H'm."

"Here, now. This'll ease yo'mind."

"You reckon?"

He stood cooling it a few moments, then raised the cup and poured the contents down his throat. His eyes were wide, startled, as if he had seen a spirit. Suddenly he began trembling violently. A moment later he was crying, his hand over his eyes. Ben and Drucilla stood before him paralyzed. Then, abruptly, his shoulders rounded, he gave a little hiccough and the coffee came out of his mouth in an ugly geyser that spouted on the floor of the porch. And when he removed his hand from his eyes and saw it there, he began crying louder.

"Lordy, Ben, look at it. See there. There it is. I told you so. They fixed me. I done puked up a varmint. What is it — a snake or a lizard? Lordy! They done fixed me. Look at it there, Ben."

His crying became louder and louder. Then, without warning, he left Ben and Drucilla in the doorway, bounded across the yard, raising his voice higher and higher, wailing insanely, and raced toward the clump beyond the stables.

Negroes began leaving the outhouses and cabins, coming into the early sun with amazed faces. One by one they started after Pharoah, pursuing him hesitantly, partly curious, partly concerned, but unable to resist following. Ben and Drucilla remained like statues in the doorway.

It was five minutes later when Drucilla went outside and recovered the cup and saucer the crazed fellow had tossed there as he left. She saw some of the black men returning from the tree clump, walking slowly.

"Catch him, George?" Ben called.

"It wasn't no use, Uncle Ben."

"Lord help."

"Done climbed a tree already. Up there barking like a dog."

"Barking, hunh?"

They went on. Drucilla went back into the kitchen. Ben stood wringing his hands. So Drucilla thought it was no more than Pharoah should expect for telling a thing like that? Telling a thing like that! Lordy, what could anybody expect. Anybody.

Ben's hands felt scaly and cold to himself. They were so thin and brittle he imagined they were like the hands of a skeleton. Still he could not restrain the impulse to pass one in and out of the other. He could not move his feet from the place where he stood on the path, either.

7

An air of mystery invaded the Virginia State Legislature. Assembled in secret session with drawn blinds and guards at every door, the men sat with bowed heads in a haze of tobacco smoke and flickering lamplight. A warm proud voice engulfed them. Subdued yet distinct in the small chamber, it laid before the group a possible solution for the baffling problem.

"*Resolved,* that the Senators of this state in the Congress of the United States be instructed, and the Representatives be requested, to use their best efforts for the obtaining from the General Government a competent portion of territory in the State of Louisiana, to be appropriated to the residence of such people of color as have been or shall be emancipated, or hereafter may become dangerous to the public safety. . . ."

At length the reading was finished and discussion was allowed. The black-clad men, intensely sober, deeply concerned, shook their heads and murmured. Somewhere in the rear a tired voice was heard saying, "Sir, not yet. The time is not ripe. Our present situation only delays the possibility of such action. There are so many angles. Perhaps slavery itself –"

Yes, the Governor told himself at Oak Lawn, it all led back to the same colossal bugbear. Why such a widespread fret about slavery? Hadn't there always been slaves? But with liberty the fad of the hour, it might well be expected. Some fanatic would always be absent-minded enough to apply his cant to the black man's condition in the American States. Whenever there was a nonsensical thing to be said, nature would provide a fool to say it. So it always went. At any rate, he was still the Governor of Virginia; his personal responsibilities had not ceased. He could at least write the President a letter looking forward to such action by the United States Congress as his own legislature was hesitant to suggest at the moment.

He walked to the window, withdrew the hangings. A frame of stars. A moment later he returned to his writing table. In the pale orchid light he took a quill and began writing: "Honorable Sir –"

Now it was different with Gabriel in his cell. He had not been returned to the hole where he had lain chained to the floor beside Mingo. Here there were chains, but now he sat upright on a stool when he wished, rolled on the floor when he felt inclined. There was a barred window, too, a frame of indigo sky with little near stars.

218

Them white folks is sure a sight. Now they's aiming to make Mingo talk some mo'. They is sure got great heads for figuring out something what ain't. They sure loves to wring and twist about nothing. Nothing going to do them now but to make somebody say white mens was telling us to rise up. Never heard tell of nobody being so set on a thing before.

When the night watch passed, Ovid walked around the corner and whistled for Midwick. Later, plowing his feet through the loose leaves, the older guard came to a pool of light near the main gate.

"Well, doesn't anyone know why she left, Midwick?"

"Don't seem to. Not unless some politician caused it – him or somebody mixed up with this insurrection business."

"Now that's a thing to blind you. I always thought that young Robin Sheppard was great on her."

"Just getting his education, I reckon." He snickered. "They say he's sparking somebody he can marry now."

"The other one was really something to look at, though. Kind of a – I suppose you call it exotic. Apricot-colored, enameled-like hair – most any man could enjoy a little recklessness with –"

"Steady, Ovid. Remember you're a –"

"Dash it all, Midwick. I'm sick of being steady. I want to do incredible things."

"Incredible?"

"Yes, outlandish, glamorous –"

"Well, now, if we go to war again –"

"Oh, you don't understand me, Midwick."

8

A week passed. The gallows-day came, and Gabriel awakened to the clatter of heels and the rattle of side arms outside his cell.

This the day all right. They is sure here early a plenty. Trying to be good as they word, I reckon. Beating the sun up so I won't get to thinking they's gone back on me. Never got up this soon in the morning to feed me, not as I can recollect, nohow.

H'm. Yes, suh, it's still night.

He curled his legs and sat upright, his hands resting on the floor to spare them the weight of the iron wristbands and chains. His naked shoulders gave a faint glow in the darkness. There was a brightness on his cheekbones, on his forehead.

Suddenly there was silence outside. A brief hush blanketed the men with the flambeaus and sabers.

Them is the mens with the milk-white horses, I reckon. I ain't seen nara one of them, but I know right well how they looks. H'm. I got a good mind how they come. I know about *them* all right, all right ... Galloping down a heap of clouds piled up like mountains. I know them milk-white horses, me.

His eyes, large, the whites prominent, turned listlessly. He was still sitting on his feet, his hands resting on the floor. Again the sabers rattled, heels clattered and a medley of gross voices rose in confusion.

Put yo' key in the lock, Mistah Man. Give the sign and come in, please you, suh. I heard a nigger say Death is his mammy. His old black mammy is name Death, he say. Well and good, onliest thing about it is Death is a man.

Come on in, suh, if you's a-mind to. I'm ready and waiting, me. I ain't been afeared of a nachal man, and I don't know's I mind the old Massa hisself. I ain't been afeared of thunder and lightning, and I don't reckon I'll mind the hurricane. I don't know's I'll mind when the trees bend down and the tombstones commence to bust. Don't reckon I'll mind, suh. Come on in.

The sky flushed as they put him in the cart, and suddenly Gabriel thought of the others, the ones who were to follow him, the ones who waited in their cells because of his leadership, these and others, others, and still others, a world of others who were to follow.

There was a long oversized box on the cart, and Gabriel knew its use. It had to be long, oversized, for a body of his dimensions. He sat on the thing, threw out his feet. A flood of color burst in the east, rose and orchid and pale gold. The cart jogged. A clatter of feet went before, and a clatter of feet came after. Sabers rattled from the belts of shadowy, uniformed men. Above their heads a score of muskets pointed toward heaven, pointed like the stiff fingers of black workers rising from their prayers.

The trumpet sounds within-a my soul.

Ditcher, even then was standing at his small window with bloodshot, sleepless eyes. His face was marked by numerous small scars. He had been a fighter. Not that he was petulant or touchy, but the nature of his work frequently got him embroiled. The nature of his reputation, before Gabriel deflated it, obliged him to meet all comers. But fighting had never been a pleasure to Ditcher; this morning, his massive hands clasping the window bars, he lamented all wars. Presently, he thought, so far as he was concerned, the trumpets would blow their last blast. The sky would flush, redden like a sea of blood, and the sun would go down on all conflict.... Presently. Presently. Outside the cart lumbered. The pale torches blossomed like white flowers.

Good-by, Gabriel. Don't nobody need tell *you* how to die, I reckon. You's the gen'l, you.

Distraught, fluttery, Mingo chewed his lips and dug his fingernails into the palms of his hands. The Book said some powerfully hopeful things about the stranger, the servant, the outcast. The Book was all for abused folks like

221

Negroes. Other books too, in fact. Mostly them men what writ books was a little better kind than them what made speeches at the town meetings.

Wagon, hunh? Bright and early, too. Gabriel be the first, I reckon. Yes, the first, all right. Toussaint was first across yonder; Gabriel's first here. The first robin going north. It was too soon for Gabriel, though. It wasn't summer. The cold caught us here, the rain and all. Toussaint drunk blood. Gabriel never had no head for such doings as that. They was the first, them two.

Ne' mind, boy.

General John was as scrawny as a hawk now. The days of waiting had drawn his face so tight and hard it suggested a bird's face. Inside his torn garment, his shaggy feathers, he twitched a rattling skeleton-like body.

Was I a singing man, I'd sing me a song now, he thought. I'd sing me a song about lonesome, about a song-singing man long gone. No need crying about a nigger what's about to die free. I'd sing me a song, me.

The horizon was pearl-gray now, but overhead a star or two lingered. A man gave the word, and Gabriel climbed the steps to the platform. For an instant he was still, his hands idle. Across some rooftops a limp flag rose, ever so lightly, fluttered a little.

They had chosen to bring him without shirt or coat. He stood, naked above the waist, excellent in strength, the first for freedom of the blacks, savage and baffled, perplexed but unafraid, waiting for the dignity of death.

"Have you anything to –"

Then an interruption, another voice.

"Would you ask that of a – of a black?"

"Well, seeing he's getting a hanging like this, I thought maybe –"

"As you wish."

Then a stuttering followed by bluster.

"You want to talk now, you a – a – scoundrel?"

No answer.

"Want to talk now, I say?"

"Let the rope talk, suh."

"No statement?"

"The rope, please you, suh – let it talk."

The vein grew big in the executioner's forehead. His face became livid. The narrow scar that was his mouth tightened, tightened, tightened. Another man, standing beside the one with the ax, stepped forward, stood on tiptoes and placed the cowl on the tall Negro's head.

Somewhere down below feet tramped. The escort jostled, wheeled and withdrew a few paces.

Like night, Gabriel thought, like night with this thing on your head.

A command to the soldiers broke the absolute stillness. A wagon moved. A horse nickered. Then, here and there, the sudden, surprised intake of breath filled the air with a tiny whispering. The sheriff's ax inscribed a vivid arc. The trap banged, and the rope hummed like a violin string. And still there was that arc, inscribed by the ax, lingering there against the sky like a wreath of smoke.

Seated in a cariole a hundred yards away, a blanket tucked about his knees, Ben saw it and gasped. Near him a small crowd of Negroes bowed their heads, covered their faces with their hands. Even when Ben closed his eyes, he could see that arc, hear that violin string.

9

Ben did not wait to see them remove the body. There were errands for him in town. Later he was expected to meet Marse Sheppard and drive him home.

So the morning was spent. Then it occurred to Ben that the sky was no longer clear, clouds were gathering. But now there was no further need for haste. Marse Sheppard was not ready. The old Negro drove his carriage down a street he knew well and remained in the seat, watching something in a corral beyond a low fence. A crowd of white men were mulling in a yard. Saddle horses were strung along all the near hitching bars; and wherever there was space, driving rigs were hitched.

Ben could see the slave block from his seat, could hear the auctioneer's voice, but he had been watching a long while before he realized that the brown girl up for bids was Gabriel's Juba, the tempestuous wench with the slim hips and the savage mop of hair. Her feet were bare. Her clothes were scant. And there was something about her figure, something about the bold rise of her exposed breasts, that put gooseflesh on a man. But her look was downcast, bitter, almost threatening.

Yet the bidding continued lively. Ben decided abruptly that he did not wish to see it through. He pulled on his lines and began threading a way through the thronged carriages of the planters. It was definitely going to rain.

Ben was waiting at a curb for Marse Sheppard when the first flurry came. Then the silvered old man, wrapped to the eyes in his cape, came out, and they started home in the downpour. When they were in the heart of town, lightning flashed, and Ben saw an array of bright red and yellow and green and purple parasols suddenly raised. Men dashed across the wet street, seeking shelter in shops. Carriages jostled. Voices called in the rain and received something better than their own echoes for answer. The clouds bore down. The air had a melancholy sweetness. But Ben could not forget Gabriel's shining naked body or the arc inscribed by the executioner's ax. He could not feel reassured about the knives that waited for him with the sweet brown thrashers in every hedge and clump. For him the rain-swept streets had a carnival sadness.

The little mare's feet played a soothing tune on the cobblestones.